False Flag

Book Four
The Boston Brahmin Series

A novel by

Bobby Akart

Copyright Information

Other Works by Amazon Top 50 Author, Bobby Akart

The Doomsday Series

Apocalypse

Haven

Anarchy

Minutemen

Civil War

The Yellowstone Series

Hellfire

Inferno

Fallout

Survival

The Lone Star Series

Axis of Evil

Beyond Borders

Lines in the Sand

Texas Strong

Fifth Column

Suicide Six

The Pandemic Series

Beginnings

The Innocents

Level 6

Quietus

The Blackout Series

36 Hours

Zero Hour

Turning Point

Shiloh Ranch

Hornet's Nest

Devil's Homecoming

The Boston Brahmin Series

The Loyal Nine

Cyber Attack

Martial Law

False Flag

The Mechanics

Choose Freedom

Patriot's Farewell

Seeds of Liberty (Companion Guide)

The Prepping for Tomorrow Series

Cyber Warfare

EMP: Electromagnetic Pulse

Economic Collapse

DEDICATIONS

To the love of my life, you saved me from madness and continue to do so daily. Thank you for loving me.

To the Princesses of the Palace, my little marauders in training, you have no idea how much happiness you bring to your mommy and me. Seeing your wiggly butts at the end of a long day behind the keyboard makes it all worthwhile.

To my friends and readers, please heed the warning of this series. A cyber attack can strike in an instant. No bombs, no bullets, no swordfights. Just a few keystrokes on a computer, and we're done. I write this book to entertain you, but also to get you ready for the coming cyber war. And make no mistake, Martial Law is a distinct probability in the event of a catastrophic event. The President's power to wield this authority transcends party affiliation or political ideology. Any President will use it as necessary.

To the Founding Fathers, whose vision and bravery built America. My apologies for what we've become.

ACKNOWLEDGEMENTS

Writing a book that is both informative and entertaining requires a tremendous team effort. Writing is the easy part. For their efforts in making The Boston Brahmin series a reality, I would like to thank Hristo Argirov Kovatliev for his incredible cover art, Pauline Nolet for her editorial prowess, Stef Mcdaid for making this manuscript decipherable on so many formats, Joseph Morton for bringing my words to life in audio format, and the Team—whose advice, friendship and attention to detail is priceless.

Thank you!   Choose Freedom!

About the Author

Bobby Akart

Author Bobby Akart has been ranked by Amazon as #55 in its Top 100 list of most popular, bestselling authors. He has achieved recognition as the #1 bestselling Horror Author, #2 bestselling Science Fiction Author, #3 bestselling Religion & Spirituality Author, #6 bestselling Action & Adventure Author, and #7 bestselling Historical Author.

He has written over twenty-six international bestsellers, in nearly fifty fiction and nonfiction genres, including the chart-busting Yellowstone series, the reader-favorite Lone Star series, the critically acclaimed Boston Brahmin series, the bestselling Blackout series, the frighteningly realistic Pandemic series, his highly cited nonfiction Prepping for Tomorrow series, and his latest project—the Doomsday series, seen by many as the horrifying future of our nation if we can't find a way to come together.

His novel *Yellowstone: Fallout* reached the Top 50 on the Amazon bestsellers list and earned him two Kindle All-Star awards for most pages read in a month and most pages read as an author. The Yellowstone series vaulted him to the #1 best selling horror author on Amazon, and the #2 best selling science fiction author.

Bobby has provided his readers a diverse range of topics that are both informative and entertaining. His attention to detail and impeccable research have allowed him to capture the imaginations of his readers through his fictional works and bring them valuable knowledge through his nonfiction books.

SIGN UP for Bobby Akart's mailing list to receive special offers, bonus content, and you'll be the first to receive news about new releases in the Doomsday series:

eepurl.com/bYqq3L

VISIT Amazon.com/BobbyAkart, a dedicated feature page created by Amazon for his work, to view more information on his thriller fiction novels and post-apocalyptic book series, as well as his nonfiction Prepping for Tomorrow series.

Visit Bobby Akart's website for informative blog entries on preparedness, writing, and a behind-the-scenes look into his novels.

BobbyAkart.com

INTRODUCTION TO *FALSE FLAG*

FALSE FLAGS THROUGHOUT HISTORY

false flag ('fols 'flag): An operation designed to deceive in such a way that events appear as though they are being carried out by perpetrators other than those who actually planned and executed them. A false flag is used as an ideological weapon to control the citizenry with the fear of a manufactured enemy.

Governments and military operations have used false flag events throughout history. They have been used to persecute a political enemy, or to enact laws in the name of security. Some governments unabashedly admit their use of the false flag concept.

Originally, the term had its origins in naval warfare as a ruse de guerre, literally translated as a ruse of war. This can be considered a military deception against one's opponent, as well as other more creative, sometimes unorthodox means, involving clever and misleading propaganda.

False flags have occurred for thousands of years. In ancient times, there is the mythical use of the Trojan Horse that the Greeks used to enter the city of Troy. The legends of false flags date back to days of Hannibal and Alexander the Great.

Then there is the most famous use of a false flag in the case of the British ocean liner, the RMS Lusitania.

For eight years, the Lusitania was the largest passenger ship in the world. When the Lusitania left New York for Liverpool, England on May 1, 1915, she was making her final voyage.

After World War One broke out in 1914, President Woodrow Wilson maintained America's neutrality which was favored by a majority of the American people. At the time, Britain was one of our largest trading partners. During this timeframe, tensions arose between the U.S. and Germany over Berlin's attempted quarantine of the British Isles. As American ships traveled to Britain, they became imperiled by the throes of war. Eventually, several U.S. flagged vessels were either damaged, or sunk, by German mines. Ultimately, by the spring of 1915, Germany openly announced unrestricted submarine warfare in the region.

The American media published warnings issued by the German government that Americans traveling on British or Allied ships in war zones did so at their own risk. One such announcement was placed on the same page of the New York Times that contained an advertisement for the Lusitania's voyage from New York back to Liverpool.

As the Lusitania departed New York's port, Germany had not formally declared the area around the British Isles a war zone. That did not occur until several days later. The Lusitania sailed without knowledge of the dangers ahead.

The Lusitania also traveled with an interesting passenger and unusual cargo. Woodrow Wilson's trusted advisor, Colonel Edward Mandell House, was aboard. He was dispatched on a secret mission to investigate the prospects of an American-brokered peace before the casualties in the War became too high. The ship was also stockpiled with one hundred and seventy-three tons of American-made war munitions destined for England in violation of several international treaties.

Crossing the Atlantic had been rough, but as the Lusitania approached Ireland, Captain Daniel Dow raised the American flag atop the otherwise British-commissioned ship. The night before, the Captain was concerned about being torpedoed. He hoped for safe passage through the German occupied waters off the coast. Out of an abundance of caution, he lowered the Union Jack and raised the Stars and Stripes.

On May 7, as the Lusitania approached England, the thirty-two thousand ton ship was hit by an exploding torpedo on its starboard side. The torpedo blast was followed by a second, larger explosion, which included the ship's boilers. Chaos ensued. The ship listed so badly that the lifeboats crashed into the passengers on deck. Reportedly, within eighteen minutes, the Lusitania quickly sank off the southern coast of Ireland. The death toll was nearly two thousand passengers, including over one hundred Americans.

The sinking of the Lusitania by the German U–boat played a pivotal role in geopolitical affairs. The sinking enraged Americans. The political fallout was immediate as President Wilson protested the attack. Months later, Germany gave assurances that passenger ships would be sunk only with prior warnings and appropriate safeguards for passengers. However, the seeds of discontent had been sown, and within two years, America entered World War One.

Throughout history, these types of events have played a pivotal role in influencing public opinion. I encourage you to review the Appendix, found after the end of the story. In the Appendix, you will find a list of fifty false flag events carried out by civilian organizations as well as covert, governmental agencies.

Previously in The Boston Brahmin Series

Dramatis Personae

THE LOYAL NINE:

Sarge – born Henry Winthrop Sargent IV. Son of former Massachusetts governor, godson of John Adams Morgan and a descendant of Daniel Sargent, Sr., wealthy merchant, and owner of Sargent's Wharf during the Revolutionary War. He's a tenured professor at the Harvard Kennedy School of Government in Cambridge. He is becoming well known around the country for his libertarian philosophy as espoused in his *New York Times* bestseller—*Choose Freedom or Capitulation: America's Sovereignty Crisis.* Sarge resides at 100 Beacon Street in the Back Bay area of Boston. Sarge is romantically involved with Julia Hawthorne.

Steven Sargent – younger brother of Sarge. He is a graduate of the United States Naval Academy and a former platoon officer of SEAL Team 10. He is currently a contract operative for Aegis Security—code name Nomad. He resides on his yacht—the *Miss Behavin'*. Steven is romantically involved with Katie O'Shea.

Julia Hawthorne – descendant of the Peabody and Hawthorne families. First female political editor of the *Boston Herald.* She is the recipient of the National Association of Broadcasting Marconi Radio Award for her creation of an Internet radio channel for the newspaper. She is in a relationship with Sarge and lives with him at 100 Beacon.

The Quinn family – Donald is the self-proclaimed director of procurement. He is a former accountant and financial advisor who works directly with John Adams Morgan. Married to ***Susan Quinn*** with daughters ***Rebecca*** (age 7) and ***Penny*** (age 11). Donald and

Susan coordinate all preparedness activities of the Loyal Nine. They reside in Brae Burn Country Club in Boston.

J.J. – born John Joseph Warren. He is a direct descendant of Dr. Joseph Warren, one of the original Sons of Liberty. The Warren family founded Harvard Medical and were field surgeons at the Battle of Bunker Hill. J.J. was an Army battalion surgeon at Joint Base Balad in Iraq. While stationed at JBB, J.J. saved the life of a soldier who was injured saving the lives of others. He later became involved in a relationship with former Marine Second Lieutenant Sabina del Toro. He finished his career at the Veteran's Administration Hospital in Jamaica Plain, where he also resides. He is affectionately known as the Armageddon Medicine Man.

Katie O'Shea – graduate of the United States Naval Academy who trained as a Naval Intelligence officer. After an introduction to John Adams Morgan, she quickly rose up the ranks of the intelligence community. She now is part of the President's Intelligence Advisory Board. She resides in Washington, D.C. Katie is romantically involved with Steven Sargent.

Brad – born Francis Crowninshield Bradlee, a descendant of the Crowninshield family, a historic seafaring and military family dating back to the early 1600s. He is the battalion commander of the 25th Marine Regiment of 1st Battalion based at Fort Devens, Massachusetts. Their nickname is *Cold Steel Warriors*. He is an active member of oathkeepers and the three percenters.

Abbie – Abigail Morgan, daughter of John Adams Morgan. United States senator from Massachusetts since 2008. Independent, with libertarian leanings. She resides in Washington, D.C. She has been chosen as the running mate of the Democratic nominee for president. She briefly became romantically involved with her head of security, Drew Jackson, aka *Slash*, on the Aegis team.

THE BOSTON BRAHMIN:

John Adams Morgan – lineal descendant of President John Adams and Henry Sturgis Morgan, founder of J.P. Morgan. Morgan attended Harvard, obtaining a master's degree in business and a law degree. Founded the Morgan-Holmes law firm with the grandson of Supreme Court Justice Oliver Wendell Holmes Jr. Among other concerns, he owns Morgan Global, an international banking and financial conglomerate. Extremely wealthy, Morgan is the recognized head of the Boston Brahmin.

Walter Cabot – direct descendant of John Cabot, shipbuilders during the time of the Revolutionary War. Wealthy philanthropist and CEO of Cabot Industries. He is part of Morgan's inner circle. Married to Mary Cabot.

Lawrence Lowell – descendant of John Lowell, a federal judge in the first United States Continental Congress. Extremely wealthy and part of Morgan's inner circle. Married to Constance Lowell.

Paul Winthrop – descendant of John Winthrop, one of the leading figures in the founding of the Massachusetts Bay Colony, his family became synonymous with the state's politics and philanthropy. The Winthrops and Sargents became close when Sarge's grandfather was governor of Massachusetts and his lieutenant governor was R. C. Winthrop. The families remained close and became a valuable political force on behalf of the Boston Brahmin. They have a French bulldog called Winnie the Frenchie. Married to Millicent Lowell.

Arthur Peabody – Dr. Arthur Peabody is a plastic surgeon in private practice. He is the youngest of the Boston Brahmin at age fifty-five. His wife is Estelle, affectionately called Aunt Stella. They are Julia's aunt and uncle. They're direct descendants of the Hawthorne and Peabody lineage.

General Samuel Bradlee – former general and Secretary of Defense. A direct descendant of Nathaniel Bradlee, one of the key participants in the Boston Tea Party. He is Brad's uncle.

Henry Endicott – great-grandson of former Secretary of War William Crowninshield Endicott. The Endicott family name is synonymous with warfare throughout the world as one of the largest manufacturers of advanced weapons systems in America. His third wife, Emily, is younger than some of his children.

ZERO DAY GAMERS:

Andrew Lau – MIT professor of Korean descent. A brilliant mind that created the Zero Day Gamers as a way to utilize his talents for personal financial gain.

Anna Fakhri – MIT graduate assistant to Professor Lau, of Arabic descent. She prides herself on her "Internet detective work." She speaks multiple Arabic languages.

Leonid "Leo" Malvalaha – MIT graduate assistant to Professor Lau, of Russian descent. He is very adept at creating complex viruses, worms, and Trojans used in cyber-attack activities. He speaks fluent Russian.

Herm Walthaus – newest member of the Zero Day Gamers. MIT graduate student. Introverted, but extremely analytical. Stays abreast of the latest tools and techniques available to hackers.

AEGIS TEAM:

Nomad – Steven Sargent.

Slash – Drew Jackson. Former SEAL Team member who worked briefly for private contractors like Blackwater. Born and raised in

Tennessee, where his family farm is located. He has excellent survival skills. He was assigned to Senator Abigail Morgan's security team that works with her Secret Service detail.

Bugs – Paul Hittle. Former Army Special Forces medic, who left the Green Berets for contract security work. He owns a ranch in East Texas, provided to him as compensation for his service to Aegis.

Sharpie – Raymond Bower. Former Delta Force, who now operates a lucrative private equity fund venture with former classmates from Harvard. He resides in New York City.

OFFICERS OF 1st BATTALION, 25th MARINE REGIMENT:

Gunny Falcone **–** Master Gunnery Sergeant Frank Falcone. Under Brad's command for years. A loyal member of the Mechanics. Stationed at Fort Devens. Primary on-base recruiter of soldiers to join the Mechanics.

Chief Warrant Officer Kyle Shore – young. Expert in sniping. Recorded two kill shots in Afghanistan at just over 2,500 yards. Stationed at Fort Devens. Also recruits members of the Mechanics.

First Lieutenant Kurt Branson – Boston native. A loyal member of the Mechanics.

SUPPORTING CHARACTERS:

Agent Joseph Pearson – special agent working for the Federal Protective Services—a division of Homeland Security. He first appeared at Fort Devens to meet with Brad in April 2016. A subsequent meeting at Fort Devens with Brad following the cyber attack became very contentious. He is now the special liaison to the Citizen Corps governor of FEMA Region I—James O'Brien. His office is located on High Street in Boston.

James O'Brien – president of the Boston Carmen's Union—one of the oldest and largest public service employees' unions in the city. O'Brien is a staunch supporter of the President and is known to have organized-crime connections. He is a fierce political opponent of Republican Governor Charlie Baker. He was named the new governor of Region I. His office is located on High Street in Boston.

Marion La Rue – Member of the International Brotherhood of Teamsters. Called upon by union leaders in Boston to undertake special union *activities*, including the orchestrated walkout of MBTA bus drivers during the St. Patrick's Day festivities.

J-Rock – Jarvis Rockwell, leader of the unified black gangs of Dorchester, Roxbury, and Mattapan in South Boston. He rose to power after the death of his unborn child during a race riot in Copley Square in April 2016.

Joe Sciacca – *Boston Herald*'s chief editor.

Malcolm Lowe – John Morgan's trusted assistant. Former undersecretary of state during Morgan's tenure as Secretary of State. He *handles* sensitive matters for Mr. Morgan.

Sabina del Toro – former Marine second lieutenant deployed to Iraq, assigned to the 6th Marine Regiment under the 2nd Marine Division based at Camp Lejeune. The 6th was primarily a peacekeeping force deployed throughout the Sunni Anbar province, which included Fallujah, just west of Baghdad. Sabs, as she prefers to be called, was seriously injured protecting children from a car bomb blast. She lost her left arm and left leg as a result of her heroics. She was in a relationship with J.J. She died in *Martial Law*, book three, during a confrontation with local residents.

Previously in The Boston Brahmin series

Book One: The Loyal Nine

The Boston Brahmin series begins in December of 2015 and the timeframe of *The Loyal Nine*, book one in The Boston Brahmin series, continues through April 2016. Steven Sargent, in his capacity as Nomad, an Aegis deep-cover operative, undertakes several black-ops missions in Ukraine, Switzerland, and Germany. The purposes of the operations become increasingly suspect to Steven and his brother, Sarge. It is apparent that Steven's actual employer, John Morgan, is orchestrating a series of events as part of a grander scheme.

Sarge continues to teach at the Harvard Kennedy School of Government. He begins to make public appearances after publishing a *New York Times* bestseller *Choose Freedom or Capitulation: America's Sovereignty Crisis*. During this time, he rekindles his relationship with Julia Hawthorne, who is also celebrating national notoriety for her accomplishments at the *Boston Herald* newspaper. The two take a trip to Las Vegas for a convention and become unwilling participants in a cyber attack on the Las Vegas power grid. Throughout *The Loyal Nine*, Sarge and Julia observe the economic and societal collapse of America.

The unraveling of society in America is evident as the chasm between the haves and have-nots widens, resulting in hostilities between labor unions and their employers. There are unintended consequences of these actions, and numerous deaths are the result.

Racial tensions are on the rise across the country, and Boston becomes ground zero for social unrest when a beloved retired bus driver is beaten to death during the St. Patrick's Day festivities. In protest, a group of marchers descend upon Copley Square at the end of the Boston Marathon, resulting in a clash with police. The protestors are led by Jarvis *J-Rock* Rockwell, leader of the unified black gangs of Dorchester, Roxbury, and Mattapan in South Boston. The march quickly gets out of hand, and J-Rock's pregnant girlfriend is struck by the police, resulting in her death and the death of their unborn child.

The Quinn family—Donald, Susan and their young daughters—are caught up in an angry mob scene at a local mall, relating to the Black Lives Matter protests. Donald decides to accelerate the Loyal Nine's preparedness activities as he gets the sense America is on the brink of collapse.

The reader gets an inside look at the morning security briefings in the White House Situation Room. Katie O'Shea becomes a respected rising star within the intelligence community while solidifying her role as a conduit for information to John Morgan.

John Morgan continues to act as a world power broker. He manipulates geopolitical events for the financial gain of his wealthy associates—the Boston Brahmin. He carefully orchestrates the rise to national prominence of his daughter, Senator Abigail Morgan.

As a direct descendant of the Founding Fathers, Morgan is sickened to watch America descend into collapse. Morgan believes the country can return to its former greatness. He recognizes drastic measures may be required. He envisions a reset of sorts, but what that entails is yet to be determined.

Throughout *The Loyal Nine*, the Zero Day Gamers make a name for themselves in the hacktivist community as their skills and capabilities escalate from cyber vandalism to cyber ransom to cyber terror. Professor Andrew Lau and his talented graduate assistants create ingenious methods of cyber intrusion. At times, they question the morality of their activities. But the ransoms they extract from their victims are too lucrative to turn away.

The end game, the mission statement of the Zero Day Gamers, is succinct:

One man's gain is another man's loss; who gains and who loses is determined by who pays.

Book Two: Cyber Attack

But who else loses in their deadly game? *Cyber Attack*, book two in

The Boston Brahmin series, begins with the Zero Day Gamers testing their skills by taking over control of an American Airlines 757. Throughout *Cyber Attack*, the Zero Day Gamers conduct various cyber intrusions, including compromising a nuclear power plant in Jefferson City, Missouri. But one of the Gamers, in an attempt to impress a young lady, makes a mistake. His cyber snooping into the laptop of Abbie Morgan following the Democratic National Convention is discovered.

Meanwhile, over the summer, the Loyal Nine increase their preparedness activities. Through some legislative maneuvering, John Morgan acquires Prescott Peninsula at the Quabbin Reservoir in central Massachusetts. The Quabbin Reservoir is the largest body of water in the State of Massachusetts. Located in the central part of the state, it was formed by the creation of dams and dikes in the 1930s and became federal government owned and was largely undeveloped. Prescott Peninsula is completely surrounded by the reservoir and was largely unimproved except for an abandoned radio astronomy observatory where the old town of Prescott Center once stood. The entire acquisition encompasses nearly forty square miles. He immediately tasks Donald and Susan Quinn with renovating the property into a high-tech bug-out location for the Boston Brahmin.

While Donald, Susan, J.J., and Sabs focus their attention on Prescott Peninsula, Sarge is making a name for himself on the speaker's circuit as a straight-talk libertarian. His relationship with Julia Hawthorne has grown, and they continue to observe world events with an eye towards preparedness.

After the hack of Abbie's computer, through some excellent cyber forensics on the part of Katie O'Shea, the Zero Day Gamers are located and contacted by Steven Sargent and Malcolm Lowe, acting on behalf of John Morgan. The three orchestrate a ruse upon Andrew Lau and his team of cyber mercenaries for hire.

Morgan has determined that America is descending into collapse, both socially and economically, and is in need of a reset. The Zero Day Gamers are the perfect tool to accomplish this purpose.

Morgan has conducted several private meetings with the

President, culminating with a face-to-face discussion in August of 2016. The two agree—a reset is necessary, and each will play a vital role in bringing America to its knees only to build the country back in their respective images. These two powerful political players navigate a complex game of chess, not realizing the unintended consequences on the people of America.

As *Cyber Attack* closes its final chapter in early September 2016, Andrew Lau is forced to make a choice. Does he watch his young proteges die by a gunshot to the head at the hands of Morgan's men, or does he push the button that will result in the end of life as we know it?

Book Three: Martial Law

Lau makes his choice, and his sophisticated cyber attack causes a cascading collapse of the Western and Eastern Interconnected Grid representing ninety percent of America's electricity. Only Texas, whose grid is not connected to the rest of the nation, is spared.

The Loyal Nine are scattered throughout the country. Each faces their own set of unique circumstances and challenges.

John Morgan, despite his meticulous, well-thought plans, makes one critical mistake—he loses track of his daughter's whereabouts. Despite his efforts, Morgan is unable to call off the cyber attack. This leads him to frantically arrange a trip to Florida to extract his daughter and bring her to safety. Just before, and immediately following the grid collapse, he communicates with Abbie's chief of staff to insist that Abbie meet him at Camp Blanding.

Abbie Morgan is in Tallahassee to give a campaign speech. Under the watchful eye of her ever-present protector, Drew Jackson, Abbie addresses a packed crowd at the Donald Tucker Civic Center. Then they are thrust into darkness. Within moments, thirteen thousand people are informed, via text messages and cell phone calls that America has been attacked and the power grid is down.

Drew, Abbie, and some of her entourage attempt to travel several hundred miles east to Camp Blanding, where John Morgan will meet them in his helicopter. First, they have to flee the inner city of Tallahassee, where nearly one hundred thousand people have congregated for the concert and a college football game.

During this night of terror, Drew and Abbie fight their way through looters, marauders, and the throes of Hurricane Danni. Within thirty miles of their destination, they run out of fuel near the small town of Lulu. This small community has been ravaged, not by the hurricane, but by escaped inmates from three of the worst prison facilities in Florida.

Daylight approaches, but the feeder bands of Hurricane Danni continue to obstruct visibility. With a borrowed car from an elderly victim of the inmates' violence, Drew and Abbie make their way to the rendezvous point. Within fifty yards of the helicopter, and safety, they are overrun by a group of attacking inmates. Drew pushes Abbie to the safety of her father, but he is savagely beaten and left for dead. As Drew reaches toward the helicopter, shouting, Abbie and Morgan leave him behind, much to the devastation of Abbie, who had fallen in love with Drew.

In Boston, Sarge and Julia are having drinks on the rooftop of 100 Beacon, having a deep conversation, when the transformers begin to explode. As the lights go out in waves throughout Boston, they immediately recognize this as a possible grid-down collapse event.

They immediately begin to implement their preparedness plan. First, they secure their perimeter. Next, they establish various means of communications and information gathering.

The first call Sarge makes is to John Morgan, who at the time is traveling to the heliport by private car. Morgan's orders are clear: gather up the Boston Brahmin and keep them safe. Sarge knows that this is his call to duty. But something else bothers him about the conversation. Morgan's words weigh heavily on his mind—*widespread, long-lasting*. For the past seven years, somehow Sarge knew this moment would come. What bothers him is the fact that so did John Morgan.

Sarge successfully gathers up the executive committee of the Boston Brahmin, but it does not go without incident. During his last pickup, Sarge is involved in a high-speed chase, with gunfire, through Chinatown. He unknowingly leads them right to the front door of 100 Beacon.

Steven and Katie are in Washington together, enjoying a few beers and shooting pool at a local hangout near the White House. As the grid collapses, they also recognize the need to get out of the major population center and return to Boston. But for Katie, work calls. She ignores her instructions to report to the Situation Room in the White House. She cannot, however, ignore the phone call from John Morgan with instructions to contact General Mason Sears, the chairman of the Joint Chiefs. Katie makes a choice to remain with Steven and loyal to her friends.

Katie is prepared for a bug-out scenario, and the two embark on a road trip through the Poconos toward Boston. They quickly learn that bugging out isn't easy, even when you are armed and prepared. They are attacked near a toll-booth exit and Steven is almost killed. Katie repels their assailants and nurses a badly injured Steven back to health.

But now their car is destroyed. Their gear and communications are lost. They only have their handguns and limited ammunition. They have to enter survival mode in a world without rule of law. Finding a car dealership, they commandeer a Range Rover and begin their trip northward. But another unexpected confrontation occurs.

Within miles of the last encounter, they see a young girl running in fear from a group of men who are chasing her through an industrial park. Steven and Katie give chase and save the girl, leaving four dead bodies in their wake.

At various junctures of their trip, the two meet people familiar with Sarge and his book. Some have tattoos of the Rebellious Flag—five red and four white vertical stripes. Several use the phrase *choose freedom* as a way of showing solidarity. Steven begins to see that Sarge's message is resonating throughout the country.

Finally, driving a FedEx delivery truck, the two make their way to Boston and the safety of 100 Beacon only to find it under assault by four Asian men. Steven, who quickly morphs into *Nomad*, despite his injuries, takes out the four attackers. The only thing standing between them and the top floors of 100 Beacon is a group of frightened residents firing wildly out of the front entrance. Not a problem for Nomad.

At Prescott Peninsula, the detailed preparedness plan implemented by Donald and Susan Quinn is on full display. They had successfully built a state-of-the-art bug-out facility on the old radio observatory site. J.J. and Sabina had grown close over the past several weeks and were officially a *couple*. Along with the Quinn's young girls, the four are enjoying a quiet Labor Day weekend away at the Quabbin Reservoir facility.

When the power goes out, the four are enjoying drinks and dinner in front of 1PP. Because of the lack of surrounding, ambient lighting, they don't realize the grid is down. Once they discover the situation, they begin to implement their preparedness plan.

Their first arrivals come in the form of the Morgan Sikorsky helicopter. Abbie is still upset over the loss of Drew and mourns for several days. As she calms down, Donald introduces Abbie and John Morgan to the sophisticated 1PP facility, which includes a gold and silver vault worth hundreds of millions of dollars.

Brad beefs up security at Prescott Peninsula. After a visit from a representative of Homeland Security, he senses that the President is about to declare martial law. Brad goes rogue and rallies the Mechanics led by Gunny Falcone, Chief Warrant Officer Shore, and First Lieutenant Branson. They systematically divert assets and like-minded troops to Prescott Peninsula. They are nearly at company strength in gear and numbers.

In the process of building up the military assets at Prescott Peninsula, Brad has to send a platoon to Boston. He gathers up the Boston Brahmin from 100 Beacon to take them safely to 1PP. Sabs, over J.J.'s objection, takes up the slack and joins the security detail at the gated entrance to the Quabbin Reservoir complex. In a confrontation with locals, she is shot.

J.J., with the assistance of Susan and Donald, tries valiantly to save his new love, to no avail. Sadly, Sabs dies on the table, together with his unborn baby, of which he has no knowledge. Susan and Donald wrestle with telling him, but the arrival of the Boston Brahmin and the upcoming address by the President puts the issue off for another day.

On the fifth night following the collapse, the President is set to speak to the nation through whatever means of communications are available. Susan overhears a conversation between two of the Boston Brahmin that leads her to believe there is something nefarious going on. Abbie, who has been having nightmares, finally comes to the realization of what happened the morning they left Drew behind. He was shouting, "He knew, he knew." *What did that mean?*

The President addresses the nation, but not with an uplifting message of hope and perseverance. It is divisive, condemning, and declarative. Through executive orders, the President quickly sets up a massive militaristic occupational force called the *Citizen Corps*. In conjunction with regional FEMA governors, the Citizen Corps will establish local Citizen Corps Councils that will fall under the control of the President and FEMA.

Then the President instructs General Sears to read the Declaration of Martial Law, which suspends the constitution and essentially revokes all freedoms guaranteed to American citizens by the Bill of Rights. *Freedom, liberty, and independence are lost.*

After General Sears reads the declaration, he receives a phone call from John Morgan. The four words that General Sears hears from John Morgan are plain and simple—yet chilling.

The end begins tomorrow.

False Flag begins now…

EPIGRAPH

The bigger the lie, the more it will be believed.
~ Nazi General Paul Joseph Goebbels
*****

Terrorism is the best political weapon for nothing drives people harder than a fear of sudden death.
~ Adolf Hitler
*****

The easiest way to gain control of a population is to carry out acts of terror. The public will clamor for such laws if their personal security is threatened.
~ Josef Stalin
*****

If tyranny and oppression come to this land, it will be in the guise of fighting a foreign enemy.
~ James Madison
*****

In politics, nothing happens by accident. If it happens, you can bet it was planned that way.
~ President Franklin D. Roosevelt
*****

It's easier to fool people than to convince them they have been fooled.
~ Mark Twain
*****

He that cries out stop thief is often he that has stolen the treasure.
~ William Congreve, English poet
*****

The smeller's the feller.
Southern Axiom

False Flag

Book Four

The Boston Brahmin Series

CHAPTER 1

Thursday, September 8, 2016
4:05 a.m.
265 First Street
Cambridge, Massachusetts

COGAS, combined gas and steam, permeated the nearly thirty-mile labyrinth of steel pipeline under the streets of Boston's government facilities, hospitals, businesses, and residential neighborhoods. The Kendall Cogeneration Station, located on the banks of the Charles River in Cambridge, was billed as a sustainable and energy-efficient alternative following the closure announcement of the Pilgrim Nuclear Generating Station.

Cogeneration is the process of combining steam heat with power by recycling waste heat and converting it into stored thermal energy. It was hailed as an environmentally friendly method of energy production that improved air quality and reduced carbon emissions. One official, who praised the project as being consistent with the President's desire to protect the environment, also proclaimed Kendall Station as the *beating heart and arteries* of the city's power generating system.

The nearly sixty-year-old Kendall Station was retrofitted with industrial jet engines, which utilized more than one million gallons of fuel oil stored at their facility across the Charles River from Massachusetts General Hospital. The French company that designed the system proudly proclaimed that the Kendall Station was positioned to jump-start the electrical grid following a blackout.

City officials pressured the company to bring the plant back online. After all, the plant was designed to function following a blackout just like this one. In the early morning hours of day five, after much of America was thrust into darkness, the Boston-based electrical engineering team at Kendall Station believed they had a solution that would refire the jet engines, immediately allowing the plant to produce two hundred fifty-six megawatts of electricity and one million two hundred thousand pounds per hour of steam. Relying upon satellite phone guidance from the expert troubleshooting team based in France, they initiated the necessary steps to return power to Cambridge and much of Boston.

As with all appliances, incidents with gas-fueled engines and turbines typically occurred during start sequences. The newer cogeneration plants in Europe—France and Denmark in particular—contained sophisticated auxiliary equipment, sensors, and control systems for the purposes of purging pressurized air within the network of piping. The latest technology incorporated into the European plants had large exhaust systems capable of handling significant volumes of stored COGAS during the restart sequence. It was recommended that forced ventilation should continue during idling of the jet engines throughout the start-up process, as high concentrations of unburnt gas could accumulate within the exhaust system and throughout the pipeline distribution network.

The team initiated the start-up sequence, but the turbines did not rotate. The engineers tried again, but nothing happened as the system misfired. They waited, heeding the warning to limit the number of start attempts. The team, and their French counterpart, was concentrating entirely on the firing of the jet engines. They did not focus on the requisite purging of combustible gases contained within the exhaust system and the pipeline network.

The team tried again and again. With each attempt, high concentrations of unburnt hydrocarbons backed up throughout the system. When the powerful jet engines finally fired for a moment, the team cheered and shared high fives. But after the engines groaned to a halt, dejection was the mood.

During the brief operation of the turbines, combustible gases were forced through the pipelines from Cambridge to the west, throughout Boston across the river. The steel pipes swelled, and the gases looked for a place to release—*to purge.*

Within minutes, the *beating heart and arteries* of the Boston power grid had an aneurysm.

CHAPTER 2

Thursday, September 8, 2016
5:51 a.m.
100 Beacon
Boston, Massachusetts

Sarge stood alone on the rooftop of 100 Beacon, staring across Cambridge in wonder of the darkness and the deafening silence that had overtaken his hometown, as Beantown was devoid of vehicle traffic. Ordinarily, Storrow Drive would be awake with commuters making their way downtown. The never-ending low hum of the vehicular traffic on the Mass Turnpike to his south would be evidence of Americans going about their lives, scurrying from one important destination to another.

Was this the new normal?

It had only been a few days since the cyber attack took away power and water from two hundred and ninety million Americans. America went from a nation enjoying Saturday night dinner dates or sporting events, to a country struggling to survive—under the specter of martial law.

Sarge was incredulous as he watched the arrogance of the President's press conference the night before. He was too wound up to sleep and took Julia's shift patrolling the rooftop and the rest of the top three floors of 100 Beacon.

Although information was limited, Sarge was privy to communications via the expansive network set up by Julia. Within a day of the grid collapse, they were fully informed. For other Americans, information was scarce. *Not knowing* consumed them initially. Then the realities that America was a *powerless* nation set in—as did the panic. On this sixth day, survival was all that mattered to most.

I knew this would happen!

Sarge's lectures at Harvard Kennedy covered a variety of subjects, including national defense, global governance, and the subject of world economics. He tried to be impartial in his discussions, but it was impossible to avoid inserting his world view when exploring these concepts. He warned his class about the fragility of society and the dangerous threats that one nation could pose to another. He talked about advanced weaponry like electromagnetic pulse weapons, bioterror, and, of course, cyber warfare. *Did his students prepare?* Doubtful. Sarge knew that most Americans who were interested enough to advanced their level of knowledge on these subjects still had enough doubt in their minds regarding the realities of these threats. Sarge had no doubt, and he prepared accordingly.

He ambled along the building's rooftop, periodically looking over the edge for signs of activity along the street. He kicked a pebble into one of the roof's scuppers and listened as it found its way down the drainpipe to the ground eleven stories below. He stopped and stared out across Boston Common to the southeast. It was completely deserted.

So this is what TEOTWAWKI looks like.

Sarge thought about this for a moment—the end of the world as we know it. *It doesn't have to mean it's the end of the world.* The situation was bad for most, but it could be worse. Sarge was exceedingly concerned about the events surrounding the cyber attack. He'd observed the increased Russian military activity along the U.S. coastal waters. Putin had amassed an army in the Arctic. All signs pointed toward a potential incursion onto American soil. It was the Russians modus operandi to use cyber attacks as a precursor to war. Estonia, Georgia, Ukraine, and Turkey had all experienced Russia's use of cyber warfare to collapse their financial institutions and critical infrastructure in advance of military action. With Americans losing hope every day, the country was weakened. Sarge hoped that the military was prepared for every contingency.

If the Russians are preparing for World War III, why is the President using American soldiers to clamp down on our constitutional rights by declaring martial law?

Sarge watched the sun begin to peek through the skyscrapers of Boston, bearing names like John Hancock, Prudential, and the Federal Reserve. Sarge doubted that John Hancock would find anything prudent about the Federal Reserve.

The situation throughout the country was dire. In the large urban centers, the impact was felt immediately. Opportunists seized the night, taking advantage of a shocked populace and an outgunned law enforcement community. As despair spread across the nation, even midsized cities felt the impact. Julia was able to confirm that although rural areas experienced the collapse of the grid, thus far they had been spared from the collapse of society.

Where do we go from here?

With the arrival of Steven and Katie yesterday, Sarge was able to lift that concern out of his mind. They had been out of communication for days, and despite Steven's extraordinary capabilities, Sarge was worried about his brother. His *making an entrance* was both theatrical and typical for Steven. *My brother is a magnet for excitement.* After a brief conversation, and some dinner, Steven started on the rest he needed to heal his gunshot wound. At some point, the four of them would have to discuss their future. There were so many issues to address.

Should they stay at 100 Beacon or travel to the rural safety of Prescott Peninsula?

If they remained in Boston, did they hunker down and react to events, or did they become active in any rebuilding effort?

But a troubling question hung over his head like a dark cloud. *Who caused this, and how long will it last?*

"Do we just try to survive?" asked Sarge aloud. He glanced down at the front entrance and then up and down Beacon Street, which was free from activity. The sun was getting brighter and he looked toward Cambridge. He wondered whether he would ever teach again.

He thought about the students he had taught over the last ten years. Then, his thoughts were interrupted.

CHAPTER 3

Thursday, September 8, 2016
6:13 a.m.
100 Beacon
Boston, Massachusetts

Intuitively, Sarge sensed it first. He felt it coming. Inexplicably, Sarge knew it would be devastating. In the relative quiet of Cambridge across the Charles River, a hissing sound filled the air. A gaggle of Canadian geese, which had been resting on the muddy bank of the river, suddenly took flight. Sarge brought his AR-15 to low ready as the first explosions shook the building.

A geyser of hot steam broke through Amherst Street, which traversed east to west through the heart of MIT. A shower of mud and flying debris rose into the dark sky until it was eye level to Sarge. The cloud of steam continued skyward and then a second explosion occurred to the east. Sarge ducked and then ran past the hot tub towards the cloud undulating into the morning sun.

The height and breadth of this explosion obliterated his view of Mass General, which was less than a mile away. The entire complex was engulfed in smoke. Drivers, apparently startled by the events, hit each other on Storrow and careened down an embankment towards The Esplanade.

Another explosion occurred across the river near the Charles River Dam. As 100 Beacon shook from the blast, Sarge ducked again and looked towards the sky. *Are we being bombed?* Then another violent eruption shook the ground. This time, a large crater formed at the base of the Longfellow Bridge connecting Cambridge to downtown Boston. A towering cloud of swirling steam rose into the sky for nearly four hundred feet.

Car alarms were sounding all around. Then another explosion came from the downtown area. Steam rose into the sky, taller than the newly completed Millennium Tower, which stood seven hundred feet above ground. For a brief moment, the rising sun was obscured by the debris, and then the winds created gaps allowing the light to shine through.

Sarge was mesmerized. It reminded him of a scene from the *Apocalypse Now* movie. The sound of collapsing concrete and steel snapped him out of his trance as he looked back towards Cambridge. Another blast widened the crater at the Longfellow Bridge. The structure had been compromised, and the central span of the bridge was giving way.

Panicked, some drivers were attempting to back off the bridge, but the steam swallowed them from view. Others frantically turned back towards the billowing steam that surrounded Mass General. Suddenly, the bridge gave way as the structure and deck of a two-hundred-foot span of Longfellow Bridge collapsed into the Charles River. At least a dozen cars sank to the bottom, only the red illuminated taillights indicating their path to the murky depths below.

A vehicle on the south side of the bridge caught fire. A pickup pulling a trailer rested precariously against the guardrail of the collapsed structure, near the burning car. Sarge could hear the screams of motorists on the bridge, attempting to escape the collapse.

"What's happening, Sarge?" screamed Steven as he ran onto the rooftop with Julia and Katie close behind. The sun was rising and their view of the carnage was getting better.

"Are you okay, Sarge?" asked Julia as she reached Sarge's side. The four of them looked from Boston to the east across the Charles to Cambridge in the west. The sky was dense with steam, silt, and flying debris. Longfellow Bridge continued to creak as it struggled to stand.

"I've counted at least a dozen explosions," said Sarge. "Look at the steam rising out of the ground." Sarge directed their attention to the massive craters left by the escaping steam and debris. Another vehicle crash distracted them momentarily.

"Were we bombed?" asked Julia. She was trembling as she hung on to Sarge's arm. She was badly shaken by this, or the culmination of the entire situation.

"No," replied Sarge. "I saw it. I mean, I felt it coming." Sarge looked at the ground, looking for the right words.

"What do you mean, bro?" asked Steven.

"I mean, I could tell something was about to happen, and then the ground began to erupt," said Sarge. He loosened his grip on his rifle and slung it over his shoulder. He turned his attention to Julia and gave her a reassuring look. "Something happened underground. It looks like a bad day at Yellowstone Park."

Moisture and debris began to fall on them from the north as the winds picked up. Steven shielded his eyes and looked around.

"Maybe we should get inside," said Steven. "I don't know what this stuff is, but it could be toxic." The four of them turned toward the stairwell when one final massive blast knocked them to the roof deck. The sound was deafening. Katie and Julia screamed as the guys scrambled to cover them.

In Cambridge, the Kendall Cogeneration Station, the latest-and-greatest innovation in green-energy production, disintegrated and took three city blocks with it. Lights out, for a long time.

Chapter 4

Thursday, September 8, 2016
8:42 a.m.
100 Beacon
Boston, Massachusetts

Julia stood at the window and watched as the clouds of debris began to dissipate. For over two hours, their views of Boston and Cambridge were obstructed. The reinforced windows Sarge had installed during the initial renovation of 100 Beacon withstood the blast, but the residents of the lower floors were not so fortunate. Virtually all of the windows on the east and north sides of the surrounding buildings were shattered, throwing bits and pieces of plate glass to the sidewalk below.

A pipeline explosion like this had happened before. In the summer of 2007, an underground steam pipe exploded during the evening rush hour at the Grand Central Terminal. Steam, mud, and pieces of concrete were hurled forty stories into the Manhattan sky. Dozens of people were injured during the blast, primarily from the panic at the busy intersection. The carnage Julia was observing was much worse. There were immense craters spewing steam in every direction of the city.

She tried not to be overwhelmed, but despair did cross her mind from time to time. She was safe, and they'd sufficiently prepared for a collapse event just like this one. But Julia wrestled with her concern for others. People aimlessly walked along the sidewalk, appearing lost and disoriented. Not only had they lost the lives they were accustomed to, but now their homes were destroyed. *Haven't people suffered enough?*

Katie joined her and stood silently for a moment, taking it all in. Finally, Julia spoke.

"This is unimaginable, Katie. Look at these buildings. This is not Ukraine or some city in the Middle East. This is our home, Boston. It looks like it's been bombed." Julia pressed her palms against the window, unconsciously trying to reach out.

"I know, Julia," said Katie. "We're very lucky." Katie put her hand on Julia's shoulder in an attempt to comfort her.

"It's not that we're lucky, Katie. We knew our country faced threats, and we prepared accordingly. But no one could have expected *this.*" Julia drew a line across the glass with her index finger, tracing the destruction from Cambridge to the north all the way to downtown Boston, where steam still billowed skyward. "We have to do something."

The stairwell door slammed, and Julia heard the guys' voices as they approached. She couldn't hide her emotions and a few tears streamed down her face. As Sarge and Steven approached, in an attempt to stay strong, she tried to cover her face.

Sarge knew her too well, however. "Honey, what's wrong?" he asked.

Julia tried, but couldn't contain her feelings any longer. She broke down crying. "Sarge, we have to do something for them." She sniffled out the words, waving her arm towards the windows. "They didn't deserve this. Is it fair for us to hide up here in our *fortified penthouses* while so many innocent people are suffering out there?" Julia couldn't hide her sarcasm.

Steven started to speak, but Katie grabbed his arm and pulled him back. Sarge took Julia in his arms and held her until she recovered. Julia had held it together during these first six days. The fast pace in which events occurred and the large amount of activity at 100 Beacon had kept her from focusing on the reality.

"I understand where you're coming from," said Sarge, breaking the tension. "This is a conversation that is overdue. But now that Steven and Katie are safe with us, let's talk. Okay?"

Julia, still sniffling, wiped her eyes with her sleeves and nodded.

The four made their way to the couches. Katie grabbed a bottle of water for Julia, who held it against her neck. Without the generator running, the interior of 100 Beacon was stuffy and warm. This had a calming effect on her.

"It's very dangerous out there, Julia," started Steven. "I've been shot a few times, but never on American soil. I knew things would suck after the collapse, but I didn't expect to be shooting at each other within days of it happening."

"I know, Steven," said Julia. "But what are we supposed to be doing?"

"Surviving," replied Steven. He slumped back into the sofa, wincing as his shoulder hit the padding.

"We are, but where do we go from here?" asked Julia. "I guess I'm just trying to get an overall view of what we're supposed to be doing." She looked to Sarge for guidance, as she was having trouble finding the words to express her feelings. Sarge rescued her.

"Listen, guys, let's not put too much pressure on ourselves right now to set a course for our lives," said Sarge. "First, let's be thankful we're still alive. Steven was shot and survived. These two were in three gunfights in five days. I was chased by people who clearly wanted to kill me—just because I made the mistake of driving through their neighborhood!"

"That's right," added Steven. "The situation is only going to get more dangerous. As people get more desperate, they will become a threat."

"And obviously, gangs are starting to form," said Katie. "The opportunists out there know there is strength in numbers. It's a matter of time before looting gets out of hand."

Julia listened to their words, but her focus was still on the injured and the people displaced from their homes. "I know all that," Julia said. "It's a matter of time before our neighbors, or thugs, try to beat our doors down. Isn't there something we can do right now, today, for the people who just had their asses blown up?" Julia shouted the last part of her statement. She could tell that the consensus was to stay put. Her gut told her she should try to help others. It would come back to them someday.

The room was silent for a few awkward moments. Sarge stood and walked towards the windows, hands in his pockets. Shaking his head, he turned and spoke.

"My, no, our number one priority is survival and staying safe. This may sound crass and insensitive, but those people out there are not our problem. Our decisions need to be practical, considering the risk versus the reward. There are—"

Julia interrupted. "What if we were the ones suffering from injuries? Look at Mass General. It's like a war zone! What's the harm in going over to offer a helping hand? I'm not saying we have to give up our food or guns or precious medical supplies. Let's just, you know, help somebody!"

Katie and Steven remained silent, and wisely so. Sarge would always be the one to make decisions for the group. This responsibility carried a heavy burden, especially after the collapse of society. Julia stared at him. She would not go against his wishes, but she would not be happy if he turned down her pleas.

"What I was about to say was," started Sarge, "there are bigger plans for us down the road. I'm not entirely certain about what caused these events, but that conversation can be held another time. I do know this. The Declaration of Martial Law by the President came quickly, as if prearranged. Steven and Katie's observations of National Guard placement in Washington was organized at warp speed. There are aspects of this that stink to high heaven. If my hunch is correct, I believe we will play a significant role in saving Boston and maybe our nation. But, in any event, we have to maintain our humanity."

Sarge walked back to the window, where the view of the city was becoming clearer. Julia joined him and held him around his waist. She whispered into his ear.

"I love you, Sarge. Let's see if we can help them. Even if it's just one."

CHAPTER 5

Thursday, September 8, 2016
10:35 a.m.
100 Beacon
Boston, Massachusetts

Sarge and Steven went over the final preparations. The group agreed that Steven would remain behind and monitor a rooftop position with the Barrett .50-caliber rifle. Sarge, Katie, and Julia were going to walk up Storrow Drive to Mass General. The walk, which was less than a mile, would take about ten minutes. Steven would provide them some cover for the first half of the trek, but after that they were on their own.

Sarge thought they could help with the victims, as well as get a sense of what was happening in the city. The martial law declaration just took effect the night before, but he doubted the more onerous provisions had been implemented already—such as gun confiscation. All three of them would carry a concealed sidearm as well as two radios to contact Steven in the event of trouble.

Sarge would never admit this to Julia, but this was a terrible idea, in his opinion. He believed in the concept of karma, to an extent, but willfully entering what looked like a war zone for an unknown purpose just didn't make sense. He needed to indulge Julia, not only because he loved her, but because she hadn't been out of the building to witness the devastation firsthand. Moreover, she had no idea how the collapse had affected people. Going to Mass General was a relatively safe way to show her the realities of a post-collapse America.

"Listen, Sarge, I need to talk to you about something before you go," said Steven. He pulled Sarge to the side, out of earshot of the girls. "It's about Katie."

"Don't worry, buddy, I'll keep her safe," said Sarge.

Steven looked past Sarge again and leaned in to whisper to his brother, "I'm not worried about Katie. I'm worried about anybody who might get in her way."

"Whadya mean?"

"Listen, when we were getting back here, she embraced this whole *without rule of law* thing a little too quickly. She's well trained and handles herself as good as you or I would in a dangerous situation. I think she might be a little quick on the trigger, if you know what I mean."

"You two went through a lot out there, Steven, she did what she had to do, right?" Sarge wasn't overly concerned, but wanted to hear Steven out.

"I agree, and she impressed the hell out of me. I'm just saying Katie didn't think twice about shooting a guy in the back because she assumed he was going after that girl to rape her or something. No *warning*. No *hey you*. No *stop or I'll shoot*. It was just *boom, done*. Another dead guy to notch on the bedpost."

"Well, did she waste any ammo in the process?" Sarge laughed, trying to make light of the situation.

"No, of course not. All I'm saying is that Katie may be turning into a *shoot first, ask questions later* kinda gal. In my experience, that is not always the best way to diffuse a dangerous situation. Gun battles should be avoided, not encouraged."

Sarge considered this statement for a moment. Steven had seen more gun battles than any human being should. He had more experience in combat than Brad. He had to respect his point of view on this. "Should we cancel this deal and maybe have a talk with her?"

"No, go ahead," replied Steven. "What could possibly go wrong between here and the hospital, right?"

"A ton, that's what. Are you saying Katie's a loose cannon? If so, this is a bad idea."

"I don't think so," replied Steven. "It could be she was being protective of me. I don't know yet. One thing is certain, though, you can count on her out there. I'd rather have a gunslinger by my side than someone afraid to use their weapon when needed."

"Okay, got it. Three or four hours, max. I'll let Julia get her fix. I hate to patronize her, but I think it's necessary for her to see what's going on out there. Plus, I want to see what's happening in other parts of the city. At some point, soon, we have to decide whether we are going to stay here or join the others out at Prescott Peninsula." Sarge adjusted his holster and covered it with his shirt.

"If it were up to me, we'd be on the *Miss Behavin'*, heading for Bermuda." Steven slapped Sarge on the back and the men walked toward the security door. "Alright, ladies, keep an eye on Sarge for me. He's not a very good shot."

"Get your ass on the roof." Sarge laughed. "Don't shoot me with that .50 cal if there's a problem."

Sarge descended the stairs with his hand on his weapon. He didn't anticipate any issues within the building, but he maintained a heightened state of awareness nonetheless. Julia stayed several steps behind him, and Katie brought up the rear, constantly surveying the doors from the other floors. They did not encounter any other residents. *Have they left?*

Stepping onto Beacon Street, Sarge stopped to scan for any hostiles, but his attention was quickly grabbed by the scene. The vehicles, including the FedEx van that Steven drove the day before, still blocked the road in front of them. Bullet holes riddled the van, and the lifeless bodies of the four assailants were lying in the road. Someone had covered them with a sheet, but birds were pecking away at the hand of one of the dead.

Julia gasped and held her hand to her mouth. As they cautiously walked toward the street, the smell of the decomposing bodies began to reach their noses.

"Come on, let's get away from this entrance before we're noticed," said Sarge. He quickly led them around the corner and towards Storrow and the Charles River.

"Katie, are those the men who were attacking the building yesterday?" asked Julia. She turned to look again, but Sarge grabbed her hand and urged her along. As they walked swiftly down the sidewalk, their feet crunched on broken glass. Sarge glanced up and to his right, noticing some residents of another building watching their movements. He could feel their eyes. *I don't like this at all.*

They crossed the median and walked along Back Street before finding the sidewalk. Sarge turned and glanced toward the top of 100 Beacon. Steven stood on the wall with his hat turned backwards. He was giving Sarge the middle finger. Yeah, *screw me too, bro.*

Dozens of stalled cars dotted Storrow as they walked briskly up the sidewalk. As they crossed Pinckney Street, some residents of a nearby building were standing on a balcony and began to shout at them.

"Hey, where are you going?"

"Do you have any food?"

"Do you girls wanna come up and party?"

Sarge moved between Julia and the fence and picked up the pace. He glanced at Katie to see if she was going to shoot them. Fortunately, she walked faster as well, but turned and walked backwards, not wanting to lose sight of the men.

Two hundred yards later, they caught their first glimpse of the river and Longfellow Bridge. The three stopped to take it all in. From the middle of the river, toward Cambridge, the bridge was gone. Both the east- and westbound lanes were collapsed. Emergency vehicles blocked the entrance ramp in front of them, but there were no officers accompanying the vehicles.

They made their way past Cambridge Street, which resembled a parking lot full of abandoned cars. The infamous Liberty Hotel, where the Bilderberg Conference was held just three months ago, was barricaded, and the entrance was manned by security personnel.

"Let's go this way," said Sarge as they entered Grove Street and followed the sign to the emergency room entrance. What they saw caused them to stop in their tracks. Hundreds of people lay in the open promenade typically used for patient drop-off and the emergency room entrance. A makeshift triage had been established for the victims of the pipeline explosion.

As they got closer, they could hear the moans and cries of the injured. The smell of burnt flesh filled the air. Julia and Katie immediately held their hands over their mouths. Julia was fighting back the tears. Sarge stopped them before they crossed Fruit Street.

He looked Julia in the eyes. "We don't have to do this. None of us are prepared for what we are about to see."

She looked at him and then surveyed the rows of temporary cots and the personnel scurrying about. "We have to try, Sarge." She pushed past him towards the barricades, where a single police officer was attempting to hold people back. A frantic hospital candy striper was attempting to check on the status of loved ones for the distraught family members gathered around.

Julia approached the officer. "My name is Julia Hawthorne, with the *Boston Herald*. We're here to—"

"Miss, no reporters," said the officer. "These folks have their hands full, can't you see that?"

"No, you don't understand," started Julia, but Katie interrupted.

"We have medical training and we're here to help," she said to the officer. "My friends and I can lend a hand wherever needed." Katie grabbed Julia's hand and pushed forward past the crowd, attempting to walk past the officer.

"You stop right there," he shouted. "Medical personnel only."

A doctor dressed in blue scrubs overheard the scuffle and approached them. "What's the problem here?"

"No problem, Doc, these people are trying to force their way in," the officer replied. "Now move along. I don't have time for this!"

The young doctor turned his attention toward Katie. "Did I hear you say you had medical experience?"

"We do," replied Katie. "All of us are trained in advanced first aid. You look like you could use a hand, or three."

The officer became distracted by a woman trying to walk around the other end of his barricade. The young doctor saw this as well and quickly waved them through.

Sarge extended his hand. "I'm Professor Henry Sargent from Harvard. These are my friends Julia Hawthorne with the *Boston Herald* and Katie O'Shea with, uhm, she works in Washington."

The doctor looked puzzled. Katie perked up and helped Sarge with the introductions.

"I'm a *spook*, or at least I used to be." She laughed.

"A what?" he asked.

Katie and Julia started laughing.

"Listen, that was another life. How can we help you, Doctor…" Katie searched for a name badge.

"Daugherty. I'm Dr. Judd Daugherty, a third-year resident here at Mass General. As you can imagine, we're a little shorthanded. This is the biggest mass casualty incident in the history of the hospital."

Mass General had a storied history. Founded in 1811 under the guidance of John Warren, an ancestor of J.J.'s, it was the original teaching hospital of Harvard Medical School. It was the third-oldest hospital in America and conducted the largest hospital-based research program in the world. It commanded the best of the best in the medical field, but it was clearly challenged by the events of the last four hours.

At this moment, Mass General was overwhelmed with the injured. The number of casualties far exceeded what Sarge envisioned, and he was glad that Julia convinced them to assist. These were Bostonians, and they needed help.

"Well, Dr. Daugherty, what can we do to assist?" asked Sarge.

CHAPTER 6

Thursday, September 8, 2016
10:35 a.m.
Massachusetts General Hospital
Boston, Massachusetts

Julia and Sarge followed Dr. Daugherty as he led the trio to a temporary scrub station. A table was manned by a nurse who was handing out clothing, gloves, and temporary badges.

"We've had our staff arrive without their scrubs or IDs," pointed out Dr. Daugherty. "Sadly, several of the injured are hospital personnel. One of the explosions occurred on the east side of the campus near the ambulance entrance. There's a thirty-foot-wide hole in the middle of Blossom Street. A part of the building collapsed and we began treating the injured in the ER." Dr. Daugherty motioned over his shoulder to the glass entrance of the emergency room.

He continued, "We lost generator power yesterday afternoon. The feds promised us more fuel, but nothing was delivered. When the injured started arriving at dawn, it was too dark inside the building to deal with the mass casualties. We had no choice but to treat the vast majority of the victims out here." Dr. Daugherty turned and looked across the asphalt entry. "Welcome to our new burn unit."

Julia tried to count the cots and the injured. She estimated three hundred injured and less than fifty hospital personnel. Some were dressed in scrubs, others were in street clothes. All wore masks to cover their nostrils from the smell.

"I've never smelled anything like this," said Katie.

"Some of the people were actually burned by fire as a result of the car accidents on the Longfellow," said Dr. Daugherty. "But the majority of the injured have been exposed to extremely high temperature steam and hot debris, which hit them without warning. I have to warn all of you, some of these injuries are grotesque. The most severe cases have been moved inside for treatment. But you will still see some third-degree burns, and you need to be prepared for that."

"How will we know what to do?" asked Julia.

Dr. Daugherty turned to the personnel manning the table and began to gather clothes, masks and gloves. He gave them each a blank identification badge and a black sharpie.

"Write your names on here and put *Daugherty* in parentheses underneath. That will let hospital personnel know that you are assigned to me. I'm going to take you on rounds and assign you to assist certain patients."

"We don't have any experience with burn victims," said Sarge. He didn't want the doctor to expect too much from them.

"I understand," he replied. "Listen, this is unprecedented for our staff. Come over here and let me give you an overview of our approach today."

Julia and Katie followed him as he walked toward some mobile racks filled with gauze, ointments, and other medical supplies. They were running low.

"Sarge," Julia whispered as they followed behind, "thank you for letting me do this. I wanted to help, but I also wanted to see. But you knew that, didn't you?" She stopped in front of him.

"I did," replied Sarge. "I'm glad we're here."

"Okay," interrupted the doctor. "Unfortunately, we have to triage these patients as if we were in a third world country or in a remote location without a hospital. Thanks to whatever it was that happened Saturday night, the medical treatment these patients will receive is not that different."

"With the power grid down, do you have to pick and choose which patients get priority?" asked Katie.

"That's true under any circumstances, Katie," replied Dr. Daugherty. "In a mass disaster event, the goal of the triage unit is to separate burn patients from trauma patients. Ordinarily, we would send them to the burn unit and others to the trauma center. What we are doing today is acting as a triage and burn unit for those who have experienced first- and second-degree burns. Although, as I said, there are some victims that indicate third-degree burns."

"How do you tell the difference?" asked Sarge.

"Well, a trauma patient has obvious life-threatening injuries, usually to the brain, internal organs, and certain extremities. We identified these patients and moved them inside to avoid exposure to bacteria."

"Aren't third-degree burns the worst?" asked Katie. They walked through the rows of patients as Dr. Daugherty stopped and looked at charts while he adjusted bandages.

"Yes. The degree or severity of most burns is determined by the depth and size of the burn. There is, technically, a fourth-degree burn where the damage caused by a third-degree burn extends beyond the skin into tendons or even bones. Clearly, that is a trauma case, and those patients are inside. Most of the third-degree burns—identified by a widespread thickness of blistered skin that has a white, leathery appearance—are also inside. We have to be careful with the third-degree victims because the damage can reach the bloodstream and affect major organs. I won't show you a third-degree burn."

Julia was fascinated by the learning experience. It would be difficult to leave the hospital today knowing that these patients required much-needed attention. Katie wandered ahead, and Julia caught Dr. Daugherty's eyes admiring Katie from the rear.

"Are you single, Doctor?" asked Julia.

"What? Uhm, yes, but please don't mistake what I was doing," stuttered the young, handsome doctor.

"It's okay, Doc, Katie is pretty, but she is taken." Julia laughed.

"No, it's not that," he said. "She's carrying, isn't she?"

Sarge stopped and looked at Julia. He had to trust this young man. "We all are, Doctor. It's not a very nice world anymore."

"You don't have to tell me that, look around you," said Dr. Daugherty. "Besides, I have a compact nine strapped to my ankle."

They walked and caught up to Katie staring down at a patient whose eyes were bandaged.

"How's he doing?" asked Katie. She brushed the hair out of her eyes.

"Sarge and Julia, I'll make this gentleman your first patient," said Dr. Daugherty. "He was brought in from the Craigie Bridge. When the last explosion took out the area east of the Kendall Square plant, steam and debris hit most of his upper torso. His eyes were severely damaged and so was his throat. We hope that he will be able to see again, but thus far he has been unable to speak."

"This is so sad," said Julia. "What can we do to help him?"

Dr. Daugherty picked up a clipboard and examined the notes. "He's due for a change of bandages and dressings. Everything you need is in the plastic bin under the bed. Do you need instructions on how to clean a wound and reapply the antibiotic ointments with loose gauze?"

Julia looked at Sarge and replied, "I think we can do that."

"All right, don't worry about his throat or eyes. I'll come back in a moment after I assign Katie a couple of patients."

"Okay," said Sarge. As Katie followed Dr. Daugherty, she shot back a glance and a smile. "She seems to be enjoying this. Well then, Nurse Julia, let's take care of our first patient."

Julia reached under the cot and pulled out the bin holding the supplies. Sarge reached in and pulled out an identification badge.

"Look, Julia, our patient has a name," said Sarge. "He's a professor at MIT—Andrew Lau. I'm Professor Henry Sargent from the Kennedy School. Hey, look at this. It's a bitcoin. Well, Professor Lau, this must have been your good-luck charm." Sarge flipped the coin into the air.

CHAPTER 7

Thursday, September 8, 2016
11:11 a.m.
Prescott Peninsula
Quabbin Reservoir, Massachusetts

Donald and J.J. stood on the front porch of 1PP and looked across the clearing, which had been filled with picnic tables resembling a medieval outdoor dining hall. The population of Prescott Peninsula consisted of sixteen Boston Brahmin, four members of the Loyal Nine, and a platoon of Marines who were constantly rotating in and out of Fort Devens.

They watched as the group ate a lunch prepared by Susan, and Mrs. Peabody. Donald had successfully assigned duties and shifts to all of the Boston Brahmin and their wives. Most were accepting the fact that their lives had changed substantially, and they needed to make the best of it. Only Mrs. Lowell seemed to be bitter, and Donald intended to find out why. Her attitude was substantially different from the other Brahmin wives.

"Donald, I've got to get out of here," said J.J., breaking the silence. "Whenever I look across the opening, I visualize Sabs sitting here with us, having a beer. Then, that helicopter comes into my line of sight. It's that contraption, and the arrogance of John Morgan for bringing it here, that got Sabs killed."

Donald stayed quiet for a moment, not knowing what to say. It was hard to find the right words to help a grieving friend. Laying the blame at the feet of John Morgan might not be fair. Intruders attempting to gain access onto Prescott Peninsula were inevitable. Sabs was a soldier, and she knew the risks of going on patrol and protecting the gate. On the other hand, Donald was proud of the stealth way he'd brought this project together over the last one hundred days. All of the OPSEC practiced by him and his team was for naught when the Sikorsky came sailing in that night.

"You can't go back to your home, J.J., it won't be safe."

"I know. I'll take a bunk at 100 Beacon. Hell, I'll take my chances on the streets or helping out at the VA hospital. Donald, I'll lose my mind if I stay here."

"I get it, buddy," said Donald, patting his friend on the back. "Let's talk about it later. They're winding up lunch, and Brad is going to bring us up to speed on what he's learned from his command." The two men walked down the porch steps and joined the others as Brad stood to address the group.

"Everyone, let me get started, if you don't mind," said Brad as he stood between 1PP and the tables full of new residents. "I think this *daily briefing*, as Donald calls it, is a great idea. We're all hungry for information. I think it's important that we hear it from one person rather than second- or thirdhand. This helps prevent the dissemination of inaccurate news and prevents undue speculation about the events going on around the country."

"First, let me address the issue of last night's address by the President. Because I am skeptical of the President's intentions, I undertook to contact my superiors to determine how much of this declaration would be put into practice and what provisions were merely designed to be a deterrent against unlawful behavior. The information I've received indicates the President is sincere in his words. He aims to create a police state and is using the cyber attack as his justification."

Donald looked into the faces of everyone to gauge a reaction. Most were shaking their head in disbelief. John Morgan remained stoic, unaffected by Brad's statement. He continued.

"The President is moving swiftly to implement his executive orders. At this point, there has begun a gradual rollout of government control over Americans. Travel is being restricted through periodic checkpoints. The Department of Homeland

Security has established VIPR checkpoints at critical bridge crossings across the country."

Art Peabody raised his hand. "What does VIPR mean?"

"VIPR stands for Visible Intermodal Prevention and Response team," replied Brad. "The VIPR teams are designed to protect critical infrastructure, transportation in particular, during times of national emergencies like terrorist attacks. I've been told that the VIPR teams are taking it one step further. They are restricting traffic between locations. For example, they're restricting traffic in and out of D.C. Local municipalities, in an attempt to restrict refugee access to their towns, are following suit."

"That's understandable," interrupted Lawrence Lowell. "Wouldn't most cities and towns want to take care of their own first, then worry about outsiders later?"

"That may be true on the local level, but there's more to it nationally," replied Brad. "In addition, the checkpoints have established a satellite communications network with the U.S. Northern Command in Cheyenne Mountain. USNORTHCOM has stepped up their assistance of state and local law enforcement in enforcing the President's Declaration of Martial Law. The checkpoints are detaining citizens based upon certain criteria."

"What are the criteria?" asked Donald.

"I don't know yet," replied Brad. "I have been summoned to meet the new Citizen Corps governor of FEMA Region I. I expect to learn more then. From what I have been told, our unit is going to perform both a security function as well as a law enforcement capacity. It's as I suspected the other day, which was confirmed last night. The Posse Comitatus Act has been ignored by this president."

"What else have you learned, young man?" asked Brad's uncle, Samuel Bradlee.

"Sir, there are rumors of crackdowns on free speech and the rights to assemble," replied Brad. "In Atlanta, a group of people carrying Confederate flags marched into the city, demanding to speak with the Citizen Corps governor of FEMA Region IV. From what I'm told, the governor sent National Guard units into Forsyth County, which is one of the most conservative counties in north Georgia, searching out certain families. They were alleged to have committed treason against the United States. They were arrested without a warrant, removed from their homes, and their assets were seized. This happened *before* the President's announcement last night."

Susan stood up and asked, "How is this happening so quickly? The government is always a model of inefficiency."

"Susan, I'm as surprised as you are," replied Brad. "I know there are mechanisms in place for continuity of government and defense of our borders. But I believe this administration has taken extraordinary measures to gain control of the population. Further, it appears that the President has a pretty good idea of which Americans will be loyal to him and which ones are a threat to his power."

Donald watched Morgan and Abbie during Brad's discussion. While Abbie seemed interested in Brad's revelations, Morgan appeared to be disinterested, almost uncomfortable by the details. He looked at his watch several times during the course of Brad's statement. *You gotta catch a train, Mr. Morgan?*

Brad continued. "There is one more thing. Apparently a steam pipeline that runs through the city from a generation plant in Cambridge has exploded." Brad paused to allow the chatter to die down.

"Was it a terrorist attack?" asked Art Peabody. His wife held his arm for comfort.

"We don't know yet," Brad replied. "I'm told that the mayor was pushing the company to bring the system back online when something went wrong. At dawn, the steam buildup was too much for the system and began to explode out of the ground. Supposedly, a large span of the Longfellow Bridge collapsed into the river. Hundreds of people have been injured."

J.J. leaned in and whispered to Donald, "I'm going with Brad to help. The hospitals will be short-staffed under the circumstances." *Great.* Now J.J. had an excuse to go back to Boston. Mr. Morgan wouldn't like the fact that their only doctor wanted to leave.

CHAPTER 8

Friday, September 9, 2016
3:00 p.m.
Citizen Corps Region I, Office of the Governor
99 High Street
Boston, Massachusetts

James O'Brien had paid his dues, and now he was being rewarded for his efforts and *talents*. O'Brien thought he'd reached the pinnacle of his career when he was elected President of the Boston Carmen's Union nine years ago. He had been into battle with lawyers, administrative law judges, and recently, Governor Charlie Baker. He always had his membership's best interest in mind, and they loved him for it. O'Brien, who stood about five feet six inches tall, was known for standing up for the little guy. Now, he'd been handpicked by the President to be one of ten newly installed Citizen Corps governors, who would have unimaginable powers and control. *It's time to rattle some cages.*

"Sir, your first appointment is here," announced a casually dressed assistant that was O'Brien's nephew.

"Let's get started, then," he replied. "Send him in." O'Brien settled his portly frame into the chair at the head of the conference room table. The seal of FEMA Region I hung prominently on the wall behind him.

"Good afternoon, Mr. O'Brien," said the gentleman from the Department of Homeland Security. "My name is Joe Pearson. I'll be your liaison to the President as we move forward."

"Well, Pearson, it's good to meet you," said O'Brien gruffly without standing or shaking hands. "Sit down, and let's get right to it, shall we? What exactly will you do to assist me in my new job?"

"Sir, the President is making certain federal assets available to you for the purposes of carrying out his Executive Order 13777."

"For example?" asked O'Brien. He leaned back in his chair and lit a cigar. *Governor O'Brien may smoke wherever he wants.*

Pearson sat for a moment before speaking. "The President's goal is to help as many as possible cope with this disaster. He's concerned about their health and safety. He wants to quickly distribute food and necessary supplies. He wants to make sure all Americans have decent housing."

"Well now, Pearson, that is the plan, isn't it? Help people?"

"Yes, it is. That's where the Citizen Corps comes in. I am here to help you establish local Citizen Corps Councils and to—"

O'Brien blew out a puff of smoke and held up his left hand. "Let me stop you there, Pearson. I'll have no trouble picking the right people to head up *MY* team. What I need to know from you is when do I get the tools necessary to take control of *MY* region. I need to implement the rules and regulations envisioned by the President to restore order. I need the food, medicine, and supplies to distribute to those Americans who get with the program, if you know what I mean." O'Brien didn't like Pearson. He was typical of all snotty-nosed bureaucrats. But, if the man delivered, O'Brien would cut him some slack.

"I understand," said Pearson, clearly uncomfortable at O'Brien's approach.

"There need to be some controls in place; otherwise there would be anarchy. Don't you agree, Pearson?"

"I do, Mr. O'Brien," responded Pearson.

"Governor," snapped O'Brien.

"Governor?" asked Pearson.

"Yes, *Governor O'Brien,*" he replied. "You see, Pearson, our country is descending into lawlessness. People who've had it the best in this country now think they can run things. They live in houses ten times bigger than what they need. They drive around in their fancy cars, not once riding the public transportation system our government provided them. They have pantries stocked with food and swimming pools full of water. These rich fools don't give a rat's ass about the little guy.

"They will learn to spread the wealth around, one way or another. They will also learn to respect my authority, as granted to me by the President. I am now the duly appointed governor, and I will be treated accordingly. Are we clear?"

"Yes, of course, Governor," replied Pearson sheepishly.

"Now, the first order of business is I need the military to help me move forward," said O'Brien. "I want you to sit tight while I meet with one of my commanders. Peter! Send in the next appointment." O'Brien took another drag on his cigar and studied Pearson. *I showed him.*

His nephew Peter opened the door, and Brad entered and immediately stopped. The cigar smoke had filled the room, making it uncomfortable for any nonsmoker.

"Close the door behind you, Peter," said O'Brien. "What's your name, soldier?" O'Brien never had much use for the military in the past. But now, they were *his* military.

"My name is Lieutenant Colonel Bradlee of 1st Battalion, 25th Marine Regiment based at Fort Devens," said Brad. Brad looked around the room before adding, "Hello, Agent Pearson. I'm surprised to see you."

O'Brien sat back in his chair. *These two don't like each other.* "Have a seat, Colonel. I'm James O'Brien, duly appointed governor of Region I by the President. I take it you two know each other."

"We do, Governor," replied Pearson. "We've met at Colonel Bradlee's office on two occasions."

O'Brien didn't rise through the ranks of the union without being able to analyze body language and know what his adversaries were thinking. If there was animosity between them, so be it. *One will keep tabs on the other for me.*

"Good," said O'Brien. "The first order of business is to establish a few ground rules. First, nothing happens in my region unless I know about it. Second, we all serve at the pleasure of the President. He has a vision for restoring our country to greatness. We will follow all of his directives, even if they don't necessarily align with our own point of view. Third, when I need something, it's as if the President himself asked for it. Are we clear?" O'Brien purposefully took a deep draw on his cigar and filled the air to the point it even nauseated him somewhat.

"Yes, Governor," said Pearson.

Brad sat silently for a brief moment, staring at O'Brien. Finally, he spoke. "What can I do to help?"

"I need security established around this building, Colonel," replied O'Brien. "Put in place your best soldiers. Once the word gets out that this office has been established, I don't want every Tom, Dick, and Harry thinking they can stop by for a chat."

"Okay," replied Brad dryly.

"There's one more thing, Colonel. I want to train my own security force to conduct the initiatives outlined by the President. In Massachusetts, I have handpicked forty-four men for this purpose. I will have them report to Camp Curtis Guild for training Monday morning. I expect you to personally oversee their training, Colonel. Pearson, I want you to make sure they receive all the equipment they need to pursue the missions required by this office. There are forty-four armories located in Massachusetts, one for each of my men. Do whatever it takes to give each of them access immediately. Are we clear?"

"Governor, the Massachusetts National Guard armories are controlled by Governor Baker," said Pearson.

O'Brien slammed his hand on the table and stood. "Charlie Baker don't run anything anymore, you hear me? I do! Why? The President said so. Now, I want the keys to those armories. My men will be equipped to conduct the business of this office. Got it?"

"I'll take care of it," said Pearson.

O'Brien turned towards Brad. "What about you?"

"I'll see your people at oh-eight-hundred Monday morning, *Governor*."

CHAPTER 9

Friday, September 9, 2016
7:20 p.m.
Citizen Corps Region I, Office of the Governor
99 High Street Rooftop
Boston, Massachusetts

O'Brien stood on the rooftop of 99 High Street and stared out across Boston Harbor. He had big plans for this city, and the rest of the states in Region I—Connecticut, Rhode Island, Maine, New Hampshire, and Vermont. Boston was the big prize for him. It was his home. Controlling Boston would be critical to establishing his power base. Then he could deal with the other states within *his region.*

"Well, look at you, Mr. Governor Big Shot!" exclaimed a voice out of the darkness.

O'Brien turned and started to laugh. "Marion, my friend!" he shouted back. "You are the only man who can get away with that. Come on over here and share a drink with me." The two men shook hands heartily, and O'Brien poured them a drink. He lit another cigar.

Marion La Rue was a longtime member of the International Brotherhood of Teamsters until he retired. He was periodically called upon by union leaders in Boston to undertake special *projects*, which included orchestrating the walkout of MBTA bus drivers during the St. Patrick's Day festivities. Most of his assignments required months of planning and were flawlessly executed. Although the death of Pumpsie Jones was unforeseen during the St. Patrick's Day project, it ultimately helped gain the MBTA union the upper hand.

"Am I allowed to call you Jim, or should I use *your highness*?" La Rue laughed. The men clinked glasses and downed the scotch. They both stood at the edge of the roof and stared off into the rapidly disappearing daylight.

"Isn't this somethin'?" asked O'Brien.

"Sure is. I'm glad you found me. I took the missus and our stuff over to my sister's place. When your guys showed up at the door, I almost shot 'em. When they told me you were the new governor, I told them to kiss it and slammed the door in their face."

O'Brien's whole body shook with laughter. "Listen, I'm still shocked by these events too. This whole situation presents a tremendous opportunity for us, my friend. Before I tell you what I have in mind, I need to know if you're in. You and I have been friends for thirty years, Marion. We need each other now more than ever."

La Rue poured another glass of scotch and drank it all. He poured each of them another glass. "Of course I'm in, Jim. But you've got all the power. What do you need me for?"

O'Brien pulled up a chair at an outdoor dining table and motioned for La Rue to do the same. "I'm a believer in turning a crisis into an opportunity. I need someone I can trust implicitly, not these mopes assigned to me by the government."

"Obviously, I'd take a bullet for you, Jim. You know that. So what's the plan?"

"Region I encompasses a lot of territory. I need to establish myself with the people of these other states, but I think it all starts right here in Boston." O'Brien tapped his index finger as he spoke. "Once I get Boston under my control and running the way I want it to run, the rest of the region will follow by example. Of course, if they don't, then we will have ways of dealing with that."

"You have a solid base of support here," said La Rue. "The unions have a strong representation in the community. We just need to get in touch with them and tell them what to do."

"Yes, that's part of it. To gain respect as their governor, I also need to give the rest of the population a reason to believe in me. Listen, power is not only what you have, but it's what your adversaries think you have. Our people, the *working men and women*, will respect us because we're the same. It's the money people, you know, the ones who bought their yachts and big houses on our backs, that need to understand who's runnin' things now."

"So what do we do about them?" asked La Rue.

"In a normal world, before the lights went out, a threat is usually more terrifying to scare people than the thing itself. For example, when the blacks invade the malls, do you see the fear in the eyes of people? Black people aren't there to rape, pillage, and burn. But the whites that fill up these malls don't know that. They think just the opposite. So they're afraid."

"Are the tactics the same now that the power has gone away?" asked La Rue.

"Not necessarily. Remember, a good tactic is one that your people enjoy doing the most." O'Brien took another swig of the scotch and winced. He was feeling good now.

"So, do you want me to round up the blacks and send them to the malls?" asked La Rue.

O'Brien laughed and toasted La Rue. "Very funny. No, what we need are some useful idiots. I don't want to get in bed with the blacks necessarily, but I do have a plan for them. Tell me what you know about the gangs of Boston." O'Brien stood and walked next to an air-conditioning unit. He began to pee while La Rue spoke.

"Let's start with the blacks who are primarily located to the south in Mattapan, Roxbury, and Dorchester. They have never been able to coalesce as a unified group until recently. At the Boston Marathon, a large group of gang members came together as part of a Black Lives Matter march. The leader of the Academy Homes gang in Roxbury is a kid named Jarvis Rockwell. They call him *J-Rock*." When O'Brien returned, La Rue took his turn at the *restroom*.

A full glass of scotch awaited his return. La Rue continued. "The Academy Homes gang, representing a large territory in central Roxbury near Martin Luther King Boulevard, has about five hundred members. J-Rock rose up the ranks starting as a runner, and graduated to enforcer by age sixteen, when he supposedly committed a double murder against an encroaching gang. At age twenty-three, he was the undisputed leader of the Academy Homes gang. At the Marathon, he marched side by side with his pregnant girlfriend and the leaders of the Franklin Field Boyz and the Castlegate Road Gang. I guess they found a common purpose. Anyway, you know how that ended. The thing got out of control and J-Rock's girlfriend lost their baby."

"Is he still runnin' things?" asked O'Brien.

"As far as I know," replied La Rue. "Afterwards, he sat down with the leaders of the rival gangs mafia-style and they all came together. Jim, they've got a small army down there."

"What about the Mexicans?" asked O'Brien.

"You mean the El Salvadorans out east?"

"Same thing."

"Kind of," said La Rue. "They're brutal. A Central American drug cartel known as *Mara Salvatrucha,* or MS-13, predominantly operates in the East Boston ghettos, though they recently started to spread out all over the city. They're headed up by a banger named Joaquin Guzman. This guy's been deported four times, but he keeps coming back."

"You say they're brutal?"

"They're rapists and conduct murders using machetes, like those ISIS radicals. MS-13 already controls the alien smuggling routes along the Mexican border. They've teamed up with al-Qaeda terrorists and run the largest Islamic terrorist smuggling network in the country."

"That's a helluva combination," said O'Brien.

"Then we have the Asians in Chinatown," said La Rue. "They're different from MS-13 and the blacks. I guess I could call them *businessmen.* MS-13 is all about demanding respect and revenge killings. They're heavy into drugs. The black gangs just want to loot and steal. But the Asians operate a huge oxycodone-running operation as well as legitimate businesses, but with an iron fist. They're led by a white guy."

"You're kiddin'me, right?" asked O'Brien.

"Nope. He goes by the nickname *Bac Guai John*, or White Devil."

"Seriously?" O'Brien filled their glasses with the last of the scotch.

"He's got quite a story, like a celebrity. Hell, they did a whole article on him in *Rolling Stone* magazine."

"Does he think he's John *the-teflon-don* Gotti?" asked O'Brien.

"Pretty close." They both sat silently for a few minutes and finished their drinks.

"Can they be controlled?" asked O'Brien.

"They're all businessmen, Jim," replied La Rue.

"Listen up, here's what I want you to do."

CHAPTER 10

Saturday, September 10, 2016
8:20 a.m.
Massachusetts General Hospital
Boston, Massachusetts

J.J. was filling his backpack with medical supplies when Katie and Steven came down the stairwell. He wanted to be left alone. Sabs was on his mind constantly, and he felt the anger come back. For years after his retirement, J.J. carried a lot of anger with him. He was disappointed in the lack of appreciation the veterans of the wars in Iraq and Afghanistan received in the media and by politicians. The mistreatment of vets at the VA hospitals made it worse.

Gradually, with the help of the Quinns, the anger over the atrocities of war and lack of respect for the soldiers who did their duty subsided. Falling in love with Sabs put his life on a new course. Then she was ripped away from him, by a bullet, on American soil. He tried to save her, but her wounds were too severe.

He hurriedly finished packing because he wanted to leave. He was not ready to engage in idle conversation.

"Hey, Doc!" said Steven. "I'm glad we caught you. We were thinking about tagging along. You know, it's really not safe on the streets alone. Katie and I've got cabin fever and were gonna check things out around the building anyway."

J.J. could tell Steven was trying hard to be chipper. It didn't matter. "Thanks, but no," he said. "I'd rather go alone." He started for the stairwell and Steven followed him.

"Listen, Doc, I know you're going through a rough time. But you are too valuable to us to get hurt by some thug wanting to steal your backpack or something."

Katie added, "Plus, let me introduce you to Dr. Daugherty. He's a great guy and really cares about his patients. I'm sure you two will hit it off, and he can help you hit the ground running. C'mon, J.J., let us walk you over there."

J.J. knew they were right, of course, so he acquiesced. Katie and Steven strapped on their weapons and made J.J. do the same. He hadn't thought of carrying his sidearm before, and he was glad they brought it to his attention. *Maybe I am in a fog.*

The trio walked quietly to Mass General, taking a different route than the day before. As they turned onto Cedar Street in the heart of Beacon Hill, J.J. was amazed at how deserted the streets were. Vehicles were abandoned in all directions. The intersection of Pinckney and Cedar was completely blocked due to an accident. But there were very few pedestrians. No one was willing to make eye contact with them, much less engage in conversation. Bostonians were scared.

As they approached the entry of the hospital, J.J. was pleased to see that the patients had been moved inside. Sarge had described the scene to him last night when he arrived at 100 Beacon. J.J. was concerned that bacteria in such a non-sterile, open-air environment could cause infection for the burn victims.

Security had been increased as well. When Katie was able to gain access by using her hospital badge, J.J. realized that bringing them along was a good idea. They quickly located Dr. Daugherty, who had only slept a few hours since his arrival on the scene Thursday morning.

"Hi, Katie," said Dr. Daugherty. He pointed up and down the corridors. "As you can see, we've moved everyone inside, but there aren't enough beds to take care of everyone. More came in throughout the day Friday, and rooms are assigned based upon severity of wounds. Also, the ER has been filling up with gunshot victims."

"It's not going to get any easier for you, Doc," said Steven, extending his hand. "I'm Steven Sargent. This is our friend Dr. J.J. Warren. As I'm sure you know, the Warren family founded Harvard Medical and were field surgeons at the Battle of Bunker Hill. J.J. was an Army battalion surgeon at Joint Base Balad in Iraq."

"Nice to meet you, Dr. Daugherty," said J.J. as the two men shook hands. "Most recently, I helped PTSD victims at the VA Jamaica Plain campus."

"Call me Judd. Without a doubt, we can use a doctor of your capabilities and experience. Our immediate need is to help the burn victims, but I have to say, I've never seen this level of despair among the patients or their family members. I don't know if it rises to the level of post-traumatic stress disorder, but it's the closest I've witnessed."

"And I'm J.J. In a nutshell, there are five types of PTSD, ranging from a normal stress response to the most severe cases of complex PTSD. The complex cases, which are also called disorder of extreme stress, are usually found among individuals who have been exposed to prolonged traumatic circumstances, such as childhood sexual abuse." The group moved against a wall as two orderlies pushing a gurney sped past them.

"My guess is that the vast majority of your patients are undergoing a normal stress response to this single event. Their response will be characterized by intense bad memories, emotional numbing, feelings of unreality, or bodily tension and distress. These patients usually achieve complete recovery within a few weeks. I suggest a group debriefing experience for both patients and family members. Debriefings would begin by briefly reliving the event and discussing the survivors' emotional responses to the event. I would put an emphasis on the survival aspect. Without diminishing their trauma, they need to be reminded that they *survived*."

"You mentioned other types of PTSD, J.J. What are those?" asked Katie.

"Well, there is acute stress disorder that is characterized by panic attacks, confusion, paranoia, and being unable to perform basic daily functions. The next level is called uncomplicated PTSD, which involves the re-experiencing of the traumatic event. Finally, there is PTSD comorbid with other psychiatric disorders. These patients already have psychiatric issues that are exacerbated by the traumatic event."

"It will be difficult to diagnose these PTSD levels in this chaotic environment," interjected Dr. Daugherty.

"That's true," said J.J. "You don't have sufficient personnel, whether trained or otherwise, to conduct a proper evaluation. The best you can do is interview and counsel the obvious cases."

"Dr. J.J. Warren, welcome to the team," said Dr. Daugherty. "Are you up for it?"

"I am if you'll have me," replied J.J. "I'm glad to be able to help."

"Judd, may I check on a few of the patients we helped the other day?" asked Katie.

"Sure, Katie. Just go to the nurses' station, flash your hospital ID badge, and they'll help you out. I'm gonna show J.J. around."

J.J. and Dr. Daugherty started down the hall.

"I'll be honest, you're the first person I've met named Judd," said J.J. "Your accent is Southern, isn't it?"

Dr. Daugherty laughed. "Oh yeah. Back home they referred to me *as J-U-Double-D Party Daugherty*. After med school, the party train pulled out of the station. Let's get you into some scrubs."

CHAPTER 11

Saturday, September 10, 2016
8:20 a.m.
Massachusetts General Hospital
Boston, Massachusetts

Katie led him to the nurses' station, where an older woman was frantically trying to help several family members locate their loved ones. Lack of computer technology and phone communications took her out of her routine. The woman was in a frenzy and accomplishing very little.

"I'm going to try to help her for a moment, and then I want to check on this list of patients Julia wrote out for me," said Katie as she stood on her toes to give Steven a kiss on the cheek. "Stand over there, stay out of the way, and if you lay eyes on any of these cute nurses, I'll crush your nuts. Fair enough?"

"Damn! I'll be a good boy and stay out of trouble." Steven kissed her back and watched as she returned to the nurses' station to offer her help. He had never been in love with a woman before. Katie was clearly someone he could spend the rest of his life with, as best they could in this post-collapse world.

A commotion at the stairwell grabbed his attention and he instinctively felt for his weapon. Some uniformed soldiers were making their way up the stairs and pushing civilians out of the way. They approached the nurses' station.

"Who's in charge here?" yelled one of the lieutenants at Katie. Steven inched closer to the desk. Clearly, these guys were in a foul mood. Two other men joined his side.

"Stop barking orders," said Katie, leaning in to see the soldier's name. "Lieutenant Rose, I'll try to help you, but you are scaring people who have had a rough couple of days."

Steven moved to the side to get a better view. *Rose! What brings you here?*

He immediately recognized Second Lieutenant John Rose, who had represented the 1st Brigade Combat Team at the exercise hosted by Camp Edwards last summer. Rose and Steven had battled it out in more ways than one during the training competition, including a simulated knife fight, where Steven made Rose look foolish. Based on attitude, Rose needed a refresher course.

He slammed a photo on the counter and stared Katie down. "We're looking for this man. Have you seen him?"

Rose was part of the 10th Mountain Division stationed at Fort Drum, New York. *What are they doing in Boston?* Steven moved to intervene. Katie stepped back from the counter with a three-ring binder containing the names of the patients admitted to the hospital.

"What's his name?" she asked.

"Mike Austin. He's a fugitive and he's wanted for questioning."

Steven walked up to Rose, and the other two soldiers moved toward him.

"Aren't you boys a little bit out of your jurisdiction?" asked Steven. "In case you haven't noticed, this is Boston, not New York."

"What?" screamed Rose, who spun around to face Steven. "Sargent, is that you?"

"Rose, you need to tone it down, pal. Perhaps you left your manners at Fort Drum."

"Shut up, Sargent, this is military police business," said Rose, pointing at the Citizen Corps patch sewn on his sleeve. "Stand down while we conduct it. Last time I checked, *you are a civilian*."

Steven got into Rose's face. "And you're still a douche bag. You wanna go for another round outside. I'd enjoy kicking your ass, again, in front of your friends."

Katie intervened. "Guys! Enough! Lieutenant Rose, there is nobody here by that name. Now please, calm down and leave."

Rose ignored Katie and stood nose to nose with Steven, who returned the glare. "It's your lucky day, Sargent," Rose hissed through his teeth.

"You need to find some mouthwash, asshole."

"Let's go, men," instructed Rose as he pushed his way past Steven. "We'll see you around, Sargent."

"You better pack a lunch and bring a few more friends next time, Rosey," Steven shouted to their backs as they walked toward the stairs. Katie joined his side as the long line of people looking for their loved ones suddenly disappeared.

"What the hell was that?" asked Katie.

"Rose is a douche!"

"Obviously you two have a history, and you can tell me all about it later," she said. "But you can't blow up the hospital, *Mr. Badass*."

Steven caught his breath and he started to calm down. The veins returned to his neck where they belonged. "Fine. You're right. I'm sorry."

"Much better, Steven," said Katie. "Let me look at this list Julia gave me and see if I can locate any of them. Hold on." Katie went back to the nurses' station and began to flip through the list of patients. She suddenly stopped and returned to Steven.

She grabbed him by the arm and pulled him to the end of the hallway past several wide-eyed patients. Steven seemed to have an effect on the onlookers.

"What's wrong?" asked Steven.

"You'll see. Come on!"

They approached a nurse who was standing just inside the patient's room.

"May I help you?" she asked. Katie showed her the hospital badge as they entered the room.

"Yesterday, I helped Dr. Daugherty attend to this man," said Katie. "How's he doing?"

"Somewhat better," replied the nurse. "His hearing has returned, but his eyesight is limited due to the burns. We've kept him under sedation until just a little while ago. He's able to respond to commands and seems coherent. A few more days, and his sight will gradually return."

"That's good news," said Katie. "May I talk to him?"

"I think so, for just a moment." The nurse remained in the room.

Steven wandered over to the window and peeked through the blinds. He stared at the collapsed Longfellow Bridge. *Everything is collapsing.*

"Andrew, are you awake?" asked Katie. Steven turned to see the patient lift his hand.

Katie gently grasped it and spoke again. "My friend was helping take care of you yesterday. The nurse says you're doing better."

He squeezed her hand once. Steven looked at the nurse, who was smiling. Katie looked nervously at him and then at the nurse.

"Oh, that's a good idea. You can squeeze my hand once for yes, twice for no."

He squeezed it again, once.

"Is this your bitcoin on the table?" she asked. No squeeze. *Bitcoin?*

"I've brought my friend with me today. Would you like to meet him?" One squeeze. Katie hastily motioned for Steven to come over to the side of the bed.

"I want you to meet Professor Andrew Lau from MIT."

Steven froze. *Are you kidding me?*

CHAPTER 12

Saturday, September 10, 2016
6:45 p.m.
100 Beacon
Boston, Massachusetts

Brad gave Gunny Falcone and CWO Shore some final instructions and sent them back to Prescott Peninsula. He needed time away from the activity of 1PP to talk strategy with Steven and Sarge. A lot had happened in the week since the cyber attack. Brad needed to have a few drinks, decompress, and come up with a plan to deal with Governor O'Brien and Pearson.

As he entered 100 Beacon, the first thing he noticed was a lack of security. He climbed the stairwell and carefully opened each door—looking for signs of life. The building appeared to be abandoned. Did everybody leave? Were they dead? At what point would he and his men be ordered to conduct door-to-door searches in a city with nearly a million people?

He activated the biometric keypad and made his way to the top floor. Julia greeted him as he entered the Great Hall.

"Brad, I'm so glad you're here." She gave him a much-needed hug and led him toward the kitchen island, where a makeshift bar had been set up.

"What's your pleasure, sailor?" Katie asked with a laugh.

"Whisky, dirty glass," replied Brad. Steven and Sarge joined the group and shared some backslaps with Brad. It had not been that long since they were all together, but under the circumstances, it seemed like an eternity. Brad downed his first glass. "Hit me again, bar wench!"

"Hey, soldier, you better be careful." Steven chuckled. "She may just knock your ass out!"

Katie filled his glass and the group made their way to the couches. Brad looked around for J.J.

"Where's our Armageddon doctor?" he asked.

"He's gonna work at Mass General for a few days as they clear the patient backlog from the explosions," replied Steven. "He really needs to clear his head anyway."

"He took her death personally, you guys," said Brad. "I'm told he reluctantly let her go out on patrol to begin with. Then, when he couldn't save her…" Brad looked into his glass before he drank it down. He stood and walked to the bar and poured himself another. *I need this.*

"We understand," said Julia. "We all loved Sabs and considered her one of us."

Steven raised his glass in a toast. "A toast to the fallen." They all clinked glasses and finished their drinks. While they were refilled, Brad walked through the room and looked into the darkening Boston skyline. He caught his breath and walked back to the group.

"There's a storm brewin'," said Brad as he sat down. "This Governor O'Brien is a real piece of work."

"Here's what I know about him," said Julia. "The paper did a background story on O'Brien years ago when he took the helm of the Carmen's Union. He's known to be hard-nosed. He's almost a throwback to the fifties era of union bullying tactics. His battles with Governor Baker over the MBTA are legendary. There is absolutely no love lost between those two. In fact, they don't speak to each other."

"He's got a Napoleon complex, from what I've seen of him," added Sarge. "In his public appearances, he's overly aggressive and domineering."

"What do you think he has planned, Brad?" asked Katie.

"He wants his own personal military force," replied Brad. "He's taking this martial law declaration very seriously. He's almost, uhm, opportunistic."

"In other words, he has an agenda and he plans to use his new power to settle some scores," said Sarge.

"You nailed it, Sarge," said Brad. "Sounds like a certain President I know who went on and on about fundamentally changing America. It's been changed all right."

"Maybe I should just take him out," offered Steven.

Brad laughed, although he was aware Steven was serious. "I'm afraid they would replace him with another like him," said Brad. "At least this guy is predictable. I also think he can be manipulated. I have a plan for that."

Brad spent the next hour talking with the group about his plan. He would be putting a lot of trust and responsibility upon one of his men. But they all agreed that it was time for them to ramp up the Mechanics and be prepared for the inevitable violent clashes with some of their fellow Americans.

"What are you hearing from our friends in the military?" asked Julia.

Brad took another sip of his drink and exhaled. "Martial law is considered a public law of necessity," he replied. "Ideally, the President will never have to declare martial law in response to a national crisis. The best scenario envisions the nation responding to such a crisis with civilian agencies in the forefront and the Department of Defense in its traditional support role. You'd really like to see the communities pull together to help each other."

"Katie and I saw that on our road trip back from D.C.," said Steven. "In rural Pennsylvania and New York, small towns seem to rally and circle the wagons around their friends and neighbors."

Julia leaned forward on the sofa. "You guys know I've been monitoring communications across the country," she said. "The cities are falling apart, and the rest of the nation is hanging tough. State and local governments seem to be doing okay, except in the mid- to large-size cities. Cities like Chicago, Detroit, and Memphis are on fire."

"The military has been ordered to enter some of these areas, but they're considered too dangerous," added Brad. "When state and local law enforcement or first responders become overwhelmed in an environment of chaos and panic, one of the President's obvious options for restoring order would be to declare martial law. We may see this response as an extreme option, well beyond what is contemplated under the Constitution relating to disaster-response actions or limited military support to civilian law enforcement authorities."

"Naturally, I'm not in favor of the President's declaration of martial law because it is too broad in scope," said Sarge. "I agree that *necessity* should be a mandatory precondition to impose a state of martial law. Necessity justifies the declaration and implementation, but it should also measure the extent and degree to which it should be employed. This President has used necessity as a justification for suspending the Bill of Rights. It's an overreach."

"I agree, Sarge," said Brad. "I've studied the Army Techniques Publication, ATP 3-39.33: *Civil Disturbances*. The Army details preparations for full-scale riots within our borders which may deem the deployment of troops a *necessity*. The ATP provides various scenarios under which the Constitutional rights of American citizens can be suspended in times of civil unrest."

"Why didn't the President use the powers granted under this publication?" asked Katie.

Sarge stood and paced the floor. "Because he has bigger plans," he replied. "It's logical that a President should be able to impose martial law to preserve the nation, even if not explicitly authorized in the Constitution. President Lincoln once asked: '*Are all the laws, but one, to go unexecuted, and the government itself to go to pieces, lest that one be violated?*'"

"In other words, if the Prez decides the Constitution should be set on fire, who are we to argue? Am I right?" asked Steven. He slammed his empty glass on the table in front of him.

"Some might argue the President should have the inherent authority, in fact, the responsibility, to preserve the nation in a time of extreme crisis, even if it means taking actions in contravention of the Constitution."

"Because he considers the action a *necessity* and in the nation's *best interests*," said Steven sarcastically.

"That pretty much sums it up," added Julia. "This is why elections matter. The President is using the collapse of our nation as an opportunity to exert his ideology on the entire nation and to stomp on his political opposition. This is much worse than the societal war we experienced between the *haves* and the *have-nots*. This is a battle for the heart and soul of America's freedoms."

Brad nodded and raised his glass in Julia's direction. *Well said.*

"People are going to have to pick a side," said Sarge. "Are you a patriot, or are you a loyalist to this tyrannical government that has arisen out of this crisis?"

They sat quietly for a moment until Steven spoke, breaking the silence. "There's one more thing. Today, I went with Katie to Mass General, and I ran into someone I know."

"Yeah, our old friend Rose," interrupted Sarge. "You need to know this, Brad. Soldiers from Fort Drum are wearing Citizen Corps badges on their uniforms. They busted into Mass General looking for a so-called *fugitive*. Do they have jurisdiction here?"

"Well, none of the normal rules apply anymore," replied Brad. "First off, it's a violation of the Constitution for any military members to be acting as domestic police personnel on American soil. But after Thursday night, as we just discussed, they ripped the Constitution to shreds and threw it out the window."

"It's going to become very difficult to determine who the good guys are under these circumstances," said Sarge.

"Yeah, but I'm not talking about Rose," said Steven as he stood up and began to pace the floor. He stared out the window, hands in his pockets, before he spoke again. "Last month, Mr. Morgan sent me on an operation with Malcolm Lowe."

"Malcolm Lowe, Morgan's do-boy?" asked Brad.

"That's the one," replied Steven. "He actually did a good job, although I'd forgotten about the details until something jogged my memory today."

"What was the op?" asked Brad.

"He sent us undercover locally to hire a hacktivist group called the Zero Day Gamers. They were the group that hacked into Abbie's computer after the Democratic National Convention in July."

"What did he hire them to do?" asked Sarge.

"We don't know," replied Katie. "But a couple of weeks ago, Morgan had Steven and his Aegis team abduct the hackers and deliver them to a warehouse."

"Then what?" asked Brad.

"I don't know," replied Steven. "Lowe handled it at that point, and his own team took over security. We were pulled out of the equation."

"What are you guys saying?" asked Sarge.

"I'm saying that I don't believe in coincidences, that's all," replied Steven.

CHAPTER 13

Monday, September 12, 2016
8:00 a.m.
Camp Curtis Guild
Reading, Massachusetts

Camp Curtis Guild, a Massachusetts Army National Guard Reservation located fifteen minutes north of Boston in Reading, was commissioned in 1916 during the First World War. CCG, known for its variety of training facilities, was widely recognized in the law enforcement community as the location of their SWAT competitions. It was an ideal location for the training of military and law enforcement personnel. Today, it was going to be used for the training of Governor O'Brien's Citizen Corps enforcement team leaders—a mixed bag of union thugs, criminals, and tough guys.

Brad and First Lieutenant Kurt Branson stood alone at the entrance of the sixty-five-thousand-square-foot maintenance facility that was ironically shaped like a stealth bomber. Brad had plans for the new governor, and 1LT Branson had to be *stealth* to make it work. As the vehicles carrying O'Brien's men began to enter the parking area, Brad took this opportunity to give Branson a history lesson.

"George Washington was a master of deception. The fight for our independence was a story of patriots and acts of great sacrifice, Lieutenant. You are about to play an important role in what I see as a similar battle against a tyrannical government."

"Yes, sir," said Branson. "I understand what needs to be done. It will be hard for me to give even the appearance of disloyalty to you and my principles. But it is necessary, sir."

"Thank you, Lieutenant. During the Revolutionary War, General Washington utilized a wide variety of intelligence-gathering methods. Some of the people who performed these missions paid the highest price in order to forge a new nation."

Some of the new arrivals shouted greetings to each other. Brad knew that this group would be tight-knit, exhibiting the kind of camaraderie necessary for a fighting force. Unfortunately, their ideals and purposes would be misguided. Brad continued.

"Washington had a passion for intelligence gathering, and he recruited the best people to spy for him. His spies developed elaborate cover stories and backed up others to protect themselves. They were adept at sending information via code and other covert methods. But they were especially successful at military deception and counterintelligence."

"I have to gain O'Brien's trust first, right, sir?" asked Branson.

"When he arrives, don't move too fast or he'll suspect something," replied Brad. "You're a smart guy. The opportunity will present itself. Play on his ego. When you meet our governor, it will be real obvious that his ego is as big as his belly."

"Yes, sir."

"As your relationship with O'Brien becomes more secure, we'll begin feeding him false information. If you're good at it, he'll believe you. If he suspects something, well, just be aware of shifting winds, Branson. Don't put yourself in danger."

"No problem, sir," said Branson.

O'Brien parked his red Cadillac ATS in the grassy area in front of the building and extricated himself with a lot of effort from the front seat. He made his way toward Brad and Branson.

"That has to be him. He walks like the Penguin character in the Batman movies." Brad stifled a laugh, as did Branson. *He was gonna do just fine.*

"Good morning, Governor," said Brad, using his best impression of greeting a superior. It took Brad a tremendous amount of effort not to show his disdain for O'Brien. "Welcome to Camp Curtis Guild, the best training facility in the Massachusetts Guard."

"Yes, it is, that's why I picked it." O'Brien bristled. "Are all of my men here?"

Brad caught his breath. "Governor, they appear to be arriving now," he replied. "We are ready for forty-four trainees. I would like you to meet Lieutenant Branson. He's our best *trainer*."

"Branson," gruffed O'Brien.

"Hello, sir," said Branson. "It will be an honor to train your men, sir."

"Good," said O'Brien. He turned as the first group began to approach.

"Sir," said Branson to O'Brien, "I would be remiss if I didn't make a suggestion."

"What is it, Lieutenant?" asked O'Brien.

"Well, sir, you're the most important person in Massachusetts and the northeastern part of the country," started Branson. "Arguably, you are one of ten critically important people in the nation, charged with the responsibility of rebuilding America."

O'Brien stood a little taller and his chest puffed out with pride. "That's true, soldier."

"Sir, you should not drive yourself anywhere," said Branson. "You should have a uniformed, military security detail with you at all times."

O'Brien studied Branson for a moment and then spoke. "You're right, young man, I should be well protected," said O'Brien. He turned towards Brad. "A man of my stature should have a *captain of the guard*. This man is only a lieutenant. I want you to elevate his rank to captain, effective immediately!"

You pompous fool! Why don't I just kick you in the nuts instead!

"But of course, Governor," said Brad, gritting his teeth. Former First Lieutenant, now honorary Captain, Kurt Branson was smiling. "Well, Captain Branson, I will get you those bars forthwith."

"Thank you, sir," said Captain Branson, saluting his colonel. Then Branson, inappropriately, but for effect, saluted O'Brien. "And thank you, Governor, for the confidence you have placed in me. I look forward to training these men and molding them into the leaders you envision."

O'Brien returned the salute. Brad could tell that he was hooked on the attention.

"After training today, Captain, you will escort me back to my offices," said O'Brien. Addressing Brad, he used the incorrect designation and said, "Commander, I want you to assign your best men to Captain Branson to act as my protective detail. Is that understood?"

"It is, Governor," replied Brad. "I'll handpick them myself." *You can count on it.*

"Sir, if there is nothing further, I'll gather the men and we'll get started," said Branson. He left as O'Brien and Brad turned their attention to an approaching Pearson.

"Good morning, gentlemen," announced Pearson as he joined them. "I wanted to attend the first day of training to make myself available to you, Governor."

Brad stood silently, attempting to avoid conversation with Pearson. Brad sensed that Pearson was always probing him, trying to determine Brad's intentions.

"I have some interesting news for you both from the Western White House," started Pearson.

"Is this something that I should have been made aware of through more direct channels?" asked O'Brien. "As governor, I shouldn't receive information *second hand*."

Pearson shifted uneasily and Brad watched the power struggle between the two men. Brad planned to drive a wedge between these two and ultimately create a rift of distrust.

"I've been told by a friend in Hawaii that the President has asked the United Nations to increase its presence here and in Mexico," said Pearson. "The U.N. has amassed troops along the Texas-Mexico border as a show of force."

"Are they going to invade Texas?" asked O'Brien.

Brad became concerned at the thought of this. Texas continued to defy the President by not complying with his executive orders or his authority in general. Governor Abbott easily tripled his Texas State Guard with volunteers. The ranchers had a sizable contingent assisting them in closing the borders with neighboring states.

"It's a possibility," replied Pearson. "Abbott's activities, and those who agree with him, are un-American. There are people in need around this country, and Texas refuses to share their good fortune. The President addressed an emergency session of the United Nations General Assembly by satellite. He asked for, and received, a resolution calling on Governor Abbott and the people of Texas to cease all hostilities against the United States. They were instructed to stand down as U.N. peacekeeping and humanitarian forces entered the state for the purposes of gathering food and supplies for the rest of America."

"It's about time!" exclaimed O'Brien. "Why should Texas have it easy? Abbott's pretty selfish, in my opinion."

Brad shifted uneasily on his feet. He wanted no part of this conversation. He'd already expressed his opinion in front of Pearson too many times in the past. He needed to tone it down, or they would use it against him.

"The President agrees with you, Governor," said Pearson. "They're calling the border with Mexico, which follows the path of the Rio Grande River, the *blue line*."

"Why not the red line?" asked Brad. "Doesn't the President refer to *crossing the red line* as a point of no return, like drawing a *line in the sand*?" *You know, like the red line he establishes and then quickly ignores once it's crossed.*

"The blue line is a media term," answered Pearson. "It refers to the fact that the United Nation's colors are blue."

"Makes sense," muttered Brad.

Pearson continued. "The U.N. is determined to keep the borders open between Mexico and the U.S. per the President's instructions," said Pearson. "The U.N. has pledged its willingness to move into the U.S. in any capacity deemed necessary by the President."

"Do you mean an occupation of America?" asked Brad, unable to contain himself. "We are perfectly capable of taking care of ourselves." Pearson and O'Brien exchanged a glance. *I knew it! They baited me into a reaction.*

"Colonel, it appears there have been mass defections across the country by our soldiers and law enforcement personnel," said Pearson. "Apparently, they felt it was important to put their needs ahead of their country."

"Have you had defections?" asked O'Brien.

"We have experienced soldiers leaving," replied Brad. "That is a real problem. I've heard this from other base commanders around the country."

"So, you would agree that a United Nations presence is necessary to keep the peace, since our military is depleted or otherwise occupied," stated Pearson.

This guy sounds like a damn lawyer. "That's not up to me," replied Brad. "First Battalion, 25th Regiment stands ready to help our country get back on its feet. We're ready to do whatever it takes." *Even if it means taking you two down.*

CHAPTER 14

Monday, September 12, 2016
6:00 p.m.
Citizen Corps Region I, Office of the Governor
99 High Street
Boston, Massachusetts

As newly *ordained* Captain Branson entered the conference room at 99 High Street, he found O'Brien pacing the floor. He took Brad's advice to heart and tried not to come on too strong with his *governor*, but the opportunity to gain his confidence worked out perfectly. O'Brien and Pearson watched the training exercises most of the day before getting bored. Captain Branson had no intention of creating leaders out of the band of thieves designated the Citizen Corps enforcement team. In fact, the physical aspect of the training today made them look more foolish than like leaders.

This was Branson's first opportunity to be alone with O'Brien and Pearson. He would have to tread lightly to further gain their trust.

Pearson announced himself as he entered the room. "Great training day, don't you think, Governor?"

Good start.

O'Brien pulled up a chair at the end of the table and crushed the cushion as he sat. "I thought so too, Pearson," he replied. "Captain, you seemed to work them pretty hard at times. These men aren't soldiers, they're leaders. I need them to understand tactics, not how to run through an obstacle course."

"Yes, sir, I understand," said Branson. "The training schedule for the week will be progressive in nature, sir. I'm trying to take a twelve-week basic-training matrix and condense it into a week or so. Certain aspects can be eliminated, but they'll be ready when I'm done with them."

"How long?" asked O'Brien. He motioned for Pearson and Branson to sit. "When will they be ready?"

"I think I can have them ready by Monday to perform basic law enforcement functions," replied Branson. "You refer to them as *team leaders*. May I assume that they will have subordinates under their command? And will they require similar training, sir?"

"I need them ready by the end of the day Thursday," said O'Brien.

"Ready for what, may I ask, sir?" asked Branson.

"Ready to do the President's business, that's what!" O'Brien sternly replied. "In case no one has noticed, there is chaos in the streets and I need a fighting force to deal with it. *My people!*"

Branson was taken back by O'Brien's sudden change in mood. He went from a normal state of mind to a much more volatile attitude. His face showed the sudden shift as well. Even Pearson noticed it.

"Of course, sir," said Branson, trying to pacify the man. "I will accelerate their program. Is there anything in particular you'd like me to focus on?" Branson was probing, trying to see what the governor had in mind.

"Arrest procedures, for starters. They need to learn how to quickly gain control of a situation and subdue someone who refuses to cooperate with their demands. I want them to learn advanced interrogation techniques as well. They also need a day of weapons training."

"Speaking of weapons, the President is insisting that we try to get all weapons off the street," said Pearson. "I can provide you some suggestions based upon successes in other jurisdictions."

"Let's hear them," said O'Brien.

He was calming down again. Branson observed these highs and lows in O'Brien's demeanor. He was an open book. This would make it easier to manipulate him. Branson had already used the *fear-then-relief* procedure earlier in the day. By playing on O'Brien's ego, he was able to elevate his importance while placing an element of fear in the back of O'Brien's mind. Branson was able to disarm O'Brien's defenses, which made him less likely to be mindful or make rational decisions. Branson had easily manipulated O'Brien into accepting him as head of his security detail.

Pearson continued. "Two things have helped in this regard. First, the governors are ordering all gun stores and pawnshops to turn over their weapons to the Citizen Corps. This not only removes a large portion of weapons off the street, but it helps arm the newly designated law enforcement personnel in performing their duties."

"How the hell does that work? Do we just send them a certified letter?" O'Brien laughed. "What's the other suggestion?"

"In my capacity with Federal Protective Services, I am able to gain access to the National Guard armories in your jurisdiction, Governor," replied Pearson. "This option is a little tricky politically and requires more time to implement. But it is an option for you."

O'Brien sat back in his chair as he clearly pondered his options. Branson didn't like either one. Arming his band of thieves with a large arsenal was not an option. He needed to buy some time and report this back to the colonel.

"Sir, may I make a suggestion?" asked Branson.

O'Brien didn't answer, but waved his hands as if to indicate *by all means*.

"Organizing a group of men to confiscate weapons from local gun shops would be a fast and effective way to get weapons for your team. We could use them to train as well. I presume that under the President's Declaration of Martial Law, you are not required to give notice of such activity. Am I correct?" Branson looked at both Pearson and O'Brien for the response he anticipated.

"Yes, we can do whatever we want," replied O'Brien. "What do you have in mind?"

"Well, sir, during tomorrow's training session, let me handpick four men for this task," replied Branson. "I will identify those men who seem to be more advanced than the others. You know, capable of getting the job done, sir."

"I like the way you think, Branson," said O'Brien. "Then what?"

"Tomorrow evening, under your authority, sir, this team will go store to store and confiscate every last weapon and box of ammunition," replied Branson. His mind was reeling. He needed to get Pearson involved somehow. "If Mr. Pearson doesn't mind assisting, he could work with the men tomorrow afternoon at Camp Curtis Guild and prepare a list of stores for the first night's work."

"Sure, I'd be glad to help," said Pearson. "I just need to know where to start."

Branson stood and walked over to a telephone table. He found the yellow pages and thumbed through to the gun shops. "Just a suggestion, but you could hit them geographically," he said. "Maybe hit the stores north of the Charles after training tomorrow. On Wednesday, hit the stores west of the city, and so on."

"Okay, I like Branson's plan," said O'Brien. "Now, what about the armories?"

"It will take me several days to gather *the keys to the vault*, as they say," replied Pearson. "But I should have everything in place by Friday."

By O'Brien accepting Branson's suggestion for confiscating the weapons from gun stores, he now accomplished the foot-in-the-door method of manipulation. He'd offered an easy solution to the problem, which was quickly accepted by both Pearson and O'Brien. Now he would manipulate them into following his lead on the real request—access to the armories.

"With respect to the armories, if Mr. Pearson wouldn't mind working with me directly, I have a couple of ideas," said Branson. This was Branson's chance to gain control of this situation and set up Pearson at the same time. "Of course, I will have to accelerate the training of the men," started Branson. "It's not ideal, but they are fast learners." Branson had command of the room.

"I'm listening," said O'Brien as he lit up a cigar.

Branson continued. "Let's face it, gentlemen, we're raiding the armories of the Massachusetts National Guard. This will be a shock to the system in that a clear message is being sent to state and local politicians—Governor O'Brien is the man in charge now."

O'Brien leaned back in his chair and let a huge puff of smoke into the air. He was clearly enjoying this moment. Branson recalled later that O'Brien resembled Boss Hog from the *Dukes of Hazzard*.

"Ironically, there are forty-four armories and support facilities in the commonwealth," continued Branson. "Some are remote, and others may not have sufficient assets to warrant our efforts. I believe that Mr. Pearson and I can work together to identify the two dozen most *lucrative* targets and hit them one by one. We'll divide the men into two-man teams and assign an armory to each. Mr. Pearson and I will make the rounds opening the facilities, and while they clean out the weapons, we'll travel to the next location."

"I like it, Governor," said Pearson. "We can do this quickly and efficiently."

"When?" asked O'Brien.

"Here's what I suggest, Governor," replied Branson. "Vehicular and pedestrian traffic drops considerably after dark, sir. Also, we don't want to throw our activities in the face of local politicians trying to hold onto some semblance of authority. If I may be frank, sir? The political struggles for power between your office and the obsolete local officials need to be fought another day. Our singular focus should be on confiscating these weapons and equipping our teams."

"I'm glad you're on board, Captain Branson," said O'Brien. "I've always had a knack for picking damn fine personnel." He took another draw off his cigar.

Chapter 15

Monday, September 12, 2016
8:00 p.m.
Citizen Corps Region I, Office of the Governor
99 High Street Rooftop
Boston, Massachusetts

Once again, O'Brien found himself alone atop the 99 High Street offices assigned to him by the Citizen Corps. He hated the FEMA offices he'd inherited within the building. They were too simple—typical government bureaucrat cubicles and cheap furniture filled every room. He was the governor of Region I, and his offices should reflect that status.

This evening would set the tone for the next few weeks in his quest to subdue Boston and create long-lasting alliances. Once that was accomplished, he could spread his influence throughout New England. His new man, Captain Branson, was a great addition to his team. He was very impressed with the first day of training, although it was focused too much on military protocol. He told Branson afterwards he needed the training sped up, and he wanted the men to learn interrogation tactics as well.

O'Brien turned as the stairwell door opened and his first *guest* appeared, escorted by Marion La Rue. O'Brien sized up his new potential *ally*, Joaquin Guzman.

La Mara Salvatrucha, or MS-13, was an international criminal enterprise that originated in Los Angeles. The majority of the gang was comprised of Central Americans, primarily from El Salvador. Known locally for their drug operations, they gained particular notoriety for their illegal immigration and human-smuggling operations.

In 2005, MS-13 began meeting with al-Qaeda in El Salvador for the purposes of assisting them with entry into the United States. Boston, in particular, became a port of entry for Islamic terrorists. One of the al-Qaeda operatives who trained the suicide bombers for the attack on the USS *Cole* was an Eastie, the nickname for those who live in East Boston.

Guzman had over a thousand hard-core gang members under his control. For decades, the Italian Mafia ran drugs in East Boston, until MS-13 arrived on the scene. Guzman had been deported four times by Immigrations and Customs Enforcement—I.C.E., only to return via their underground smuggling network. His feats were legendary, and the loyalty of his MS-13 soldiers was undeniable.

As he approached O'Brien, Guzman observed Boston Harbor. He looked nervously around the rooftop, then turned his attention to his host. O'Brien spoke first.

"My name is Governor O'Brien. I trust that Marion explained to you the purpose of this meeting?"

"Yeah," replied Guzman. "Am I the only one here?"

"For now, but we're waiting on one more."

As the stairwell door opened, Guzman abruptly swung around and felt the back of his waistband for his gun.

"Here's our other guest," said O'Brien. Captain Branson led a man across the roof through the dark. When the man's identity was known, Guzman reacted.

"Yo! What's he doin' here? Nobody said nuthin 'bout that jerk-off bein' here!"

"Calm down, Guzman," said La Rue. "We're all friends today. This is a meeting that will benefit us all."

"Rockwell, I take it you two know each other," said O'Brien. "Captain, you can leave us now."

Branson moved in to respond. "Sir, these men are notorious gangbangers and murderers," he said. "The purpose of this meeting is none of my business, and as the head of your security detail, I am sworn to secrecy. But there is no way in hell, sir, pardon my French, that I'll leave you alone with these two."

O'Brien laughed. "Okay, Captain, but I need you to stand over there to observe but not listen," he said. "Some conversations are on a need-to-know basis."

Branson nodded as he stepped away after giving the men another glance.

Jarvis Rockwell, known within the black gang community as *J-Rock*, had become the undisputed head of the newly unified black gangs of the south Boston neighborhoods of Dorchester, Roxbury, and Mattapan. Typically, the black gangs were divided along geographic turf lines. In Boston, there were no national gangs like the infamous Bloods and Crips.

The previously hostile gangs came together following the death of J-Rock's unborn child during a clash with police at the Boston Marathon. He used the event as a catalyst to lead a wave of black violence against law enforcement, especially white cops.

"What up?" said J-Rock as he nodded to Guzman.

Guzman glared in response.

"This meeting won't take long," interjected O'Brien. "I asked La Rue to bring you here so you can hear my words and know what it is I expect from you in return."

The two men relaxed and turned their attention to O'Brien and away from each other. Although they had never crossed paths, having kept the peace throughout J-Rock's rise to power, they represented wholly different cultures and approaches to *business.*

"Okay," said Guzman.

O'Brien walked to the edge of the roof and looked to the street below, which was virtually empty. He reminded himself that a good tactic was one your people enjoyed—Alinsky's *Rules for Radicals*, number six.

"We find ourselves in difficult times, but a situation that is full of opportunity," started O'Brien. "I share a point of view with our President that focuses on the needs of the many against the survival of the few. Under the circumstances that we face, I don't believe it is fair that a bunch of rich people get to save themselves because they have their own bunkers or a house stocked with food."

Guzman and J-Rock listened intently, but remained silent throughout.

O'Brien continued. "I know that your people are suffering out east, Guzman. The same is true down your way, Rockwell. I want each of you to resist the urge to turn on each other to survive, and especially not on your own. I think there is a better way."

The men glanced at each other and nodded.

"We're listening," said J-Rock.

"We will be working hard to get food and supplies from Washington, or whatever source they have available," said O'Brien. "But the government assistance may be slow in arriving. We need to look at ways to help ourselves.

"I believe there is a way to help your people survive, and erase injustices, prejudices, and other atrocities that you have endured by our society. I have no interest whatsoever in preserving the wealth and greed of Boston's rich for it to proliferate again when the power comes back on. This is our opportunity to even the playing field."

"What do you have in mind?" asked Guzman.

"These are dangerous times, as I'm sure you both have witnessed," replied O'Brien. "The scenarios your people face are too grim for us to talk about. I believe it is better to all die trying to survive together, saving one another, than to allow the majority of working men to die so a minority of rich people can survive."

Both Guzman and J-Rock were nodding in agreement. O'Brien liked the way this was going.

"Here's what I propose," he continued. "I believe in justice and fairness. If our survival cannot be achieved without achieving a level playing field for all, it's not worth it. We need to achieve the greater good through whatever means are necessary."

"How do we do that?" asked J-Rock.

"I control the military and law enforcement for the entire New England region," replied O'Brien. "There are parts of Boston full of food and supplies that can help save the lives of your families and neighbors. I don't have the personnel to get these things, but you do." O'Brien walked to the roof's edge again and then spoke, with conviction.

"I am telling you to gather your men, enter the neighborhoods of Boston's wealthy, and take whatever you want. None of my people will stand in your way. I guarantee you safe passage and the ability to right the wrongs that have been forced upon you by this country since it was formed. These reparations are long overdue, gentlemen!"

O'Brien basked in the excitement of these two former adversaries, who were thrilled at the opportunity given them. He was, however, completely unaware that Captain Branson overheard every word.

CHAPTER 16

Tuesday, September 13, 2016
10:10 a.m.
Prescott Peninsula
Quabbin Reservoir, Massachusetts

Morgan listened as Donald finished up the morning briefing for everyone. He'd requested that Donald reduce the amount of detail associated with the collapse, as it was having an adverse effect on the morale of the Boston Brahmin, and their wives in particular. Mrs. Lowell appeared to be especially hard hit with the change in lifestyle and circumstances, and Morgan intended to address this with Lawrence in a moment.

He motioned for Donald to join him at the edge of the clearing. "Mr. Quinn, I have only spoken with Henry one time in the ten days since the attack. I expected to see him here by now. Is there a problem?"

"No, sir," replied Donald. "Sarge is working closely with Steven and Brad to keep tabs on our new governor. It appears that O'Brien is taking his job to heart and his newfound power is being wielded at will."

"Don't you think I'm entitled to a report on these activities?" asked Morgan. He was not concerned with a perceived slight. Morgan was starting to feel excluded. He was never one to become overly suspicious to the point of paranoia, primarily because he was always in control of a situation.

"Yes, sir, of course," replied Donald. "At this point, the governor is attempting to disarm the citizenry first, with the further goal of centralizing law enforcement activities under his command. We'll continue to monitor this as it develops."

Morgan studied Donald closely and then shrugged and walked away. He didn't see Donald let out a sigh of relief.

"Walter, Lawrence," shouted Morgan across the yard to his two most trusted members of the inner circle, "may I have a word?"

The two quickly left their conversation with Art Peabody and approached Morgan.

"Yes, John," said Lawrence Lowell. "Is everything okay?"

Morgan nodded and gestured for them to walk with him. He led them down a well-worn path through the woods that made a one-mile loop to the south of 1PP. Before he spoke, he allowed the lead member of his security detail to rush past them to lead the way. The second member trailed dutifully behind. Since the attack on the front gate that led to the death of Sabs, Morgan insisted that two men accompany him when he was away from camp. Out of precaution, Donald kept a two-man team on Morgan at all times.

"Lawrence, we have several things to discuss, but I must address a personal matter with you first," started Morgan. "It's not so sensitive that Walter must be excluded. In fact, he has noticed the issue as well."

"What is it, John?" asked a concerned Lowell.

"Your wife has been acting strangely, Lawrence," said Morgan. "I understand that the attack and the resulting lack of power has caused angst and stress for us all. But Constance seems very angry at our circumstances. Mary has noticed it as well, am I right, Walter?"

"Very true, John," replied Cabot. "Everyone responds to a crisis differently, but all the wives have pulled together to make the best of it. Constance has not. She seems to be holding a grudge of some sort. Haven't you noticed this?"

Lowell walked along quietly and put his hands in his pants pockets. Pride and force of habit caused Lowell to continue dressing as if he were headed for the office. He shook his head as he spoke.

"I've made a mistake, my friends," said Lowell. "It was out of love and emotion that I said too much to Constance. When the event occurred, she was very frightened for us, but also for our children and grandchildren. I tried to calm her down the best that I could, but in my efforts, she saw through my façade. She forced me to admit that I was aware that the cyber attack was preplanned."

The three men walked silently for nearly twenty yards. Morgan knew the stability of their group would be in jeopardy if they became aware of his involvement. Constance Lowell had the ability, in her emotionally charged state, to expose his scheme to the others.

"Can you control her, Lawrence?" asked Morgan.

"I think so, John, but can you tell us how long this might last?" asked Lowell.

"I don't know, Lawrence," he replied. "There are a lot of factors to consider. What can we do to ensure Constance doesn't cause a disruption?"

"Honestly, John, she'd prefer to be around family," replied Lowell. "I must assume that bringing them here is not an option."

"No, I'm afraid not," said John.

"I could take her to Hyannis Port, where our daughter lives," suggested Lowell.

Morgan pondered this for a moment. He couldn't guarantee the safety of his lifelong friend, but it was perhaps a better option than having his potentially unstable wife, and an unforeseen complication, remain at Prescott Peninsula.

"Lawrence, my old friend, it won't be safe for you out there," said Morgan. "Hyannis Port is a long way from the cities, but eventually it will be affected by desperate people." Morgan placed his arm around Lowell, who was clearly shaken by facing this reality.

"I understand, but I don't know what else to do to help my wife," said Lowell. "She is so angry at me, at us. Perhaps a change of scenery will make it better. Truthfully, I'm at a loss."

The men walked further as Morgan weighed his options. He didn't want to lose his friend, but he couldn't tolerate a mutiny either.

"Allow me the opportunity to discuss this with Colonel Bradlee," said Morgan. "Perhaps he has some suggestions for your security.

Now, there is something of importance I need to discuss with you both."

Suddenly, the soldier stopped in front of them and dropped to one knee. He held his fist up, indicating that the men stop as well. They also moved to an area of cover just off the trail. The second member of their security detail ran quickly but quietly past them and joined his fellow Marine. Morgan's heart raced as he listened. From their right, they heard the sounds of twigs breaking on the forest floor. Leaves rustled as something approached the trail. The soldiers, now slightly separated, raised their weapons and waited for the approaching intruder.

Morgan peered around an oak tree and watched as a nearly one-thousand-pound moose lumbered across the trail about thirty yards in front of them. Nearly six feet tall at its shoulders, the enormous member of the deer family walked across the open path and across to the other side, where he stopped for a snack of *browse*—the twigs and new growth that is the preferred diet of moose.

The three men exhaled and began to laugh. The soldiers quickly resumed their positions and awaited Morgan and his friends to continue on their walk. Once the group began moving up the trail, the moose decided to move deeper into the woods to seek protection.

"I don't know, John, this place seems like it's pretty dangerous too." Cabot chuckled. "Did you see the size of that animal?" Cabot lifted his arm over his five-foot-ten-inch frame.

"I guess it could have been worse, Walter," added Lowell. "It could have been a bear!"

Lowell and Cabot laughed, enjoying the moment, which eased the tension between the men. The laugh was short-lived.

"That's why I brought you on this walk, my friends," started Morgan. "I'm afraid the Russian bear has come out of hibernation, and it is roaring." Morgan proceeded to detail the news he'd received from General Sears about recent Russian troop movements and incursions into U.S. territorial waters.

Over the previous twelve months, Russia had expanded its

presence in the Arctic as well as its submarine activities off the U.S. coast. In the past, the Kremlin held the advantage on the ocean surface, but the Pentagon dominated beneath the waves. But that, Morgan explained, had changed.

General Sears shared intelligence with Morgan about a new high-speed drone submarine that was capable of delivering a nuclear warhead developed by the Russians. Even when the U.S. defense capabilities were fully functional, the nuclear-tipped, torpedo-shaped weapon, nicknamed *Kanyon,* was capable of avoiding their customary response.

Morgan added, "This new weapon is designed to damage our nation's coastal areas by creating wide areas of radioactive contamination that would render our coasts uninhabitable. This is a concern for your family, Lawrence, and anyone who lives within fifty miles of the shore."

"How does it avoid our naval defenses, John?" asked Cabot. Cabot Industries was the world's premiere shipbuilder and a major supplier to the U.S. naval fleet.

"The speed and depth of the drone would be massively in excess of the capabilities of any manned submarine in the world, much less those of our Navy," replied Morgan. "A drone submarine with these characteristics would be invulnerable to interception."

"What about our ground-based missile systems in Alaska and California?" asked Lowell. They were approaching the end of the mile-long loop on this trail, and Morgan stopped them to finish the conversation.

"We've been obsessed with the North Koreans, so those missiles are pointed at the DPRK missiles and the Iranians," replied Morgan.

"What are the Russians up to, John?" asked Cabot. "Are they going to kick us when we're down?" Both Cabot and Lowell were looking to Morgan for reassurance.

"I don't know, but I will find out," replied Morgan. "I'll make contact through our usual backchannels. At this point, I can't rule out anything."

"What does the President think?" asked Lowell.

Morgan, for the first time, looked distressed during the conversation. He kicked at a few stones lying on the path.

"I don't know, Lawrence, he has stopped taking my calls."

CHAPTER 17

Tuesday, September 13, 2016
1:00 p.m.
Chinatown
Boston, Massachusetts

Sarge navigated through the stalled vehicles on Stuart Street as he cautiously approached the roadblock manned by members of the Asian gangs of Chinatown. He chose to drive his Mercedes G-Wagen despite the risks associated with driving an expensive vehicle around the streets of postapocalyptic Boston. After his made-for-TV chase last week following his last foray into Chinatown, he deemed it prudent to leave the Toyota OJ40 at 100 Beacon. "No sense in getting our collective asses shot up before we hit the checkpoint," he'd mused to Julia and Steven as they pulled out of the garage earlier.

He'd hesitated to bring Julia with him, but her background in China and her ability to speak fluent Chinese should assist them in getting through safely. Once they met with the head of the Asian gangs, the language barriers would evaporate.

They approached the intersection of Washington and where Stuart became Kneeland Street. Large panel trucks formed a V, blocking access. Armed men motioned for Sarge to turn left onto Washington. This area was beginning to look all too familiar to Sarge as he momentarily relived the chase scene. When they approached Beach Street to turn into Chinatown, four large Asian men with AK-47s approached the vehicle.

Sarge rolled down all of the windows in the G-Wagen and instructed Steven and Julia to make their hands visible to the guards.

He looked to Julia to take the lead in conversing with the men.

Although Julia was fluent in both Mandarin and Cantonese, she told the guys that she would use the more common Mandarin dialect, as it was typically favored among Chinese speakers. After several minutes of conversation and waiting while they relayed the purpose of the Loyal Nine's visit to Chinatown, they were instructed to follow a lead vehicle to their destination.

This trip down Beach Street allowed Sarge to see things from a different perspective, rather than the tension-filled ride last time. Along the walls of the worn row houses and above the formerly bustling shops and restaurants were the faded plaster markings of the houses and restaurants that were here before the collapse. Rooflines remained, defined in weathered brick that shifted from deep red to charcoal black, but they were now inhabited by wandering guards dutifully standing watch over the streets below.

Near the end of Beach Street was Ping On Alley, where immigrant Chinese workers first settled in the 1870s. Gone were the double-parked trucks and sidewalk vendors hawking clothes and vegetables. There were no scantily clad women standing near the pay phones, which were topped by green and yellow pagodas. Closed were the late-night restaurants with the brash neon marquees shouting *Dim Sum, Cocktails*. A yellow sign that read *Jeannie Beauty & Hair* was hanging by its last nail from a wooden roof canopy. Two weeks ago, Jeannie, a Malaysian woman, offered facials and foot reflexology. Today, the shop was empty, and Jeannie was dead.

There were seven thousand residents of Chinatown squeezed into forty-six acres between downtown skyscrapers, two highways, and a sprawling medical complex. In addition, thousands of Boston-area Asians maintained close ties with this neighborhood, many of whom came to escape violence and oppression in their homelands of China, Vietnam, Cambodia, and elsewhere.

Prior to the cyber attack, Chinatown was thought of as a vibrant neighborhood, a safe place to raise a family, and a place where gangs still ruled the streets. The gangs were accepted by all as a necessary evil. Today, it was a close-knit group of survivors sharing what they had with others similarly situated. This was their heritage, as their ancestors had all been through situations like this before.

The vehicle caravan stopped just short of the Chinatown Gate in front of the Gourmet Dumpling House. At the end of a short stretch of brick buildings was a door that led to a basement social club where men would once gather late into the night to play mahjong, a game in which bets were placed on matching tiles. Now, it was the safe haven of John Willis, the only Caucasian in Chinatown and the undisputed head of the Ping On gang. He was known as *Bac Guai John*, or more commonly as the *White Devil.*

Willis was born in the working-class Boston neighborhood of Dorchester, which was known for hockey-playing Catholic kids and the birthplace of the famous Wahlberg actors. The path of his life would more closely follow another famous resident of the old neighborhood—gangster Whitey Bulger.

He grew up fatherless, and after his mother died when he was fourteen, he found himself alone and struggling to survive. Willis learned to protect himself by bulking up his body with an extreme weightlifting program and the use of steroids. At seventeen, he was stronger than most adults and easily landed a job as a bouncer at an after-hours Asian nightclub. While working late one night, he helped save the life of a high-ranking member of the Ping On gang who had come under assault. This landed him in their good graces, and Willis was essentially adopted by the gang.

Over time he rose through the ranks and became the leading oxycodone importer from South Florida—a three-billion-dollar-a-year industry. He also became known as the White Devil. Now, the days of organized crime were over, and the fear of being hunted by the feds had passed. Willis had one goal in mind, and that was to preserve Chinatown for those he considered family.

"This way," said a short, stocky guard in Mandarin. He swung the rifle barrel like it was a policeman's traffic baton. Julia, followed by Sarge and Steven, descended the stairwell into a dimly lit bar. They were greeted by several other men who immediately separated the three members of the Loyal Nine and frisked them. One of the men became a little too friendly with Julia during the process, but she gave Sarge a reassuring look.

"Come sit down," came a voice out of the darkness past the pool tables. A faint red candle burned on a table in the corner. The sound of a chair sliding on the floor indicated they were going to greet their guest.

Sarge was amazed at the size of Willis. He towered over Steven, who stood six feet three inches. He wore a black polo shirt that barely contained his biceps. The White Devil looked more like a *white elephant.* Sarge spoke first.

"My name is Henry Sargent, but you can call me Sarge. This is my brother, Steven. This is Julia Hawthorne."

Julia, who knew the White Devil's story from years of media coverage, immediately engaged him in Mandarin. This proved to be an excellent way to break the ice, and Willis relaxed.

"Please, call me John," he said laughingly. "Only my wife does anymore, and the lawyers, of course."

"Thank you for seeing us," started Sarge. "You don't know us, and we only know you by reputation. I believe you are a devoted husband, and I know that you have a heartfelt sense of community. Your choice of career is none of our business."

Willis laughed again. "I can say this with absolute certainty. Whatever has happened in this country sure is bad for my business. Nobody could buy my *products* even if I could manage to find any to sell!"

Sarge humored the notorious gangster by laughing with him. *We need this guy's help—for his muscle.*

"Let me get right to the point because time is an issue for us both," said Sarge. "There has been a new governor appointed by the President. He is power hungry and will stop at nothing to control anyone who resists his demands."

"What does he demand?" asked Willis. He leaned on the table, clearly interested in Sarge's information. His muscular arms bulged as he flexed his fingers.

"He intends to enforce the martial law declaration announced by the President last week," replied Sarge. "He has recruited an army to help him with the task of confiscating weapons, food, and supplies from any source available, including people's homes."

"What kind of army?"

"The kind that poses a direct threat to you and those that you are attempting to protect," replied Sarge. "He gave a blank check to La Mara Salvatrucha and the unified black gangs out of the south led by Jarvis Rockwell to enter Boston without fear of retribution by law enforcement."

"I know J-Rock," said Willis. "He's a punk. Guzman heads up the Hispanics. He's crazier than those ISIS jerkoffs. How do you know this?"

"We just know," replied Sarge. He couldn't give away too much information received from their new mole—Captain Branson.

"What does this have to do with me?" asked Willis.

"The Callahan Tunnel is shut down," replied Steven. "The only open route across Boston Harbor is through the Ted Williams Tunnel. Get the picture?"

"Yeah, by the time the MS-13 clear the Fort Point Channel, they'll be right here at our doorstep."

"Exactly," added Sarge. "We need your help to stop them or at least thin their ranks before they can roll into Boston and make life rough for all of us. J-Rock will be our responsibility."

Willis leaned back in his chair to stretch. He looked at Steven as a boxer would assess his adversary. "Just who are *you*, exactly?"

"We're just a group of people who love Boston and our country," replied Julia. "We don't want to see our city destroyed by people who would take advantage of others during this crisis. Despite our differences in ordinary times, we share a common purpose now. Protect our homes and the people who are vulnerable to opportunists."

Willis sat quietly for a moment and then spoke to Sarge. "You know they call me the White Devil, and there is a reason for that. You're asking me to take on those head-choppin' assholes from El Salvador, which I'm capable of doing. But I'm supposed to count on you to take on J-Rock and his boys. I can get on board with *the enemy of my enemy is my friend* thing. J-Rock and his kind won't hold back, and you don't look like no White Devil to me."

"I'm not," said Sarge, pointing to Steven. "But he is."

CHAPTER 18

Thursday, September 15, 2016
8:00 p.m.
630 Washington Street
Boston, Massachusetts

Steven gathered the group leaders of the Mechanics in the Boston area for the first time. The city was becoming more dangerous by the day, and the level of desperation of ordinary Americans was unprecedented. People who were self-reliant were being targeted by those who had not prepared or by a newly burgeoning criminal element of hopeless survivors. Those who were used to accepting government handouts were still given a preference but demanded more. Lawlessness became the norm, and Steven knew it was by design. *The takers were getting even with the makers.*

They chose an iconic location in Boston that was full of symbolism. The forty-three-thousand-square-foot building located at 630 Washington Street was centrally located and bordered their new allies in Chinatown, who provided round-the-clock security.

The first floor, formerly the home of Dunkin' Donuts, contained a full kitchen, which Steven had equipped with a generator that utilized the building's exhaust system to vent the fumes. The second floor was a large open space furnished with tables, chairs, and large chalkboards. This was ideal for large gatherings, like the one this evening.

The third floor was used for office space prior to the cyber attack, but it was now retrofitted to conceal supplies and weapons for the use of the Mechanics. A thorough search might reveal the hiding places Steven devised, but a cursory examination by the untrained eye would not.

The fourth floor provided barracks and sleeping quarters for displaced members of the Mechanics and their families. Because of its close proximity to downtown, the fourth-floor barracks was originally considered temporary housing. The fifth, or top floor, provided Steven's hand-chosen leaders a permanent place to live. Following the new alliance with the White Devil, many members of the Mechanics now called 630 Washington Street their home.

It was the symbolism of this location that was ironic. It was the site of the famous Liberty Tree. At the time of the revolution, a great elm tree stood in front of a grocery store here. It had wide spreading beautiful branches, and for many years was the center of business in Boston's original South End. Several large elms grew nearby, and this area was known as the Neighborhood of Elms.

On August 14, 1765, this particular tree was selected for hanging the effigies of those men who favored passage of the detested Stamp Act. On September 11th, a three-by-two-foot copper plate, with large golden letters, was placed on its trunk bearing the inscription *The Tree of Liberty.*

Thereafter, nearly all the great political meetings of the Sons of Liberty, and their insurgent arm known as the Mechanics, were held in this square. Embedded in the wall of the building located at 630 Washington Street was a tablet marking the spot of the historic landmark, bearing the inscription *Sons of Liberty, 1766.*

The British made the Liberty Tree an object of ridicule. During the siege of Boston in August of 1775, a party of British Loyalists defiantly cut it down. The Liberty Tree, which was planted in 1646, stood strong for one hundred and twenty-nine years. It was at this spot that the seeds of liberty were sown by the original Loyal Nine.

Steven looked at these brave men and women who comprised his modern-day Mechanics. All were prepared for this eventuality, but none could have imagined the battles would be in defense of their freedoms. It was time to get the evening started, so he quieted down the crowd.

"Listen up, everybody, we need to get started." The raised voices died to a murmur as the Mechanics gathered around. Steven continued. "First, let me thank Don Scott, the regional supervisor for the REI sporting goods outlets in the Boston area, for gathering up these BaoFeng radio units and the Goal Zero portable solar panel chargers. Let your employer know how much we appreciate their generosity."

Scott stood up and received a few pats on the back. "No problem." Scott laughed. "I paid them with a check when I dropped off the keys to the stores the other day."

"Just add it to your expense report, Don," said Steven. He laughed as he watched Sarge hand out the new frequency codes. "Radio comms are critical to us now more than ever. We are all going to be involved in armed confrontations. Not only will the radios allow us to report intel, but they will enable you to request help if you are overrun."

"These are your new active channels," interjected Sarge. "Prior to the cyber attack, we all communicated through MURS channel 3, 151.9400. Those of you are active HAMRs know this to be a common channel utilized by like-minded patriots around the world. Steven and I believe that the government knows this as well." Sarge stood back and yielded the floor to Steven.

"The bottom line is that we can't trust them," started Steven. "I believe people like us are being targeted by the government, especially in light of the martial law declaration. We have to be mindful of shortwave listeners, other ham operators, or Citizen Corps personnel monitoring conversations via radio scanner." Steven took one of the frequency flyers from Sarge and held it face forward to make his point.

"As you know, there is no such thing as a secret frequency," he continued. "Anyone with a scanner can push the seek button and lock onto your conversation within minutes. We believe the government may be utilizing spectrum analyzers or scanner features like Close Call and Signal Stalker to monitor frequencies. Don helped us put together an SOP—standard operating procedure—for comms."

Scott stepped forward and added, "Never give away your location if at all possible. Pay particular attention to the channels I've identified here as *tactical*. If you face a possible capture situation, or in the event of suspected eavesdropping, announce your desire to go to our backup frequencies, which you will find attached as page two. These should be committed to memory. In that event, announce the change to everyone using the code word *Brady*. Think of Tom Brady calling an audible during a play. This will alert everyone to the fact that our tactical frequencies have been compromised, and to utilize 151.600 until we can assign new tactical channels." Scott stepped away and gave the floor back to Steven.

"On the next matter, it turns out we correctly anticipated the moves of our new *governor*," said Steven as he was greeted with a chorus of boos. He laughed until they subsided. "Staging the break-ins at Atlantic Tactical, Boston Firearms, and the other local gun stores was genius. This left his Citizen Corps goons walking out of the stores with nothing but their pricks in their hands." Steven shared high fives with the Mechanics. It was important to establish esprit de corps, a sense of enthusiasm and devotion, amongst the Mechanics. They would begin to risk their lives for their families, neighbors, and country tomorrow. This camaraderie would help keep them alive.

Steve went on to describe the mission of the Mechanics for Friday night. Using his most trusted lieutenants, he divided them into groups and assigned the highest-capacity armories to each. He and Brad determined it would not be possible to stop all of O'Brien's men on their raids of the Massachusetts Guard armories Friday evening, nor did they want to. As Brad said, sometimes you had to give a little to avoid suspicion. Three-quarters of O'Brien's men would not return on Saturday, having been abducted and locked up at the former federal prison facility at Fort Devens. The President had ordered, through Pearson, the inmates there released. Brad intended to fill it back up with O'Brien's thugs.

Before he gave Sarge the final words of encouragement, he added, "All we can do is delay the governor and his Citizen Corps butt-buddies. At some point, the President will order the military into

Boston to shut down dissent and our insurgent activities. I hope that our soldiers will obey their oath to the Constitution and stand down. As a soldier, I would never turn on my fellow Americans. Let's continue to be a gnat in their ear. Let things play out. Above all, survive. Always live to fight another day."

"Choose freedom!" came a shout from the rear of the room. Yells of *choose freedom* echoed throughout the room.

CHAPTER 19

Thursday, September 15, 2016
9:00 p.m.
630 Washington Street
Boston, Massachusetts

Sarge took in the whole scene for a moment. These three dozen plus strangers were taking up arms to fight a tyrannical government, just like his ancestors had done two hundred and fifty years ago. It was a humbling experience for Sarge as the Mechanics shouted choose freedom. When he began writing the book one year prior, he never imagined that its words would inspire Americans to this level of patriotism. Based upon the reports they were receiving all across the country, freedom-loving Americans were surviving and standing up for their rights. Now, he was doing the same.

Sarge raised and lowered his arms, motioning for everyone to quiet down. Although chairs were available, no one sat in them. Their adrenaline and excitement ran high—much like it did for the colonists during those historic meetings at the Liberty Tree.

"My friends, America is the most exceptional nation in the history of the world because our forefathers had vision. That vision guided them in creating the United States Constitution and the Bill of Rights. They are unequivocally the greatest political documents ever written.

"Our founding documents provide something vastly different than almost any people of any government has believed in human history. Most governments in the past have believed that *might makes right.* The king or ruler has all the power, and the people are expected to be dependent subjects. Out of fear of repercussions, most of the dependent class accepted their fate.

"Not in America. Our Founding Fathers said *no*. They believed that God gave us our inalienable natural rights. No government, or the individuals who are responsible for its operation, could possibly possess the power to violate these God-given rights.

"Government was never intended to be the source of our rights, and the Constitution was never meant to be interpreted as a source of giving a greater power to one man in Washington or an unelected tyrant over here at 99 High Street!" The Mechanics cheered Sarge's words. They were looking for a leader. In this moment, Sarge knew it was time for him to fill the role that so many encouraged him to assume.

"In our country, over time, the rule of law and the freedoms to which we have grown accustomed have been lost. With few exceptions, Americans were too ignorant and unconcerned to do anything about it. The more often the rule of law was set aside, the more difficult it became to reestablish it. Now, the rule of law envisioned in the Constitution ceases to exist except as a distant memory.

"The reality is that a cloud of tyranny has descended upon America. Our President, and those who think like him, recognizes that for tyranny to be successful, the American people must first be disarmed.

"As history has proven time and again, a disarmed populace can easily be led to slaughter. But unlike the tens of millions executed in ethnic, religious and political cleansings of the last two centuries, Americans have a rich tradition of personal liberty and the right to bear arms. It is embedded in our culture and guaranteed by our Bill of Rights.

"Even before the attack of September third, those who would ignore the Constitution within the halls of government knew that if they pushed too far, they might incite a revolution. After the declaration of martial law, the time to revolt may be upon us.

"The Second Amendment wasn't enacted just to arm hunters, as this President would have you believe. It is there for the American people to defend themselves against the criminal element, to protect themselves against terrorists and radical ideology, and it's also there to push back against a tyrannical government that has overreached its power.

"This President does not trust the law-abiding American citizen, especially in this time of turmoil. His solution is to disarm us, but I submit to you, my friends, this has caused a revolution in America, the seeds of which are happening in buildings like this one all across the nation." Sarge paused to allow some applause and shouts of encouragement to subside.

"We are not the enemy. The law-abiding gun owners in this country and the freedom-loving patriots like those in this room are the solution to the problems facing us in these difficult times. The enemies are the terrorist group who caused our power grid to collapse and an overreaching government who intends to profit from our nation's demise.

"James Madison, one of our Founding Fathers, once wrote that the United States Constitution preserves the advantage of being armed. This is a fundamental right all Americans possess over the people of nearly every other nation, where governments are afraid to trust their people with arms. This right holds true two hundred fifty years later.

"This President believes that the circumstances we face oblige the government to form an army of those loyal to the government, the so-called Citizen Corps. That army can never be allowed to violate the liberties of the American people. Such infringement will never happen for so long as there is a large body of like-minded patriots who stand ready to defend their rights and those of their fellow Americans.

"We are not alone. The Mechanics are all over the country. Steven saw them in Pennsylvania and New York. We talk to them from California to Florida, and from Maine to Washington State.

"Know this, during the American Revolution, the active forces in the field against the king's tyranny never amounted to more than about three percent of the colonists. This small group gave their lives to protect their God-given natural rights to liberty and property.

Never underestimate the abilities of a small group of committed citizens to change the course of a nation. In that respect, history can, and will, repeat itself."

Sarge looked into the eyes of these brave men and women, true American patriots. Many were clearly moved by his oration.

"I will leave you with these words from Thomas Jefferson:

"The strongest reason for the people to retain the right to keep and bear arms is, as a last resort, to protect themselves against tyranny in government. Jefferson asked, *what country can preserve its liberties, if its political leaders are not warned from time to time that the people preserve the spirit of resistance? Let them take up arms against us. The tree of liberty must be refreshed from time to time with the blood of patriots and tyrants.*"

"Hear, hear!"

"Choose freedom!"

CHAPTER 20

Friday, September 16, 2016
7:00 p.m.
Massachusetts Guard Armory
275 Union Street
Braintree, Massachusetts

Following the Civil War, the U.S. government was becoming increasingly concerned over the possibility of widespread civil unrest and class warfare. In 1877, the War Department authorized the construction of fortified armories to be used by local militia, the predecessor to today's State Guard units. The early armories were often ornate, redoubt-like structures. One of the first in the nation, built in Rhode Island, resembled a castle. At the turn of the twentieth century, the predominant architectural philosophy was that a building should proclaim its purpose. Churches should be welcoming, jails needed to appear oppressive, and armories should be suggestive of a fortress.

Armories were intended to be gathering places for the local militia to train as well as to store their arms and munitions. Today, armories—or their more recent politically correct designation, readiness centers—were used by the National Guard and military reserve units for the same purpose as contemplated in the 1800s.

The facility at Braintree was one of the largest armories maintained by the Massachusetts Army National Guard and held the same purpose as their original nineteenth-century counterparts, the storage of arms. It was a prime target for Governor O'Brien as a means to arm his Citizen Corps.

But Braintree was also a stronghold for the Mechanics. Settled in

1625, the town of Braintree was the birthplace of John Adams, John Quincy Adams, and John Hancock. Its residents were patriots and loyal to the Mechanics.

Steven and his team waited on the caravan led by Pearson and Captain Branson to arrive. Based upon their early morning meeting with Branson, a plan was set in place. The Braintree Police Department across the street would appear abandoned. In fact, their chief of police, Walter Russell, and two of his officers would assist Steven. Most of the homes in the area of Union Street and Williams Court were evacuated, as families were told to stay with friends temporarily. Steven and Chief Russell didn't want anyone hurt by stray bullets.

The intelligence received by Steven was invaluable in planning this operation. But the lack of radio communication with Captain Branson in the four hours prior to the caravan's arrival provided an unexpected, yet complicating, surprise.

"Brain One, this is Brain Trust, do you copy?" said Steven into the BaoFeng's microphone clipped to his olive drab, plate-carrier vest created by 5.11 Tactical. Brad had assigned similar kits to everyone participating in tonight's mission. They contained ceramic armor plates and were relatively lightweight.

Steven missed Slash and the other members of the Aegis team. Tonight, no other member of his team was active duty or ex-military, as this operation could not involve Brad's men and the mission could go awry. Only one other person had post-collapse *combat* experience. Katie insisted on being part of the action, to no one's surprise.

The operation was fairly straightforward. There were four teams of two strategically placed around the facility. Steven and Katie took up a position that gave them unobstructed views of both the entry gate and the rear of the facility through which the arms would be removed.

At the rear of the armory, another team was hidden underneath a tarp in a parked M35 Deuce and a Half cargo truck. The M35 was delivered by Brad's men earlier in the day and would also be used to transport their prisoners to Fort Devens.

Chief Russell had two teams on the ready. One team would block the entrance with a City of Braintree garbage truck after Captain Branson and the other vehicles left for their next pickup. They would then cover the front entrance. Chief Russell's second team would cover the south side of the building on Williams Court and assist with the surprise raid on O'Brien's men.

"Roger, Brain Trust," Chief Russell replied. His men wore comparable olive drab tactical gear rather than their customary black law enforcement issue. Captain Branson knew that O'Brien would insist upon ballistic protection, and that his only source of this type of gear was the Boston Police Department. To avoid friendly fire and prevent confusion, Steven followed Branson's suggestion and issued the military-style gear. "We have them in sight. They are about a mile up Pilgrim's Highway. ETA, two minutes. Over."

"Roger, Brain One," replied Steven. "Showtime, people. We'll go on my signal. Nice and smooth." Steven flexed his fingers and took a deep breath. He hadn't performed his role as Nomad since he led the team into Frankfurt back in May, a career he thought he'd left behind.

"Target approaching." Chief Russell's voice was heard over the radio units. Steven rolled his head on his shoulders and released some tension. He raised his SCAR 17 and flipped the caps off his FLIR night scope. He carefully followed the lead vehicle, a military HUMVEE, as it came into view. The right turn signal was on as it approached the gated entry.

"Great," Steven muttered.

"What's wrong?" asked Katie. She raised her M4 to sight the incoming vehicles as well. "Is that a Cadillac?"

"Yeah, that's what's wrong," replied Steven. "Branson and I worked out a prearranged signal if something was not according to plan. He would use his blinker when he entered the compound if there was a potential change. The Caddy probably contains our illustrious governor."

The vehicles entered the oversized parking area one by one and took a wide swing in order to point outward. Captain Branson's

HUMVEE drove within a few yards of Steven and Katie's position, who quickly ducked under the thick underbrush to avoid detection. Following O'Brien's Cadillac were two twenty-four-foot-long MBTA Red Line maintenance vehicles, which resembled U-Haul moving trucks. Each contained three men. The remainder of the caravan was comprised of similar vehicles labeled green line and red line maintenance.

As the vehicles came to a stop, Captain Branson and Pearson exited first. O'Brien stayed in his vehicle until Branson approached and opened the door for him, not out of courtesy, but more likely to indicate it was safe to come out. Pearson motioned for the two maintenance trucks to back up to the rear of the building.

Steven swung his rifle around the perimeter of the armory. He was relieved to see that the occupants of the remainder of the caravan stayed with their vehicles, which were parked along Union Street, but still running. *They won't be here long.*

"Stick to the program," said Steven into his mic. "This dog and pony show will pull out soon enough." He took a deep breath and settled into the brush as Katie did the same.

"Do you think O'Brien will be with them all night?" asked Katie. She took a drink of her water bottle and adjusted her vest. "This thing is heavy."

"It'll keep you alive," said Steven. He rolled over so that he could face Katie, who he could barely see in the dark. All of the members of the team wore camouflaged face paint. "Listen, no hero crap tonight. I want to take these guys without firing weapons. This whole operation will create a buzz around the city as it is. We don't need the optics of an armed assault."

"I'm not trigger-happy, Steven. Do you think I enjoyed killing those guys on the way back to Boston?"

"Yes," he replied dryly.

"Okay, well, maybe a little," said Katie. "Listen, it all happened so fast and it was remarkably easy. I guess my adrenaline took over, and my mind knew what needed to be done. But I haven't second-guessed myself once. They had it comin'."

"I don't disagree, but we don't know anything about these men. For all we know, they're just trying to feed their families and will do whatever the governor asks to survive."

"Well, that's a load of bull." She raised her voice, prompting Steven to place his hand on her shoulder in an attempt to calm her down. "People made choices before and after the collapse. They're cleaning out this armory to kill people like you and me. There are no rules of engagement anymore. There are no more rules. You said it yourself."

"Yeah, but there is a moral compass."

"Maybe for you and me, but not for them. Nobody is going to say *hands up or I'll shoot.* We're not gonna get the benefit of *halt, you're under arrest.* Now, it's all about *shoot first, and ask questions later. Kill or be killed.*"

Steven didn't respond and sat in silence for a moment, contemplating what Katie said. He was a trained killer. Within days of the collapse, he was almost killed for no reason, other than to take their car and what meager supplies it contained. They'd witnessed men chasing a defenseless girl with the intent to rape her and ultimately kill her. He'd killed four men who were firing upon the residents of 100 Beacon. *All in the first few days! Maybe Katie's right?*

He allowed his mind to drift momentarily while the nameless faces of the people he'd killed crossed through his memories. How many had there been? *A hundred. A thousand. There will be more.*

The sound of raised voices brought him back to reality. Steven rolled back into position and looked through his scope. O'Brien led Pearson and Captain Branson back towards their vehicles, proudly carrying an M16.

"This one goes with me," O'Brien shouted as he swung the weapon wildly from side to side. Katie inched forward in her hide and trained her M4 on O'Brien.

"Let me shoot him and get it over with," said Katie.

"Forget it. Trust me, a preemptive strike on this guy is tempting, but now is not the time. Captain Branson is looking around. He can feel our presence."

"They're getting in," said Katie. O'Brien dropped himself into the front seat of his Cadillac. Captain Branson brought the big 6.2-liter diesel engine to life and eased the truck out of the parking lot. Without using his turn signal, he turned right onto Union. They left for their next destination, where more of the Mechanics would be waiting.

*****

"Brain One, this is Brain Trust. Radio check, over," Steven whispered into the microphone attached to his kit.

"I read you lima charlie," replied Chief Russell. "The street is quiet."

"Brain Trust, this is Brain Two. In position." They were located on the south side of the building. As soon as the convoy pulled out, they cut their way through the chain-link fence.

"This is Brain Three. Ready, on your signal." Brain Three consisted of two former security guards who worked for CitiBank. They were positioned in the back of the M35.

Steven looked at Katie and nodded. She was ready.

"Moving," he said to the team. He and Katie left the cover of the underbrush and made their way across the parking lot towards the rear corner of the building. Chief Russell and his partner approached the front door to secure any possible exits. To Steven's right, Brain Three was barely visible underneath the tarp, but their guns were clearly leveled on the back entrance. The cloudy night helped reduce visibility.

As they reached the corner of the armory, Steven signaled for Brain Three to cross the parking area while Steven covered their movement. They immediately took up positions in front of the MBTA truck.

The plan was for Steven and Katie to enter the building first. Unfortunately, they had limited information on the interior layout. Chief Russell was familiar with the front of the building, which was accessible to the public, but not the storage rooms and the vault in the back. They would have to go in blind. The element of surprise was critical.

"Brain Trust, moving," whispered Steven as he and Katie walked in a low crouch along the back side of the building toward the double steel doors, which had been propped open by two folding chairs. They ducked under two windows covered with iron bars to avoid detection.

"Move," replied Brain Two, who could barely be seen on the far side of the building. Steven had had a few hours earlier in the day to train the other three teams. Thus far, there were no hiccups.

"Brain Trust in position," said Steven. *Moving* was the response on the radio as Brain Two joined them on the other side of the entry. At this point, hand signals would be used. The two teams would move into the building, with Steven and Katie entering first and taking the left side of the building. Brain Two would clear the right side, and Brain Three would push through the middle to keep the hallway clear of O'Brien's men.

Steven moved inside and rapidly paced up a thirty-foot hallway and assessed the building's layout, determining that the vault was ahead and the walls on the right were partition walls made of drywall. He could hear muffled voices coming from a large open area ahead, but he wanted to clear the rooms that appeared at the end of the corridor.

Steven entered the room on the left first, immediately scanning for targets in a ninety-degree arc from left to right. It was uninhabited. Although he was oblivious to anything that was not a human being until he was satisfied that the room was empty, he did notice the room was full of clothing and nonlethal military gear.

"Clear left," he whispered into the mic.

Brain Two followed suit, clearing the room on the right side of the hallway. The six members of Steven's team moved forward in unison until a loud thump struck the concrete.

"Damn," exclaimed the voice. "This stuff's heavy!" The dim glow of a battery-operated lantern illuminated three men attempting to move ammunition crates onto a dolly.

Steven moved toward the entry with Katie in tow. Two men moved along the right side of the hallway with them. *Where is the fourth guy?* If this was an Aegis operation, these three would already be a heap of dead bodies. But his team consisted of rookies and amateurs. He could not afford a firefight. He held his fist up to signal the others to wait. He turned and whispered to Katie.

"I can only see three of them. The fourth guy needs to be located before we make our move. Cover me."

Steven quietly moved into the room, hugging the wall next to the crates of ammunition. He swung his weapon side to side, looking for the fourth man.

Bingo! "I've got the fourth hostile. Keep eyes on the other three."

"Roger," said Katie.

The fourth man was examining an M203 under-barrel grenade launcher, which was designed to be attached to either an M16 or M4. Steven shouldered his SCAR 17 and switched to his silenced sidearm. He had to get up close and personal to avoid alarming the other three men. Catlike, Steven snuck up behind the distracted man and placed the barrel to the back of his head.

"You don't need to die tonight, pal," Steven hissed. "Very slowly, and quietly, set that down. Remove your weapon and remain face forward. Are we clear?"

"Yeah, yeah," said the man as he began to breathe rapidly. He complied with Steven's request and kept his hands spread apart.

"Hands on top of your head and slowly turn toward your buddies," said Steven. "Nobody has to die tonight, got it?"

"Okay."

"Brain Trust has one secured," said Steven. "On my signal, let's wrap this up."

Steven guided the man towards the center of the vault. Once he had a clear field of vision of the other three men, he said, "Go!" The sounds of shuffling feet caught the men's attention, but their reaction time was too slow. Katie yelled first.

"On the ground, assholes! Now!"

"Down," shouted another member of Steven's team.

Steven yelled, "Hit the ground now!"

The confused men swung towards Steven's voice and then fell to their knees. They were stunned by being caught. Steven pushed his captive to the floor.

"Hostiles secured," he announced into the radio. "Frisk these guys, then zip-tie their hands and feet. We still have work to do." He looked around the armory's vault. He was glad O'Brien didn't get his hands on the contents.

"We got 'em," said Katie, breathing heavily from the adrenaline. "Are you impressed?"

"Hell yeah," replied Steven. "You did great, and you didn't shoot anybody." He laughed.

"They didn't deserve it."

CHAPTER 21

Sunday, September 18, 2016
9:00 a.m.
Prescott Peninsula
Quabbin Reservoir, Massachusetts

Abbie's life revolved around politics and climbing the imaginary ladder of success. She was near the top rung, the likely next Vice President of the United States, and the ladder was abruptly pulled out from underneath her. She didn't have a partner, that significant other, to act as her sounding board or a shoulder to cry on. His lifeless body was left in a heap on a rain-soaked patch of St. Augustine grass in Florida.

For two weeks, Abbie mourned the loss of Drew. She hadn't dated anyone since her breakup with Sarge over a decade ago. They maintained a friendship, but any sign of intimacy was gone. Now she was alone, deserted on the Prescott Peninsula with her father and his friends. She had no sense of purpose.

There was so much uncertainty in the country, which diminished her feelings of self-pity. Reports were coming in daily of looting, riots, and murderous gangs taking over the city. Law and order was rapidly disappearing, only to be replaced by a Citizen Corps that used its newfound power for personal gain.

Donald was winding up the morning briefing—long on despair and short on hope. *He can't fake it anymore.* Donald and Susan approached her and sat down on top of the picnic tables. Abbie managed a smile before she spoke.

"Gee, Donald, you really know how to liven up a crowd."

Donald laughed as he replied, "Yeah, I'm a little short on material today, or every day, for that matter." Susan put her arm around Donald and smiled as she looked into the eyes of her husband. He added, "How are you holding up today, Abbie?"

"I'm better today, thanks," Abbie lied. She searched for a subject that might take her mind off her loneliness. Texas. "What are you hearing out of Texas, Donald? Are they still closing their borders?"

"As a matter of fact, there is a little bit of news that I picked up last night from a few ham radio operators," replied Donald. "The governor continues to defy the President. He is refusing to allow anyone into the state that can't prove their residency. The Texas Rangers have expanded significantly and are essentially deporting anyone, American citizen or otherwise, from the state. It's getting ugly, but Abbott feels like he has a duty to protect his citizens first."

"Greg plays hardball," said Abbie. "Before all of this happened, he was pushing his *Texas Plan*, which was part of several proposed amendments to the Constitution."

Susan perked up and asked, "What is the Texas Plan all about?"

Abbie enjoyed the opportunity to discuss politics with her friends. She missed the campaign. She missed the head of her security detail even more. Abbie sat on the picnic table opposite the Quinns and explained the plan.

"Governor Abbott was fed up with liberal, activist courts infringing upon states' rights," she began. "He was attempting to strengthen the Tenth Amendment, which provides that the powers not delegated to the federal government by the Constitution were reserved to the states and its citizens. It was Greg's opinion that our Congress had become neutered by a President who consistently acted in violation of his Constitutional authority. I'm sure the Declaration of Martial Law sent him into circuit overload!" The three laughed, although the serious topic was anything but funny. This felt good to Abbie, so she continued.

"The President's increased use of executive orders to circumvent the authority of Congress was destroying the foundation upon which America was built. Our Congress began to accept these actions as commonplace, which eroded the people's confidence in our government. Greg's solution was to propose several amendments to the Constitution and officially called for their ratification at a Constitutional Convention."

"I like his approach," said Donald. "Unfortunately, the crap hit the fan before we could fix the fan itself."

"It was a long shot anyway, Donald," said Abbie. "Greg thinks like a revolutionary. You might recall that the President issued several executive orders last year restricting gun rights. He took to the airwaves and town hall meetings to exploit the deaths of innocent people to further his political agenda."

"I remember that," interrupted Susan. "Governor Abbott issued a tweet in Greek—*Molon Labe*—which stands for *come and take it.* I admire him for taking a stand."

"Yeah, me too," added Donald. "Abbie, what do you think the states should do when the federal government usurps their power?"

Morgan joined the conversation and sat next to his daughter. Abbie didn't mind her father's presence. She was in her element now.

"It's an interesting dynamic," replied Abbie. "There are occasions when a state carries out resistance to the federal government's unconstitutional use of power. Texas closing its borders is a prime example. If a particular state takes an action that the federal government doesn't like, but that has the support of the people of that state, the federal government can't do anything about it unless it is willing to use force."

"Have we gotten to that point?" asked Susan. "I assume the President is sending troops to intervene, and we know the UN has amassed their so-called peacekeeping forces along the Rio Grande."

"There may be a war, Susan," replied Abbie. "I hope it doesn't come to that. Ordinarily, when several states oppose an unconstitutional encroachment by the federal government, the states can organize a powerful means of opposition. The citizenry can refuse to co-operate with the federal officials. Also, the state legislatures can enact laws to thwart and impede the federal government from furthering its unconstitutional schemes."

"James Madison wrote about this in *The Federalist Papers,*" interjected Morgan. "Madison wrote that not all states will necessarily oppose unconstitutional overreach by Washington. Nevertheless, this should not impede those states that do. It was originally envisioned by the Founders that the states could choose not to implement the federal government's directives. This changed over the years with the carrot-and-stick approach to government."

"What do you mean by that?" asked Susan.

"Over time, as the federal government grew, lawmakers found a way to centralize power in Washington," replied Morgan. "During the Civil War, Congress sought a way to fund the expenses. They established the Commissioner of Internal Revenue, who was given vast powers to collect taxes on behalf of the federal government. As the decades passed, those in Washington began to realize they could control the states by making the money available to them—for a price."

"A hefty price," said Abbie. She admired her father in moments like these. He was knowledgeable, confident, and spoke with conviction. Over the years, he had shielded her from the details of his business and political dealings. *Plausible deniability*, he would say to her. Despite her misgivings about his methods, she always respected his successful results. She studied him as he spoke. He looked tired, as if he was holding onto an inner pain. Her beloved father had aged considerably over the summer. *If he would open up to me, I might be able to help.*

"That's right, dear," said Morgan. "Washington made the states increasingly dependent upon federal coffers to operate. The money, whether raised in taxes or through the operation of the printing press in later years, was available to those states that toed the line. If a particular state resisted the federal mandates placed upon them, they wouldn't get their share of the pie. As a result, their citizens suffered in some cases, which brought political heat on state lawmakers."

Donald attempted to sum it up. "So, the *carrot* is the almighty dollar and the *stick* is the government's threat of *my way or the highway*."

"Very eloquent, Mr. Quinn." Morgan laughed. Donald smiled as he earned another hug from his wife. "The President has divided our country by cultural regions. While it is true that his new Council of Governors is based on FEMA regions, he has strategically placed people loyal to him in each position of power. I suspect he will use the same carrot-and-stick method to bring those regions politically opposed to him into the fold."

"What do you mean?" asked Susan.

"Let's use the southeastern part of the nation as an example," replied Morgan. "This is FEMA Region IV. Those eight states represent the vast majority of the old Confederacy and almost always vote Republican in presidential elections. The President sought to appoint an insider to the governor's position that would be, shall I say, *tolerable* to the Southern point of view."

"So centrist-democrat Congressman Jim Cooper, from Tennessee, was his choice," said Abbie.

"That's correct, but Cooper is not *cooperating*," said Morgan. "He's not *toeing the company line*, as they say. I suspect he will be replaced with someone more heavy handed soon."

"The carrot-and-stick approach is not working with Cooper?" asked Susan.

"No, Mrs. Quinn, it is not," replied Morgan. "It has not worked in Texas either. I believe the President is going to make an example of Texas."

"These are difficult times," said Donald. "How will Texas stand by itself against a President who has more power than any of his predecessors?"

"I don't know, Donald," replied Abbie. "But the world is watching."

CHAPTER 22

Sunday, September 18, 2016
8:00 p.m.
Citizen Corps Region I, Office of the Governor
99 High Street
Boston, Massachusetts

Brad rode in silence as he took in the decaying landscape of Boston. Broken glass littered the streets, as did the abandoned vehicles. Some roads were impassible as the city, or the governor, took no effort to tow them out of the way. Brad marveled at how quickly things had unraveled.

Dealing with the dead was an even bigger problem. Now that the nation was in its third week of the collapse, Americans began dying of natural causes due to dehydration, disease, and starvation. Brad verily believed that murders were the leading cause of death, and suicide was on the rise due to the lost hope of the people.

The widespread belief corpses posed a major health risk was inaccurate, especially if death resulted from trauma. In third world countries, dead bodies were likely to cause outbreaks of diseases such as typhoid fever, cholera or plague. In a postapocalyptic America, decomposing bodies might transmit gastroenteritis or food poisoning syndrome for survivors if they contaminated streams, wells or other water sources. In Boston, nobody was taking steps to dispose of the dead, whether by burial or cremation.

Gunny Falcone slowly maneuvered the HUMVEE towards the headquarters of the new Citizen Corps governor. Brad and Captain Branson were summoned to meet with O'Brien. Although Brad expected a tongue-lashing of some kind, he didn't care. Under the circumstances, their plan worked, as twenty-six of the forty-four armories were protected. Brad had a prison full of O'Brien's men under armed guard at Fort Devens, and their own armory at 1PP was capable of equipping a battalion. He was anxious to see how the governor was handling this setback.

"Wait here, Gunny, but stay frosty. Everyone should be considered a hostile."

"Yes, sir!"

Brad entered the lobby, which looked more like Don Corleone's men who had *hit the mattresses* than the offices of the regional governor. Clearly, the governor was on edge. Brad knew it was a matter of time before O'Brien called upon the President for help—probably in the form of an outside military presence. Brad was frisked and then escorted up the stairs. Captain Branson and O'Brien were waiting for him in the conference room.

"You're late," gruffed O'Brien.

Brad didn't respond.

He motioned for Brad to sit down by waving his arm in the general direction of a chair. Brad kept his eyes trained on O'Brien. He intended to use the stare as a form of intimidation. Plus, he wanted to study O'Brien further, as this was only their second meeting. Captain Branson had effectively become the liaison between Brad and O'Brien, but Brad wanted to establish his own connection with the man.

"Colonel, Mr. Pearson will not be joining us," offered Branson. "We need to discuss a few things that will not involve him."

"May I speak freely, Governor?" asked Brad, playing the part of dutiful soldier.

"Go ahead."

"Prior to the cyber attack, Mr. Pearson was insistent upon moving my regiment's assets to other locations outside of your region, sir," said Brad. "I voiced concern to my superiors that Mr. Pearson did not have our unit's best interests at heart."

"What are you thinking, soldier?" asked O'Brien. He leaned back in his chair and clasped his hands on his belly. Brad thought he looked *bigger* than their first meeting.

"Pearson is a civilian, sir, and as such, he might have loyalties and interests elsewhere."

"Like where, Colonel?"

"Region II, sir. I've received word from Fort Drum that they are gearing up for a major offensive into New York City to restore order. Once that has been achieved, the governor of Region II will be installing a new mayor." O'Brien listened intently as Brad spoke. *The seeds of doubt were planted.*

"You think Pearson is a part of that?" asked O'Brien.

"I have two pieces of intel for you, Governor. First, Pearson is a native New Yorker and his former boss at Federal Protective Services is the governor of Region II." Brad stood and pulled three photos out of his jacket. He slid them across the table to O'Brien, who picked them up and examined them. They depicted three Green Line Maintenance trucks driving up to a checkpoint where Interstate 90 crossed the Hudson River.

"What are these?" he asked.

"They were taken by a checkpoint security cam outside Albany, New York, sir. Your men and your weapons are en route to Fort Drum."

"This guy took my guns?" asked O'Brien. "Where the hell are my men?"

"We believe your men may have received a better offer, sir," replied Brad. "But I have a solution." *Time for the pitch.*

"I'm listening."

"My Marines are loyal to their country, sir. They are willing to die for her. But they also have families that they want to care for and protect."

"That's understandable," O'Brien interrupted.

"Throughout the military, troops have abandoned their posts to go home," said Brad. "The same is true at Fort Devens. I believe I can persuade them back to active duty if we could make room for their families and give them priority access to provisions and supplies." *I'll give you an army—my army.*

"I don't see a problem with that," said O'Brien.

"With your permission, sir, I'll reassemble my regiment under the promise of food, shelter, and safety for them and their families."

"Do it," O'Brien said as he stood. He added, "Branson, give the colonel whatever he needs to expedite this."

"Yes, sir," said Captain Branson. Brad and Branson stood to leave when O'Brien walked toward the window overlooking a rain-soaked Congress Street.

"One more thing," said O'Brien. "Issue a treason warrant. Bring me Pearson!"

CHAPTER 23

Tuesday, September 20, 2016
6:00 p.m.
Town Hall
Belchertown, Massachusetts

Residents of Belchertown, Massachusetts, shuffled their way across Belchertown Common toward the makeshift stage. In Small Town, U.S.A., war memorials were defining features of the landscape. They usually featured iconic statues that served as focal points in, and sometimes symbols of, the town's hub—its center of activity.

The defining feature of the Belchertown common was the commanding presence of a Civil War monument. Standing twenty-six feet tall, including the Union Civil War soldier, the monument cast a long shadow as the sun set to the west. Illuminated by the sunset, a bronze plaque on the west side of the base read:

ROLL OF THE HONORED DEAD WHO WENT FROM BELCHERTOWN AND FOUGHT IN DEFENCE OF LIBERTY AND THEIR COUNTRY

The residents of Belchertown were about to be encouraged to wage war, in the name of their country, by its newly appointed town chairman of the board of selectmen, Ronald Archibald.

"Gather around, folks, we'd like to get started so that you folks can get home before dark," shouted Archibald, the head of the Central Massachusetts Citizen Corps office. "We have a lot to discuss, and then there will be a brief question-and-answer period."

A week after the Declaration of Martial Law, Archibald was

contacted by Pearson, who was acting on behalf of Governor O'Brien. Archibald was one of five selectmen on the board, but not the chairman. After several lengthy interviews that day with Mr. Pearson, it was determined that the politics of the chairman was not a good fit for the Citizen Corps, and he was summarily dismissed. Archibald, an environmental law attorney and president of the Belchertown Lions Club, was a perfect substitute.

Pearson approached the stage and sat in a folding chair behind Archibald. Although there had been several informal gatherings of the Citizen Corps team leaders with Pearson, this was the first opportunity to address the residents as a whole. The turnout was around five hundred people, mostly men.

"Thank you, everyone, thank you," said Archibald. "As many of you know, our President is doing everything in his power to protect the citizens of our nation and small communities like this one. When I was asked to head up the Citizen Corps council in Hampshire County, which now includes the entirety of the Quabbin Reservoir, I was concerned that I couldn't achieve the lofty goals set by our President. With the help of our new governor, James O'Brien, and the folks at FEMA, we have been able to secure some fresh water, food, and medical supplies for those of you who have chosen to work with me in the rebuilding effort. I know it isn't much, but it's a start. I've been assured that there will be more to come." Archibald had lived in Belchertown his entire life and was acquainted with nearly all of its residents. He relished this opportunity to shine in front of *his* constituents.

"I know we've encountered a few rough patches, and the supplies will start coming in again. In the meantime, we need to band together to help ourselves," continued Archibald. He held a printed flyer over his head and turned from left to right for effect. "After my appointment, I distributed flyers and posted them in prominent places around the county as well. I wanted everyone to have the opportunity to voluntarily comply with the President's declaration. We are all in this together, my friends, and it isn't necessary that we become at odds with our neighbors."

The flyer stated the primary directives of the Declaration of Martial Law requiring weapons and ammunition surrender, the turning over of excess food and supplies, and a pledge of allegiance to the spirit and intent of the Citizen Corps.

"Unfortunately, not all residents have been cooperative in our efforts to gain compliance with the President's declaration," he continued. "We are now entering our third week of this disaster, and it is time to move toward the next phase of implementation. I commend those of you who joined us in our efforts, and you will be rewarded. But I must ask one more thing of you.

"I've divided my region into ten geographical parts, each with an appointed Citizen Corps team leader. These team leaders have been given the written authority to conduct house-to-house searches of their neighborhoods to ensure compliance with the President's directives. They have been given the requisite weapons, manpower, and promised support to effectuate this purpose." Archibald paused as the attendees mumbled amongst themselves and began to shift nervously on their feet. He had anticipated this reaction.

"This action could have been avoided had our friends and neighbors simply complied with the flyers I distributed. But hostilities can still be avoided in another way. I need your help in identifying those among us who selfishly hoard food and supplies for themselves. Those who are unwilling to share their bounties put you and your families at risk. Further, anyone who refuses to relinquish their weapons as required for the safety of the community puts us all at risk.

"More food and supplies are on the way. Our government is here to help us. As an incentive to those of you who cooperate with me today, you will be earmarked for additional shares of the supplies."

The crowd's demeanor picked up, and nods of approval were abundant. He created an army of snitches.

"After the meeting, the Citizen Corps team leaders will disperse throughout the common and hold up a sign indicating their assigned subregions of Hampshire County. Please introduce yourself to them and have comfort in knowing that any information you share with them, or me, will be held in the strictest confidence." It was time to take a few questions. The residents asked a variety of questions, for which Archibald had no answers. *When was the power going to be restored? What about outsiders trying to move in? Somebody stole some of my chickens, what can be done about that?*

The last question, asked by one of the residents, needed to be addressed, and he had prepared a response.

"What's going on at Prescott Peninsula? Are you gonna do anything about Jimmy Fulks, who was shot in cold blood?"

Pearson leaned up in his chair and got Archibald's attention. "What's this about?"

Archibald nodded and mouthed *I got this.*

"I know this has been on everyone's mind and I appreciate your concern," said Archibald. "As you know, Prescott Peninsula has been converted into a community for the protection of abused families. But we know very little about it. I don't know if the families are safe, how many are there, etc."

A resident shouted, "Maybe they have extra food and supplies to share with the rest of us?"

"Yeah, we need to know this, right, Archie?" *Archie* was used as a nickname by Ronald Archibald's friends.

"I agree, everyone, and I intend to broach the subject with them," replied Archibald. "Prescott Peninsula has been designated part of my territory, and therefore, they must comply with my rules. We'll deliver that message loud and clear first thing tomorrow morning."

Chapter 24

Wednesday, September 21, 2016
8:00 a.m.
Prescott Peninsula
Quabbin Reservoir, Massachusetts

The Citizen Corps contingent of eight men led by Archibald approached the front gate of Prescott Peninsula, which was manned by CWO Shore and three of his men. On Brad's instructions, none of his personnel wore uniforms during patrols. Khakis, camo pants like those made by Wrangler, and solid-color T-shirts in black, olive, or green were suggested.

CWO Shore immediately saw he was outmanned and contacted 1PP to send another team to the front entrance. He quickly instructed his men to spread out and take defensive positions on both sides of the gate and near the guardhouse. His military training sensed a potential conflict, and he wasn't gonna lose another man. Shore took Sab's death pretty hard because it happened on his watch. He didn't give a rat's ass about the local who raised his gun to shoot her.

As the two SUVs skidded to a halt in the gravel, Shore raised his weapon to low ready and stood firm in front of them. He trusted his men and knew that they would tear these locals to shreds if they considered raising their weapons in his direction. The driver of the lead vehicle stepped out of the GMC Yukon, as did his companion in the passenger seat. The other men began to open their doors when Shore shouted at them.

"That's enough! This is private property. Remain in your vehicles." Red dots appeared from all directions as his men lit up their targets. They were sending a message to the visitors.

"Now, there's no reason for all of this animosity, my friends," said Archibald. "My name is Ronald Archibald from nearby Belchertown. I need to speak to the person in charge here."

Shore stood firm and repeated his warning, "This is private property. You need to return to your vehicle and leave now!"

"Are you boys military?" asked Pearson, but he didn't receive an answer. After a few moments of awkward silence, Shore heard the sound of approaching four-wheelers with his requested reinforcements. "My name is Joseph Pearson with the Federal Protective Services. Mr. Archibald has the full authority of the President to enter these premises."

"Back in your vehicle, sir," said Shore, instantly recognizing the name. He was glad he was wearing his Oakley sunglasses. "I won't ask again."

"Or what?" shouted one of the men from the other vehicle. "You gonna shoot us like you shot Jimmy in cold blood?"

The four additional soldiers arrived and quickly dispersed, taking positions behind the HESCO barriers. The sight of the additional security personnel caused the visitors to cower behind their doors or return to their vehicles.

"I don't know what you think you're doing here, but let's get one thing straight," said Archibald. "I am the head of the Citizen Corps in this area, and Prescott Peninsula, hell, all of Quabbin Reservoir, comes under my jurisdiction. You tell your superiors that I will be back tomorrow. They will speak with me. They will obey my instructions." Angrily, Archibald reached into the truck to grab something, which caused all of the red dots to be trained on him. He had a stack of flyers and threw them on the road in front of Shore.

"You give this to your boss and tell him I'll be back tomorrow with a whole lot more questions than I had when I got here," shouted Archibald, shaking his head and shoulders side to side with a swagger as he turned to walk back to his truck. "Let's go!"

CHAPTER 25

Wednesday, September 21, 2016
3:00 p.m.
Prescott Peninsula
Quabbin Reservoir, Massachusetts

Aside from world leaders, top government officials and longtime family friends, only a few people could elicit a personal response, much less a face-to-face meeting, with the President of the United States. This President had many close advisors, including Rex Tillerson, the ExxonMobil chairman; Andy Stern, outgoing president of the Service Employees International Union; and Billy Tauzin, the head of the Pharmaceutical Manufacturers of America. *Big Oil—Big Labor—Big Pharma.* Then, there was Victoria Blanchett, *the gatekeeper* of the President's circle of confidants.

They were part of an elite group of American political movers and shakers capable of directing the highest levels of government to do their bidding. The stature of America's elite power brokers was determined by a variety of factors, including legislative victories, overall lobbying expenditures, and the number of visits to the White House. *After all, can one really be a power broker without multiple trips to 1600 Pennsylvania Avenue?*

Morgan had never visited this President at the White House. He preferred to remain in the shadows. He considered himself a lobbyist, *of sorts*. He had an incredible knack for determining a politician's true agenda and then manipulating their goals to mesh with his. Sometimes, Morgan would create opportunities for the Boston Brahmin based upon the politician's blind spots.

The cyber attack was the most strategic and ambitious of these opportunities. However, Morgan underestimated the President, a mistake that he would attempt to rectify. Morgan considered himself a close confidant of the President. He was instrumental in placing him into office in 2008. But now the President was more than aloof, he was avoiding Morgan.

In August, he met with the President, who was vacationing in Morgan's home on Martha's Vineyard. The two agreed to pursue this course of action—*the reset.* They also pledged to do so in concert with one another. The message Morgan sent to the President's Chief of Staff was clear—*we need to continue our Martha's Vineyard conversation.*

"Mr. President, it has been some time since we've had an opportunity to speak," started Morgan.

"That's true, John, but I've been a little busy." The President bristled.

"Then I'll get right to the point. We need to discuss bringing this to an end, Mr. President. Our companies are ready to deliver the computer servers, transformers, and the overseas personnel to restore power across the country. We're prepared to fulfill our end of the bargain. I need your approval to set things into motion with DARPA."

DARPA, an acronym for Defense Advanced Research Projects Agency, was an agency of the Department of Defense responsible for developing new technologies for the military. Created in 1958 under the authority of President Eisenhower, scientists at DARPA had produced hundreds of technologically sophisticated tools used by the government in every capacity.

Companies controlled by the Boston Brahmin, as an integral part of the military-industrial community, worked closely with DARPA program managers. One of the projects initiated in the past year was known as RADICS—Rapid Attack Detection, Isolation and Characterization Systems. The project, still in its infancy, was designed to provide early warning of impending cyber attacks on critical infrastructure as well as rapid forensic identifications of cyber threats. The RADICS project was also expanded to include mitigation and damage control following a successful attack by isolating unaffected networks, repairing damaged ones, and coordinating efforts to replace damaged electricity transmission components, like transformers.

Morgan knew that billions of dollars would be made from the cyber attack, and not just in the United States. Every advanced nation in the world would pay handsomely for the innovative technologies and the response protocols established by the Boston Brahmin's companies.

"There's still work to do, *John*," said the President, placing emphasis on Morgan's name. "You'll make your money now let me finish what I started." This conversation was not going the way Morgan intended. The President was surly and combative. *He's mocking me.*

"Our goals may have differed, Mr. President, as we discussed at Martha's Vineyard. But we both agreed on what brought us here. We've made our point, and the American people have suffered enough. It's time to give them the hope and change that you envisioned many years ago. It's an opportunity for you to cement your legacy among world leaders." Morgan was trying to exploit the President's vanity.

"Let me be clear, John. We've only begun this process. You, and privileged white Americans like you, don't understand the plight of the common man. You don't understand what my people have experienced for hundreds of years."

Morgan was incensed. *My people?* "With all due respect, Mr. President, this is not the time for political rhetoric," said Morgan sternly into the satphone. "We need to bring this to an end."

The President ignored him, shouting into the receiver, "White people don't have to worry about their race being targeted by police as they walk down the street. White people have been unjustly enriched for centuries on the backs of people of color. White people don't have to worry about being passed over for a job interview because they have a black-sounding name."

Morgan had had enough. "What is your point, Mr. President?" asked Morgan. "Not so long ago, someone with a self-described *funny name* was elected President. White people like me supported that President. The President I supported pledged to bridge the racial divide in this country, not widen it. So, what is your point?" Morgan repeated the question, this time shouting.

"My point is, John, that the time has come for the reset you seek, but it will fulfill my vision, not yours. I envision a country in which everyone is equal—*socially, economically, and politically*. This country became rich by invading, occupying, and looting poor countries around the globe. In the name of capitalism and free markets, this country has achieved its power by economic plunder. This stops now. It's true that I pledged to bridge the racial divide of this nation. I also pledged to fundamentally transform America. The job is not done."

The line went dead.

CHAPTER 26

Wednesday, September 21, 2016
6:00 p.m.
Prescott Peninsula
Quabbin Reservoir, Massachusetts

Morgan suddenly felt clammy and light-headed. He found his way to a chair in the small bungalow and sat down. No one had ever spoken to him that way. "I'm John Morgan," he unknowingly said aloud.

The numbness he was experiencing in his jaw and extending down his left arm was not new. Although there was no history of heart disease in his family, his cardiologist had diagnosed him as being hypertense. It had been developing gradually over several years as he developed sleep apnea. His first concern was that the stress of his *job* was the cause. His physician assured him hypertension had little to do with stress and a lot to do with issues surrounding his kidneys, thyroid, and sleep issues.

Recently, his prescription was changed to an ACE inhibitor called lisinopril. Morgan failed to communicate this change to Susan, who was responsible for maintaining the pharmacy at 1PP. Morgan ran out of his lisinopril a week ago and began taking a generic diuretic class of blood pressure medication instead. His body was not handling the transition well.

His shortness of breath subsided, and he wiped the sweat from his face and neck. Morgan was able to make his way to a pantry cabinet and found the low-dose aspirin. His hands shook as he took the aspirin, quickly chasing it with water. *This cannot be happening to me. I've got to calm down.*

He lowered himself into his nearby bed and thought about the conversation with the President. The President had avoided him, and that was telling in itself. The emotional outburst revealed the President's true feelings. He had violated rule number one, which was never let them know what you're thinking.

Perhaps the President was blinded by his anger, which would prevent him from thinking clearly. But Morgan could not take any chances. They would be in danger now. The President would consider Morgan a threat and take steps to minimize his influence. *Or worse.*

Morgan had recovered from his episode and was seeing the situation with more clarity. It was time to move forward. He used the satphone to place a call to General Sears. After a brief tussle with a new aide, General Sears came on the phone.

"Hello, John."

"Mason, this won't take long," said Morgan.

"I appreciate that, but I'm here for you, John."

"In your dealings with the President, is his focus on repairing the damage to the nation or something else?" asked Morgan.

"I would call his actions and attitude *strategic scheming*. As you know, I am not part of his inner circle. I become involved in the process once his decision has been made."

"Who are his primary advisors?" Morgan paced the floor and glanced out of the windows of the bungalow. Susan and the girls were gathering pine tree nuts near the edge of the woods.

"The usual suspects, including Giles and Blanchett, are always by his side. But he's brought back an old friend—his favorite general."

"Are you talking about Cartwright?" asked Morgan, who suddenly snapped to attention.

"One and the same. James *Hoss* Cartwright, former vice chairman of the Joint Chiefs, is back and has become an integral part of the President's advisory team."

"You had him stripped of his security clearance when he leaked the details about Stuxnet," said Morgan.

Cartwright had conceived and ran the cyber operation known as

Olympic Games, which included Stuxnet and other highly sophisticated pieces of malware aimed at the Iranian nuclear effort. Stuxnet entered Iran's nuclear apparatus through hacked suppliers. The Stuxnet worm was introduced into five component vendors that were key to Iran's nuclear program, including the one that developed the centrifuges. These firms became unwitting Trojan horses for Stuxnet. Once the malware infiltrated the Iranians' network and compromised the data at the critically important Natanz plant, it set back the Iranian nuclear program several years.

"I was told privately that the President urged Hoss to release the information to the media," said General Sears. "The administration authorized the leaks in order to increase the President's *bona fides* on national security prior to the last election. Of course, the White House denounced the leaks and demanded an investigation. The fire storm was then dumped in my lap. I had no choice but to recommend his security clearance be stripped."

"How can he possibly advise the President without the necessary security clearance?" asked Morgan.

"The President isn't following the rules anymore, John," replied Sears.

Morgan chuckled. *He never has.* "Mason, what is the consensus within the military?"

"Most are angry, especially at the dictates coming out of the White House," replied Sears. "Morale is in the tank, and trust in the President's decisions is minimal at best. Nobody wants to take actions against peaceful Americans trying to survive, but the orders from the President are more directed toward the law-abiding than they are against those wreaking havoc in our cities."

With the Declaration of Martial Law, the President exerted the most extreme assertion of domestic executive power in the history of the republic. Morgan anticipated this, but the heavy-handed approach against those who disagreed with him was surprising. There was no functioning Congress, and the President was not taking steps to reconvene one. The courts were closed, with no plan to bring them back into session. The President was wielding power without any checks and balances. Morgan took a deep breath and chose his next words carefully.

"Mason, we may be approaching a constitutional crisis in our country. You need to carefully compile a list of those high-ranking officers who would stand with us if the President needs to be removed from office."

"John, are you suggesting a coup d'état? This will be a difficult subject to broach with anyone under my command. Remember those three words—*duty, honor, country.*"

"Of course I remember them," said Morgan. "I pledged them myself many years ago."

"Honor is a commodity in short supply these days outside of the military," said Sears. "Our military is the single greatest fighting body in the world today because of this one word."

Morgan interrupted. "I am keenly aware that the men and women of the U.S. military take their oath seriously when they pledge to support and defend the Constitution."

Sears fired back. "We also pledge to obey the orders of the President of the United States and the orders of the officers appointed over us. According to regulations found in the Uniform Code of Military Justice, that last part is important. The UCMJ Article 92 requires all members of the United States military to obey lawful orders."

Morgan didn't like arguing with General Sears. One confrontational phone call was enough for today. But he had to pursue this option. "Do you consider the President's actions to be a lawful order?"

"Article 92 works to define what a lawful order is, but in a nutshell, it's any order given by a superior authority in good standing."

"Unless," added Morgan, "that order conflicts with the Constitution, U.S. law, standing lawful orders, or is issued by someone who does not possess the authority to issue that order. I'm also familiar with the UCMJ's loose definition of an unlawful order."

"But, John, removing the President from office, forcibly or

otherwise, is not our job. Nor do we have the requisite constitutional authority. We'd be just as guilty as the President if we initiated a coup."

Morgan remained quiet for a moment as he realized the *overthrow option* was not viable. He knew the law prohibited it. Article II of the Constitution established the President as the Commander in Chief. Regardless of the actions of a sitting President, unless he was legally removed from command, he was in charge. The honor of the military precluded them from doing anything against their commander, regardless of their personal opinions. The nation as a whole might believe a President had no honor at all, but that was what made our military better than him. They did have honor. Ultimately, they might not like what he was doing, but they would stand with their honor intact and continue to obey all lawful orders issued by their commander.

"Mason, you're right," started Morgan. He knew a commander unfit for duty could be removed from office. But there was a process required by the Constitution. In the case of the Commander in Chief, that task resided with Congress. The House of Representatives must impeach him, and the Senate then had to enforce that impeachment, passing sentence and removing him from office. "A military coup would not be constitutional and thus a violation of the oath every service member takes upon entrance to the U.S. military, and that just isn't going to happen. Our military members are too honorable to stoop to extra-constitutional measures regardless of the consequences."

"That's right, John," said Sears. "But let me put your mind at ease about all of this. The men under my command are not blind. They see what the President is attempting to do, and they want no part of it. Let's just say the commanders in the field are initiating a *work slowdown*."

Morgan felt relieved that he had not alienated the most important asset available to him in government. It was time for him to reassure Sears.

"Mason, thank you for hearing me out. I apologize if my concern for our great country led me down the wrong path in search of a solution. We face a monumental task. It will take great leadership to put the country together again."

CHAPTER 27

Wednesday, September 21, 2016
8:00 p.m.
Prescott Peninsula
Quabbin Reservoir, Massachusetts

Donald led the entourage along the southernmost shore of Prescott Peninsula. Brad walked alongside him while Gunny Falcone, CWO Shore, and Captain Branson walked twenty yards behind. Not that the contingent needed protection, but simply due to protocol, two seasoned Marines brought up the rear.

Initially, when Donald, Brad, and Steven discussed creating a safe haven for the Boston Brahmin on Prescott Peninsula, they enjoyed the illusion created by Donald to discourage curiosity seekers from encroaching upon their extraordinary bug-out location. Prescott Peninsula met all the most important criteria for creating a secure survival retreat.

First, it was close enough to Boston that they could get there without refueling or encountering significant resistance.

Second, it was a good distance from the major population areas, which enabled them to avoid the resulting social unrest and the likelihood of a medical crisis, which could result from lack of resources or sanitation.

Third, the Quabbin Reservoir provided them an excellent water source, which was one of the most important considerations when choosing a bug-out retreat. The Peninsula was surrounded by the largest body of fresh water in Massachusetts, but also included fresh-water springs and underground well water.

Fourth, 1PP was well concealed from outsiders. Centrally located in a heavily wooded area, the current residents could move freely around the compound without fear of detection from those across the shore. Donald did stress the practice of light discipline out of precaution. As fall approached, the leaves would drop, and their cover would gradually disappear.

Fifth, Prescott Peninsula offered them the ability to survive by adopting a self-sustainable lifestyle, which typically involved hunting, gardening, and raising livestock. Freshwater fish was abundant, as well as a variety of wildlife, which they could hunt as a future option. Their food stores were sufficient to maintain the Boston Brahmin and the growing military contingent for about a year. Planting the gardens would become a priority in the spring if the power outage continued.

Other factors typically considered were the threats of natural disasters and the prohibition of local governmental entities pursuant to zoning regulations and ordinances. Under the present circumstances, the county zoning restrictions were the least of their problems, which was why Donald brought them down for this conversation.

"Here we are," said Donald. It was nearly a full moon, providing excellent visibility across the reservoir toward Little Quabbin Island and the mainland, known as Quabbin Hill. Donald pointed toward the southeast. "There. Do you see the boat launch?"

"Yeah, just around the point," replied Brad. He lifted his 6 x 50 mm Bushnell night-vision monocular to his right eye and panned the shore across the lake. He slowly surveyed the banks from the boat launch to the west towards Belchertown. He saw the draw of a cigarette create a bright red cherry. "Someone is smoking on the bank near Belchertown." Brad lowered the monocular and handed it to Gunny Falcone, who looked as well.

"What's that structure across the way?" said Gunny Falcone. He lowered the monocular and pointed due south from their position to the top of a concrete building sitting on top of Quabbin Hill. "It looks like the top of an air traffic control tower. Is there an airport over there?"

"It's not an airport," replied Donald. "It's the Quabbin Reservoir Observation Tower." Built in 1940, the eighty-four-foot tower provided spectacular views of the Quabbin Reservoir watershed and the surrounding landscape.

"Let me see," noted Brad, who missed the structure the first time. He took another look through the monocular. "The leaves are dropping already. When they all fall over the next week or so, someone in the tower could have a clear line of sight to 1PP. How far is it from the Observation Tower to 1PP?"

"Approximately five miles," replied Donald.

"Too far for a sniper," mumbled Brad, "but not for a Stinger."

Gunny Falcone nodded.

"Belchertown is about a mile from the shore," continued Donald, pointing toward the southwest.

At Prescott Peninsula, Donald coordinated security while Brad dealt with Governor O'Brien. Frequently either Gunny Falcone or CWO Shore were pulled away to perform their *official duties*. Brad confided in Donald that he was having difficulty juggling the security of Prescott Peninsula with the duties assigned to him by his superior and the monitoring of O'Brien. Donald was taking a bigger role in the defense of their bug-out location.

Donald continued. "They've been watching us. I'll show you on the topo map when we return, but I thought it would be useful to see the topography in person."

"It's possible that Pearson recognized me at the gate this morning," said CWO Shore. "I had my sunglasses on and tried to use my weapon as a distraction."

Brad interrupted him. "Don't put this on yourself, Shore. It doesn't matter how we change our attire; even a hack like Pearson will recognize military, whether undercover or fully dressed out."

"Also, this has been going on since the shooting at the front gate," added Donald. "I believe the local residents are getting curious and might take it to the next level."

"They also appear to be organizing patrols by boat," added Shore. "We confronted two fishermen along Rattlesnake Den Road on the west side this afternoon, but they weren't fishing."

"They were observing our reactions to their presence," said Brad.

"That makes sense," Donald interjected. "It appears we're being stalked, gentlemen." The men remained quiet as Brad took another turn using the monocular.

"We always knew this would be tough to defend because of its size," said Brad. "Before the cyber attack, we defined the perimeter as a restricted area by providing a physical and psychological deterrent to unauthorized entry. This served notice to the locals that entry was not permitted. But it has piqued curiosity, and the shooting incident didn't help."

"The security fencing at the top of the peninsula has worked well," said Shore. "We haven't had anyone attempt to breach it. It has helped that the team we have in place up there is permanent. They know that fence, trust me. We've all logged hundreds of miles walking it."

"The luxury of our permanent personnel will be tested soon," said Brad. "As far as my superiors know, and our new *governor*, most of my men are AWOL. Branson is in a strategic position and can't be pulled out. Falcone will always be with me. Shore, you are very important on that fence. We are still vulnerable along the shoreline. I need more eyes on the water, to free up my men to conduct the actual patrols and be a quick-response force in the event the locals try something."

"I have an idea," said Donald. "I have a lot of warm bodies at 1PP who are bored out of their minds."

"Are you gonna put the old people in the patrol boats?" Captain Branson laughed.

"No, but why can't they be equipped with radios and binoculars," replied Donald. "It will give them a sense of purpose and free up your Marines to conduct patrols and nighttime security."

"That could work, Colonel," said Gunny Falcone.

Brad thought for a moment and then nodded. "Pick the most trainable ones, Donald. Radio discipline and situational awareness will be critical. By adding the extra eyes on the water, we'll have a better chance of dealing with any hostiles."

"I'll put it together tomorrow," said Donald. "What about Pearson?"

"We need someone to infiltrate the good people of Belchertown and find Pearson at the same time," replied Brad. "I think I know two spooks that are available."

CHAPTER 28

Friday, September 23, 2016
6:00 p.m.
100 Beacon
Boston, Massachusetts

Brad dismissed Gunny Falcone and advised him to take Captain Branson back to Prescott Peninsula. A combination of the increased patrols and the volunteers from the Boston Brahmin enabled his officers to monitor the activities of the nearby residents. Their activities on the water and the banks of the Quabbin Reservoir were increasing. The residents of Belchertown were preparing for something. He hoped his plan would work.

J.J. greeted him at the door and was in good spirits. Apparently, his time away from 1PP and the terrible memories of Sabina's final hours had subsided. J.J.'s self-imposed therapy was helping others. This helped him cope with his own psychological issues.

"Greetings, Colonel," said J.J with a salute and a laugh. Clearly, he was in a good mood. "Thank you for meeting with us in our humble abode."

"Shut your cock holster and listen up," replied Brad as he gave J.J. an unexpected hug. The two men had never been best buds, but now they shared a common bond—a fallen comrade.

"Very funny, Brad," said Julia as she approached him with an adult beverage. "After your visit with our illustrious governor, I suspect you could use one of these."

"Roger that," said Brad. "The man is a real piece of work, but the fact that he is an open book plays to our advantage." He took off his gear and laid it on the floor under the wall of televisions.

"What's the latest?" asked Sarge. He pulled up a bar stool and swiveled back and forth. "Dealin' with that guy must be a challenge."

"It is, Sarge," replied Brad. "His mood swings are incredible. One moment, he's leaning his fat ass back in a chair, puffing on a cigar. The next minute, he's enraged. Face red. Veins pulsing out of his neck. Then he'll go back to *Mr. Chill Governor*."

"You have to wonder," started Katie. "Maybe he's bipolar?" She opened two beers and handed one of them to Steven. They clinked bottles before drinking.

"I'm no psychobabble guy, but he definitely is volatile," replied Brad. "This enables me to read him and manipulate his decision making, which is one of the reasons I'm here tonight."

"Oh, we thought you were excited to watch another riveting address from his highness, the President." Steven laughed.

"Well, there's that," said Brad. "Actually, I have a job for you, my friend, and Katie, too."

"The dynamic duo." Sarge laughed.

"Superman and Wonder Woman!" shouted Katie as she jumped down off the bar stool and struck a pose.

"I was hoping for Mr. and Mrs. Smith—Brad Pitt and Angelina Jolie," said Brad.

Steven started laughing hysterically. "Yeah, I want Angelina Jolie!" he shouted.

"How about I beat your ass, Commander!" came the response from Katie, who chased him around the sofa a couple of times.

"Seriously, guys," interrupted Brad as he tried to bring the group back to business. "We have a problem developing out at Prescott Peninsula."

Brad went on to explain the events of the last several days, including the appearance of Pearson at the front gate and the increased activity of the locals on the banks of the Quabbin Reservoir. He relayed his plan to the group.

"I've secured O'Brien's approval to hire Steven and Wonder Woman here to locate and apprehend Pearson, a man now wanted for treason." Brad pulled flyers out of his kit and handed one to everybody. They resembled a wanted poster from the nineteenth century.

"How did you manage this?" asked Sarge as he studied the flyer.

"With the help of my man, Branson, we convinced O'Brien that Pearson was responsible for the failed attempts to secure the weapons from the armories," replied Brad. "I provided him images of the MBTA vehicles traveling toward Fort Drum in New York. O'Brien took the bait."

"What's our role in this?" asked Steven.

"We're going to kill two birds with one stone," replied Brad. He handed a letter to Steven on Citizen Corps stationary, which included the signature and seal of Governor O'Brien. "This letter will provide you safe passage through any government checkpoints. I also had Branson secure several blank copies of the sealed letterhead. You never know when they'll become useful."

"Hey, Nomad, we get to kill somebody!" exclaimed Katie.

Steven shot her a look. Brad knew that even amongst the Loyal Nine, he didn't like his Aegis code name mentioned.

"Not exactly," interrupted Brad, effectively saving Katie from the death stare. "We need to lend the appearance that he is being brought in for questioning. I don't want to raise suspicion with the people of Belchertown, or the governor, as to our motivations. I prefer to look at this as an abduction."

"Where do we take him, Fort Devens?" asked Steven.

"Yes. We'll lock him up with the rest of O'Brien's thugs," replied Brad. "At some point, we've got to come up with a plan for those guys. I can't hold them forever. Hell, I can't feed them forever."

"Okay, this is doable," said Steven. "What else?"

"While you're there, see what you can learn," said Brad. "This fellow Archibald, a former attorney, is the head of the Citizen Corps in the region. I believe he might be planning an assault on Prescott Peninsula."

"We'll find out what's going on," said Steven.

"I've got the best of the best out there running security, but we're outmanned," said Brad. "The front gate is relatively secured by the fence and the team I have in place, but the shoreline perimeter is massive. If they come at us all at once or in a concentrated location, we'd get overrun. Try to get a feel for their numbers. Are they training? How will they come at us? You know the drill."

"Got it," said Steven.

Sarge stood and walked toward the window and cleared his throat. Brad knew his friend was analyzing their conversation.

"What do you think, Sarge?" asked Brad.

"Sun Tzu, in *The Art of War*, argued a brilliant general was one that could win without fighting," he replied. He returned to the group. "I just wonder if there is a way to get Belchertown to stand down."

*****

The group weighed their options on dealing with Belchertown and also traded information on what was going on around the country. The President was scheduled to address the nation at 9:00 p.m. Because of the late hour, Sarge did not want to risk firing up the generators just for the privilege of watching the President on the Hughes satellite network. They were still diligent in practicing light and noise discipline in the evening. Julia brought in the radio, and she tuned it to the local emergency broadcast station that was recently activated.

"Here we go," she said. Everyone gathered around the radio, a scene reminiscent of the 1930s.

"Good evening. Tonight, my fellow Americans, and citizens of the world, I come to you with information about the source of the vicious cyber attack perpetrated upon our nation and its critical infrastructure.

"During my address of two weeks ago, I pledged to you that we would identify our attackers and bring them to justice. We now have credible evidence that the attack on our nation was undertaken at the behest of the Russians.

"As a nation, we are at a crossroads between war and peace, between disorder and hostility, between hope and fear. Around the globe, we have received an outpouring of support from our allies and from some unlikely sources. Over the years, our country has inserted itself into the affairs of others, and one might think that this act of aggression against us is well deserved.

"It is not for Russia to act as judge and jury on the sins of our past. Recently, Russian aggression in Europe recalls the days when large nations trampled smaller ones in pursuit of territorial ambition or economic gain. They have their own cross to bear.

"Despite this act of aggression against us, the United States must continue to meet our responsibility to observe and enforce international norms. It is my belief that we gain more from cooperation than conquest.

"Over one hundred years ago, a World War claimed the lives of many millions, proving that with the terrible power of modern weaponry, the pursuit of an ever-expanding empire ultimately leads to the graveyard. Some suggest that it might take another World War to roll back the forces of imperialism, the notions of racial supremacy, and nationalistic aggression to ensure that no nation can subjugate its neighbors and claim their territory.

"Now is not the time for such a war, although the actions of the Russians clearly justify it. I have a vision for this world as one in which a nation's borders cannot be redrawn by another. Whatever the motivations may have been for the Moscow government to undertake this attack upon our nation, America must defend herself." The President paused for a moment, and the radio broadcast went silent. He continued.

"Tonight, I am invoking Article Five of the North Atlantic Treaty, which provides that an attack on one member state shall be considered an attack on all. I am asking NATO member nations to join us in the defense of America against the hostilities initiated by Russia.

"Further, I have formally invited the United Nations peacekeeping forces into the United States for the purposes of law enforcement activities to quell social unrest. This will free up our military to protect our borders against further Russian aggression. I have already spoken with Secretary-General Ban Ki-moon, who has all available forces in route to our shores. Their presence will be felt immediately, and they will be on prominent display.

"Until this threat passes, we must maintain order on our streets. The most vulnerable among us will suffer if we do not. Together, in concert with our NATO allies and the UN peacekeeping forces, we will meet the challenges we face. We will take concrete steps to address the danger posed against our nation from outside our borders as well as from those within our borders.

"Tonight, I ask every American to participate in this effort. Those who have joined their local Citizen Corps office in rebuilding our community will find their lives fulfilled and their family well fed. For our citizens who refuse to comply with the reasonable guidelines I have established for the protection and rebuilding of the nation, I suggest that the future of this nation belongs to those who are prepared to rebuild, not destroy. That's an immediate challenge to you, my fellow Americans, and it is the first challenge we must meet.

"Join me, so that we may focus our attention on the enemy who put us in these inexplicable circumstances. If you refuse, you risk suffering the same fate as our enemies."

CHAPTER 29

Saturday, September 24, 2016
7:26 a.m.
100 Beacon
Boston, Massachusetts

Brad joined Sarge on the roof with a cup of coffee. Sarge was finishing up his shift on perimeter patrol of 100 Beacon. He took the mug and inhaled the aroma.

"Good morning," greeted Sarge as he took his first sip. He looked out across an increasingly quiet Boston cityscape. One of the oldest cities in the nation, and the twenty-fourth largest, was desolate. Three weeks into the collapse, people were dying from dehydration caused by dysentery, lack of food, and, now increasingly, murder. "Normally, the roar of commuters into downtown would be deafening. Today, you can actually hear the geese on the Charles. I have to be honest, in a way, I like it."

"Most of us never stop to appreciate the things around us because we create busy lives for ourselves," said Brad. "Even when we take time off from our jobs and activities, most of us insist upon having the television on or an iPad attached to our arms. It was nearly impossible for many Americans to sit still, much less quietly. Some of our new recruits were counseled for sleep disorders when they first joined our unit."

"Why?"

"They were unable to fall asleep without a TV going," replied Brad.

"What did the counselors suggest?"

"Exercise." Brad laughed as he took a sip of his coffee. "So I ran their asses off before bed every night until they passed out. Problem solved."

The two men stood in silence for another moment as the sound of an ambulance siren wailed in the distance. Sarge put his rifle down on the table next to his coffee. He rolled his neck and shoulder to ease the tension in his muscles.

"Dammit, Brad, I saw something like this coming. We all knew it was a possibility. During my lectures, I would talk about the various threats our nation faced. I discussed it with people when the publisher sent me on book signings. Hell, I even engaged people in conversation on Facebook. I just wonder if it sank in to anybody."

Brad patted Sarge on the back and responded. "Of course it did, Sarge. It rubbed off on me. Listen, with what I've seen in combat, I know the horrors of collapse. But I could've ignored the warnings because I was surrounded by tanks and troops. You opened my eyes, and I'm sure that you opened the eyes of your students, readers, and yes, your Facebook friends too."

"I wanted to change people's perspectives through facts," said Sarge. "I'll never forget the debate—no, argument—I had with another Harvard professor. He called me a *fearmonger*."

"You've gotta be kidding."

"Nope. He said that my lectures on economic collapse, cyber warfare, and the threats of an EMP attack were nothing more than an attempt to scare my students into following my political ideologies."

Brad laughed. "Let me guess, you're also part of the *tinfoil-hat crowd*."

"Yep, that too," replied Sarge. "Isn't it incredible that a group of people so intent upon teaching tolerance are the first to demean and call names?"

"Oh yeah," replied Brad.

"Think of the stigma attached to the term preppers," Sarge continued. "One time, I went to Google to research the prepper's mentality. I start typing in the letters and then Google auto-populates *preppers mental illness* and *preppers mental disorder*. Google doesn't lie."

"That's a joke!" shouted Brad.

"Well, maybe their algorithm doesn't lie. Most people's perceptions are developed through the news media, television, and movies. The mainstream media reports typically portray the preppers in a negative light. It's hard to lead a preparedness lifestyle when you are constantly vilified for it."

"Look around us, Sarge," said Brad. "You saw this coming, and you made sure all of us were ready. We owe you a debt of gratitude."

"Thanks, Brad. But we all have played an important role in surviving this collapse, now I think we might end up playing a bigger role in putting the country back together. Something inside me says that our work is yet to come."

The rooftop door opened, and Steven emerged with Katie in tow. "Hey, we're ready to shove off."

"Yeah, J.J. is coming with us too," added Katie.

"Really? I thought he needed more time," said Sarge.

"Julia spoke to Susan," replied Katie. "I guess Penny Quinn is having trouble with her braces. J.J. is now our Armageddon orthodontist too." The group laughed.

Steven pulled Sarge aside and whispered, "You guys got this? It'll be just the two of you for a couple of days."

"Yeah," Sarge replied. "There are reports from the Mechanics of black gang activity towards the South End in Jamaica Plain, around Fenway, and especially on the South Boston Waterfront. I guess MS-13 got frustrated with the tunnels being guarded by our new friend the White Devil. They took to the water as an alternative. So far, nothing has happened in Back Bay or Beacon Hill."

"Okay, bro. If you're scared, I can leave Katie behind to protect you." Steven slapped his brother on the back with a hearty laugh.

"Screw you," replied Sarge. "Take care of yourself out there. No heroics, okay?"

"Yes, dear." Steven scampered off as Sarge pretended to draw his .45 from its holster.

*****

After Brad left with the others, Sarge found Julia in the kitchen, cleaning her sidearm. He admired her beauty for a moment. Just three weeks ago, they were having an intimate conversation about their future. Then the lights went out, and the world turned upside down.

"You look really sexy right now," said Sarge as Julia put her gun back together. "You know, we're alone for the first time in several weeks. Maybe we should…"

"Forget it, horn-dog." Julia laughed as she evaded his grasp. "I want to go downstairs and check on our neighbors. We've been able to help them with some food and water, but they have to be running out of supplies."

"Fine," replied Sarge with a pout. "But afterwards…"

"Maybe, big boy. Let's go see."

Unconsciously, Sarge and Julia exhibited the new norm as they prepared to leave. Each of them checked their handguns and holstered them. Whenever they left the safe confines of the top three floors, they carried their weapons of choice in the building—the KelTec PLR-16. The PLR, an acronym for *pistol, long range*, was perfect for close-quarters encounters. It used the same magazine and ammunition as their AR-15 platform rifles. Julia preferred it for its light weight at just a little over three pounds. Sarge liked it because it was well balanced and provided him the same firepower as his beloved Smith & Wesson AR-15.

As they reached the security door, Sarge looked through the peephole to check for any surprise visitors. It was clear. He turned to Julia and spoke.

"Remember, everyone is a potential threat. Behind every unopened door, there could be a weapon pointed at us."

"Got it," she replied. "We'll start from the top and work our way down."

Sarge led the way as they descended the stairs. He understood Julia's compassion, but he didn't like taking unnecessary risks. In times of desperation, even your neighbors could turn on you. He argued this point with her before their first *visit* to the remaining occupants, to no avail. She insisted on looking after the neighbors.

A vibrant building with an interesting history, 100 Beacon consisted of forty-one-hundred-square-foot floors, which contained multimillion-dollar residences. Now, most of the units were abandoned. The opulent furnishings remained in the upscale units, but were now enjoyed by ghosts.

Sarge and Julia worked their way to the bottom floor, only encountering three occupied flats along the way. Patrolling the bottom floor was Sarge's least favorite attorney, the man who had paid him a little too much lip service when he was helping the Winthrops and Peabodys into 100 Beacon following the cyber attack.

"Good morning, Mr. Marshall," greeted Sarge. Attorney Jase Marshall and Sarge were able to set aside their differences, finally, and were on speaking terms. But not on a first-name basis. "How is your new gun working out?"

"Much better, Professor," said Marshall. "The Garand was clearly inadequate for the war zone in which we live. This shotgun makes more sense for what I'd use it for. Fortunately, I haven't had to use it since your brother arrived that day. Knock on wood, it's been pretty quiet."

"Do you have help with your security?" asked Julia. She handed him a bottle of water out of her backpack and a pack of thirty-six-hundred-calorie ER Bars. He smiled and nodded his thanks. He glanced through the front door before setting his shotgun down to accept the gift.

"I do, but it isn't much," he replied. "There's another resident on the fifth floor next to my place that comes down from time to time, but he isn't doing so well. He's been losing a lot of weight and is very weak."

Sarge and Julia exchanged concerned glances.

"Did he leave the building today?" asked Sarge. They'd knocked on all of the doors as they came down, and nobody answered on the fifth floor.

"No," Marshall replied. "He took the night shift and I replaced him a few hours ago."

Sarge nodded. *That must be it.*

"The building is mostly abandoned now," observed Julia. The three snapped to attention as a car drove slowly in front of the building before speeding off. "I hope the other residents have located safer surroundings, perhaps with family outside of the city?"

"Mostly," replied Marshall. "To be honest, I've lost track. I've located keys to their units in the super's office. I'm ashamed to admit that I've gone through their kitchen cabinets, looking for food and drinks. I'm at a loss otherwise."

Sarge was witnessing firsthand the effect of the power outage. People were starving. They were losing hope. They were disappearing without notice. This once fully occupied building was down to three residents besides themselves. Eighty percent of his neighbors were gone after just three weeks.

"Mr. Marshall, how well do you know your neighbors?" asked Sarge.

"Pretty well. I was the head of the building's association of residents. You wouldn't know that because you never attended any of our meetings."

Sarge let the comment pass. He continued. "I mean, not the ones who remain, but the residents who have left."

"We're all acquainted with each other, if that's what you mean," said Marshall. "But I don't know where they are."

Julia gave Sarge a puzzled look.

"What if I told you I could bring you some help? I have some trusted friends, good people, that could temporarily occupy these abandoned units and lend a helping hand in the process. Do you think your, I mean *our*, neighbors would allow them to stay in their homes until this situation gets better?"

Julia whispered, "What are you thinking, Sarge?"

"The Mechanics."

CHAPTER 30

Saturday, September 24, 2016
11:06 a.m.
Town Hall
Belchertown, Massachusetts

Archibald and Pearson leaned over the conference table in the property assessor's office. John Whelihan, the director of assessments, brought out another stack of maps from the plat cabinet.

"This is very confusing," said Whelihan. "There haven't been any permits pulled or licenses obtained on Prescott Peninsula since the radio observatory was constructed out there decades ago. Here are the plats for the entire peninsula, including the specific area around the observatory." Whelihan pointed to the observatory, the present location of 1PP.

Archibald took the plats and rolled them out across the table, using hardbound copies of the *Massachusetts General Laws Annotated* to hold them down flat. He and Pearson studied them further. Archibald summoned the three men directly reporting to him that had military experience. There were other retired military personnel in the community, but they refused to volunteer their assistance to the Citizen Corps. Archibald told Pearson they would be dealt with after the Prescott Peninsula situation was resolved.

"What have they built out there?" asked Pearson. He leaned back from the table and rubbed his temples. It was his curiosity regarding the activity at Prescott Peninsula that kept him in Belchertown an additional day. He needed to get back to Boston.

"Supposedly, it's a safe haven for families fleeing an abusive relationship," replied Archibald. He stood up and threw his pen on the maps. "I was there for the ribbon-cutting ceremony back in June. Hillary was there, as was Senator Morgan. The press was everywhere. Then, that was it."

"What do you mean?" asked Pearson. He leaned against the wall and folded his arms.

"I mean there wasn't any more press. Nobody has been past the security detail since the gate and fence were constructed. The only people observed going in or out are military personnel."

Pearson's first thought was CIA. There was something wrong with this picture. *Why would a home for abused mommies need military-style protection?*

"Also, the helicopter," added Whelihan.

"What helicopter?" asked Pearson.

"Most of us heard it the night after the power went down," he replied. "As far as we know, it never left."

"Was it military?" asked Pearson.

"We don't know," replied Archibald.

This stank to high heaven. He was about to ask another question when two of Archibald's men entered the room with a flyer.

The room became quiet as Archibald reviewed it. Pearson saw that the two men stared at him continuously, and he became annoyed. Archibald looked up at him.

"Archie, what's going on?" asked Pearson. He moved forward to get a better look at the paper.

"This was delivered through our Citizen Corps mail system," replied Archibald. "Seems you are in a bit of trouble, Joe." He handed Pearson the flyer, which indicated he was wanted for treason. It was signed by Governor O'Brien. He started laughing, which caught everyone in the room off guard.

"This is ridiculous and obviously fake. What the—?" Pearson protested as he reached for his jacket and satphone. Two men moved to block him but he tried to push past them. "I'm just getting my phone to call the governor!"

"Check his coat," ordered Archibald. The men produced a satellite phone, but no weapon. "Pat him down too." Archibald stood firm while his men confirmed that Pearson was unarmed.

"C'mon, Archie, this is some kind of joke or something," pleaded Pearson. "Let me call the governor now and sort this out. There's no need for all of this."

Archibald studied him for a moment and then handed him the phone. "Fellows, give me a moment with Mr. Pearson," he said. The room cleared, leaving Pearson alone with Archibald. "Look, Joe, I like you. You've been a straight shooter with me. This could be a hoax, or our governor has gone off the rails. I've learned that he's like that."

"It has to be something like that, Archie. Let me call him and find out, okay."

Archibald studied him for another moment and then leaned in to whisper, "I'm going to give you the benefit of the doubt. By the same token, I don't want any part of the conversation that you're about to have. I'll wait outside."

"Fair enough," said Pearson. He dialed O'Brien's number after Archibald left the room. The phone rang several times and there was no answer. He checked the number and tried again. Same result.

He began to sweat in the enclosed room with no ventilation. He looked around nervously, searching for answers. Pearson had seen enough of O'Brien to know that he was nothing more than a union thug with a lot of newfound *peon power*. If this flyer was real, and it certainly appeared to be, he wasn't going to submit himself to an idiot like O'Brien.

Pearson walked to the window that overlooked the two-hundred-year-old, historic Clapp Memorial Library. The parking lot and grassed area leading to the building was empty. *I've got nothing to lose.* He quietly opened up the wood-clad window and lowered himself to the sidewalk below. Within moments, he escaped into the woods bearing the colors of fall.

*****

Steven slowly approached the security barriers at the intersection of Mill Valley Road and Washington Street. Several vehicles blocked the three-way stop, preventing him from continuing. He and Katie had experienced a similar roadblock entering New York from Pennsylvania. This time his arm wasn't in a sling and the guards of the fine hamlet of Belchertown weren't proudly saying *choose freedom.* Citizen Corps patches were prominently displayed on every jacket of the men who approached their car with weapons drawn. This was undoubtedly enemy territory.

"State your business!" the lead guard shouted at Steven from a safe distance.

Steven was careful to show his hands to all the men who surrounded Sarge's Toyota Bandeirante. He pulled O'Brien's letter from the dash and handed it through the window. The lead guard took the letter and examined it. He backed away to use a two-way radio, but Steven was unable to hear the conversation. After a few moments, the guard returned.

"Out of the vehicle, and slowly," the man ordered.

Steven looked at Katie and nodded. Both of them exited simultaneously, keeping eye contact on the welcoming committee.

"We have weapons," announced Steven. "We're both going to remove them and allow you to search our vehicle. We don't want any misunderstandings here. Nobody needs to be a hero or get killed. Fair enough?"

"Remove your weapons and place your hands on your head," ordered the lead guard.

Steven and Katie complied. After a few moments, their vehicle had been searched and the lead guard was satisfied that there were no surprises. "Come with me, please." He led Steven and Katie to a panel van and opened the side door to allow them in.

"Mr. Archibald, the chairman of our board of selectmen will see you. Your vehicle and weapons will be returned to you afterwards."

Steven and Katie dutifully complied. There was no reason to escalate hostilities with the townspeople. This was a time to learn and observe.

Their driver continuously looked in the rearview mirror at his passengers while the man in the passenger seat kept a handgun pointed at them. Katie decided to play the ditzy-girlfriend card.

"Oh, honey, isn't this town quaint? I'd love to live here after this is all over. What do you think?"

Steven tried to stay serious, but he knew Katie was trying to break down the barriers with their guards. "Absolutely, look at that beautiful old Victorian. I bet those trees are hundreds of years old." Steven wondered if Katie was impressed with his knowledge of architecture.

"Sir, are these homes reasonably priced?" asked Katie of the guard.

He laughed at her. "Lady, nothing's for sale anymore. Most of the town's residents have moved on and left their places behind. The rest of us are here to help Mr. Archibald."

Katie leaned forward in the seat to allow the driver to notice her figure. "Do you think he might need some more help?" she asked innocently. "I mean, we kinda hate the city now. It's not as safe or pretty as here."

The guard lowered his weapon somewhat as he flirted with Katie. "Well, young lass," he started, assuming Katie's Irish heritage. "there is always room for one as pretty as you." He grinned, exposing a few missing teeth.

The driver wheeled the van to the front of the town hall, and they were greeted by two police officers. They slid open the van door and motioned for Steven and Katie to get out.

"Come with us."

Steven and Katie, sandwiched between the four armed men, entered the town hall, and the first thing they saw was the large contingent at the end of the hallway by a door labeled conference room.

"Wait here," said one of the men as he entered the large, open space. He spoke with Archibald, who motioned for Steven and Katie to enter. He immediately extended his hand to greet Steven, who shook it in return.

"My name is Ronald Archibald. I understand the governor sent you folks," he said. While Steven spoke with Archibald, Katie wandered around the room, appearing nonchalant.

"Nice to meet you," replied Steven. "Thanks for taking the time to meet with us. You look very busy, so I'll get to the point. Governor O'Brien has instructed us to locate Mr. Joseph Pearson. The governor's office believes he is in Belchertown."

Katie continued to wander around the room, making small talk with the men reviewing the maps and plats spread on the large conference table.

"He was here, but has since disappeared," replied Archibald.

Steven saw that Katie was making progress with the men in the room, so he took his time with Archibald. "When did you see him last?" he asked.

"It's been several hours. We discovered he was wanted for treason. Because we weren't sure of the authenticity of this paper flyer, we allowed him the opportunity to call Governor O'Brien." Archibald handed Steven the flyer issued by O'Brien. Steven examined it briefly and then set it on the table. He saw that the men were studying various maps of Prescott Peninsula.

"Are you organizing a search party?" asked Steven, glancing around the room.

"No, we've got bigger fish to fry, as they say," replied Archibald. "Pearson never caused me any problems, and my constituents' needs rise above a manhunt for an alleged traitor."

Katie had toured the entire room and caught Steven's eye. She nodded that she was finished.

"Is there anything you can tell us, Mr. Archibald, that might assist us in finding this Pearson fella?" asked Steven.

"Not really. He never returned to his hotel room. He didn't carry a weapon either. The only thing he left here with was a satellite phone."

*****

Pearson sat in the woods and stared across the lake. With the darkness and the mist of the rain obscuring his view, he was unable to see any activity. The falling rain caused him to shudder, or maybe it was nervousness as he awaited a call from the assistant director of Homeland Security.

Pearson's superiors had no knowledge of any treason charges against him and were just as surprised as he was to learn of the impending warrant. They were very interested in Pearson's theory of what brought the charges in the first place, as well as the mystery surrounding the Quabbin Reservoir. It was pouring down rain now, and Pearson tried to take cover at the base of an oak tree, but the leaves were sparse. *Come on! I know it's Saturday, but someone needs to straighten this out.*

Finally, the satellite phone rang, and Pearson, in his haste to answer it, dropped it in the wet leaves. He quickly snatched it up.

"Hello," he answered, out of breath. For several minutes, Pearson listened to the caller and only occasionally spoke. "Yes, sir. I'm on my way, sir."

The line went dead, but Pearson found new life. He started south along the shore at a quick trot. *There you have it! I knew he was up to something!*

CHAPTER 31

Saturday, September 24, 2016
2:49 p.m.
Prescott Peninsula
Quabbin Reservoir, Massachusetts

The most common orthodontic problem in children is called malocclusion, or simply *bad bite.* Sometimes this is genetic, other times it can be caused by the early or late loss of baby teeth. The Quinn's daughter, Penny, began to exhibit evidence of misalignment when she was eight years old. Her orthodontist, Dr. Daniel SinClair, suggested dental braces for Penny as her adult teeth came out. After two years, her braces were beginning to give her problems and needed to be removed. Naturally, under the circumstances, Dr. SinClair was unavailable.

"Okay, Penny, J.J. is going to take care of your braces," said Susan as she cupped a worried Penny's face in her hands.

Donald leaned down next to their daughter to reassure her. "Honey, you'll be in good hands with J.J. When he finishes up, you'll feel great and your smile will be worth a million bucks!"

"Thank you, Daddy. I just wish Dr. SinClair was here to do it."

Donald patted her on the head and he whispered to J.J., "We'll go downstairs when you're done."

J.J. nodded. "Okay, my good little Prim and Proper Penny Pincher—" J.J. laughed as he knelt down next to the nervous young girl "—the most important thing you can do for me is hold still, okay?"

"Okay, J.J.," replied Penny. She looked up to Susan and added, "I've got this, Mom."

Donald thought to himself that this world was no place for children. His girls were very fortunate compared to the horrors other children were facing *out there.* But Penny was growing into a confident young woman, just a week before her eleventh birthday, which fell on October twenty-first.

He got his daughter settled on the surgical table while J.J. adjusted the lights. He gave Penny a kiss on the forehead. J.J. gathered a few instruments, including one not normally used in a medical context.

"Susan, please keep Penny still for me," said J.J. "It will be a natural reaction for her to flinch. A little bit will be okay."

Susan nodded and looked to Donald for reassurance. He gave her a thumbs-up.

"I can't believe I missed this," interjected Donald. "I'm sorry, J.J., I thought I was pretty thorough and thought of everything."

"You did pretty good, Donald," said J.J. "Look around us."

Donald looked around the room full of medical devices and instruments. Everything here was readily available online or at local medical supply stores. The most expensive item was the portable defibrillator that J.J. had used in his attempts to revive Sabs. Hopefully, that would not be needed again.

"I would think about the mundane tasks people performed each day," started Donald. "I then thought about how those tasks could be achieved in a grid-down scenario. We talked about women's health issues at length, didn't we, honey?"

"I think we were very thorough in most respects," replied Susan. "Typically, women and children are most affected by poor sanitation conditions. I thought of everything from personal hygiene to birth control."

"That's right," added Donald. "And even though we don't personally agree with its use, we even included the Plan B morning-after pill in the medicine cabinet over there." Donald pointed to a large, locked corner cabinet.

"Don't feel bad, you guys," said J.J. as he produced a set of needle-nose pliers from the instrument sterilizer. A tear came to Susan's eyes as she saw the tool.

"I look at our baby's sweet mush every day," said Donald, becoming emotional at the sight of Susan's tears. "I could have purchased a pair of ortho pliers for around fifteen bucks on Amazon. How could I have missed that?"

"Hey, hey, you two—" J.J. laughed "—this little girl is way tougher than you two wusses. Do I need to clear *my* O.R.?"

Both of the Quinns laughed as J.J. and Penny looked at them.

"Okay, sorry," replied Donald, speaking on Susan's behalf. *Nervous parents.*

"You did have the foresight to print hard copies of *Where There is No Dentist* from the Freedom Preppers website," said J.J. "Also, the introduction to orthodontics book is a huge help."

"I'm ready, J.J.," interrupted Penny. Everyone laughed at the child's desire to get it over with.

"Okay, Penny Pincher," said J.J. He put on a pair of surgical magnifying glasses, which included an LED headlight. "Open wide."

Penny obliged.

"Obviously, you don't want to grab the tooth, as it may crack. Dental brackets have a groove close to the tooth face designed to make their removal easy. I'm also going to use my finger to support the back side of the tooth, which has the added benefit of keeping the patient steady. Let's take care of the first one."

After removing the rubber bands from the dental brace structure, J.J. took the pliers and squeezed the bracket at the front of the tooth. He gave it a slight torqueing motion.

"You only need to give the braces a gentle squeeze. You don't want to pull forward." The first brace came loose after another wiggle. J.J. was separating the brace from the bonding glue, which was very strong. After twisting the brace, the glue remained on the tooth. J.J. continued to work his way around Penny's mouth until all of the braces were removed. There was only a little bit of bleeding, which he dabbed with a Q-tip.

"That wasn't so bad, was it, Penny Punkin'?" asked J.J., who had a wide variety of nicknames for the Quinn girls.

"Nope, but my teeth feel funny," replied Penny. "They're rough."

"That's the glue used to hold the braces in place," said J.J. "Dr. SinClair would have a solvent for you, but we have to improvise."

"What can we do about the glue?" asked Susan. She helped Penny sit up and gave her a wet washcloth to bite down on, helping ease the discomfort.

"The glue could take years to wear off completely," started J.J. "But I have some pretty simple instructions for you. He walked over to the counter and grabbed a box of baking soda and peroxide. "There are hundreds of uses for baking soda, and this is one of them."

He mixed a paste from two teaspoons of baking soda and one-half teaspoon of peroxide. Peroxide caused the baking soda to bubble, so he mixed the two slowly to avoid a mess.

"Sit up straight, Penny," instructed J.J. "Susan, hold this towel under her chin to keep from creating a *mad-dog foamy mess*, right, little one?"

Penny grinned and nodded her head.

"Don't swallow this, Penny. Let the mixture spill out, okay?"

Another nod.

J.J. took a battery-powered toothbrush and began to move the mixture over Penny's teeth for a moment or two. During this process, J.J. explained that brushing with the peroxide and baking soda softened up the glue, which enabled him to scrape it off with a dental pick. He cautioned to use care when scraping to prevent accidental removal of the enamel, which could lead to tooth decay.

"Spit it all out into this bowl, Penny, and then we'll rinse your mouth out a couple of times."

"It's yucky."

"I know. Now, I need you to floss for me, okay? After that, let's rinse again, please." J.J. directed his attention to Susan as he washed his hands.

"This will help remove the glue, but it certainly isn't the perfect solution. Once a day, have a brushing, picking, and flossing session with Penny. Be sure to rinse her mouth out thoroughly to get rid of loose dental glue and residue."

"Thank you so much, J.J.," said Susan, giving him a hug. "She was so uncomfortable. I didn't know what we would do."

"Well, this has been a first for me, I can assure you," said J.J. He handed her a small tube of Orajel. "She will have a little discomfort around her gums for the next couple of days. This will help numb the pain."

"All done," announced Penny with the biggest smile she'd shared in a long time. "How do I look?"

"Like a princess!"

*****

Donald and J.J. descended the stairs into the lower levels of 1PP. It had been two weeks since J.J. left for 100 Beacon, and Donald had been busy on a project. He was anxious to share the details with his friend.

"Thank you, J.J.," said Donald as they reached the bottom floor of the former radio observatory. "Susan was worried."

"It was a simple procedure. The key is to take your time and not get aggressive with the brackets. Fortunately, the removal wasn't complicated by gum disease or TMJ pains. She should heal up nicely."

Donald reached into his pocket and pulled out the keys to the locked steel door. Certain rooms remained locked and inaccessible, like this one, the weapons room, and the vault full of a billion dollars in precious metals. This particular room had become Donald's workshop and *man-cave.*

"What've you been working on?" asked J.J.

Donald led him into the room and closed the door behind them, turning the bolt lock as well. He moved past J.J. and switched on the lights over his long workbench. Tools were organized on a pegboard wall, and there were charging stations for his lithium ion batteries.

Donald's shop was designed to perform a number of functions, including weapons cleaning and repair. There was a Hornady reloading press and several bins filled with a variety of cartridges.

Donald had acquired all of the essentials for ammunition reloading, including dies, a priming tool, and a powder scale.

The large center worktable contained drawers filled with a variety of nuts, bolts, and screws acquired at Lowe's during the build-out of 1PP. Donald was a hands-on supervisor during the process, thinking of useful tools and construction materials to benefit them in a postapocalyptic world.

"I'd like you to meet our force multiplier," said Donald proudly. He lifted a device off the workbench and set it on the table for J.J. to see.

"What the hell is this thing?" asked J.J. as he walked around the table and studied the device without daring to touch it. On a small square bracket with rubber feet, Donald had welded an eighteen-inch-diameter satellite dish. Attached to the dish were several electronic components with wires interconnecting them. A black rubber handle was located behind another box, which contained a toggle switch and a red push button.

"This is an RFW—a radio frequency weapon," replied Donald. "If all goes well, it will be the first of three that I will build in case we need it."

"Are you out of your mind?" asked J.J.

"Not at all. Listen, radio frequency weapons, also known as directed-energy weapons, use electromagnetic energy on specific frequencies to disable electronics. The principle is similar to that of high-power microwave weapons used by the military. These military systems tend to be much more sophisticated and are more likely to be in the control of technologically advanced nations.

"The RFW, by contrast, is simple and low voltage enough that it can be deployed by anyone. I found a detailed schematic online. I purchased the necessary components on Amazon, at Radio Shack, and at the local electrical supply. Instructions for assembling the components and how to use the RFW were available online as well." Donald leaned back against the workbench and folded his arms.

J.J. studied the RFW for a moment before speaking. "You've built an EMP device?"

"The force multiplier," replied Donald. "is capable of causing damage to targeted electronics. It is intended to be a highly capable nonlethal weapon. It's designed to be focused on a particular target, but can be used safely from a distance. That's why RFWs are also called directed-energy weapons. It has the capability of rendering an attacker's electronics useless. Just like an EMP."

"Donald, this has a lot of potential. We could use it defensively against attacking vehicles or boats. We could also use it covertly against a facility that had power restored or is operating through a generator." J.J. picked up the force multiplier. It was fairly heavy at seventeen pounds, but remarkably balanced. The bracket holding the components protruded underneath the handle, enabling the operator to use the base as a counterweight. The toggle switch and push button were within easy reach of the operator's thumb.

"What are all of these parts?" asked J.J. as he gently set the device back down.

"After I obtained the plans, I set about finding the parts listed on various websites," replied Donald. As he spoke, he pointed to each of the components. "I purchased the Sharp magnetron on eBay. This is called the *waveguide assembly*, which I obtained from a microwave oven. This is an eighteen-inch aluminum dish made by CETC. This PAPST fan is designed for computer servers and compact air conditioners. It will keep the magnetron cooled down if it has to be used for long periods of time."

"How long do you have to use it for it to have the desired effect?" asked J.J.

"Short bursts are sufficient for most buildings and vehicles," replied Donald. "Aircraft require a longer burst." He looked J.J. in the eye to study his reaction.

"You can disable an aircraft with this?"

"I think so," said Donald. He continued with the *tour* of the force multiplier. "This is a high-voltage YEO transformer that I bought from Sears. Everything is wired together, including the capacitor. Then it is properly grounded, or it won't work."

"Have you tried it yet?" asked J.J.

Donald put his hands in his pockets and shook his head. "No. I'm afraid to around here. What if it works better than I thought? I don't want to fry our own electronics!"

CHAPTER 32

Sunday, September 25, 2016
3:55 p.m.
100 Beacon
Boston, Massachusetts

"It's been quiet around us until now," said Julia as she and Sarge stood on the rooftop of 100 Beacon. "That gunfire is from down the street, Sarge." From the top of the building, they had a clear line of sight to the east toward Boston Common. Smoke began to rise from the vicinity of Starbucks and DeLuca's on Charles Street.

Sarge leaned over the roof's edge to get a better perspective with his binoculars, but his view was obstructed by the Greek Consulate. The commotion to their west concerned him more. The sounds of breaking glass and gunfire were common now, but this was dangerously close.

"I knew we weren't going to be insulated from the violence," said Sarge. "The respite of the last week or so wasn't going to last. That's why the idea of relocating some of the Mechanics to our building is important. I thought we could wait until Steven and Katie returned."

"Sarge, look," yelled Julia as she pointed west on Beacon Street. "Those men are shooting the plate-glass doors of the Branson Museum and going in. There are at least six of them." Gunshots rang out again on the north side of Beacon as another group of men stormed a brownstone apartment building.

"They're wearing football jerseys, the Oakland Raiders," said Sarge. An NFL team's attire held a special appeal to gangs. Typically the gang would adopt a color and then find an NFL team that coincided with them. Black had always been popular, which related back to the early Westerns when the bad guy was always dressed in black. The Raiders jersey was highly symbolic for gang members, who were drawn to the black and silver colors together with the swashbuckling pirate logo. "These guys are part of J-Rock's crew."

Now screams filled the air as more gunfire was heard, closer this time. *Not good.* Sarge and Julia didn't have much time. They left the rooftop and descended to the eighth floor, which contained their armory. Steven and Katie were due back soon, and the best they could do was hold off the approaching gang members. Sarge and Julia both put on tactical body armor vests. Sarge inserted the quarter-inch steel plates and pulled their cummerbund-style closures tight. These vests could withstand a range of ballistics up to .308 rifles and .44 Magnum handguns.

After grabbing an AR-15, they filled their utility pouches with magazines. They inserted a sixty-round magazine for starters. Sarge outfitted Julia's vest with a two-way radio, and he did the same.

He looked her in the eyes and then he kissed her. "I love you, Julia. We can do this."

"I love you too. You need to get across the street before they get closer. We have to turn them away, Sarge."

"They'll seek the path of least resistance. Right now, nobody is standing up to them. We just cannot let them enter the building." Sarge led her to the stairwell and gave her gear one last check.

"I'm ready. We've got the high ground, and they're cowards; otherwise they wouldn't be doing what they're doing. Now go. I'll wait for your signal."

Julia left and bounded up the stairs toward the rooftop. Her job was to keep the gangbangers from entering the fenced courtyard of 100 Beacon, where they could benefit from some cover. If they entered the building, then Sarge would have to clear every floor on his own.

Sarge went down the stairs and found his attorney friend, Mr. Marshall, manning the front entrance alone. He was sweating profusely from nervousness.

"You've heard the gunfire," started Sarge. "Marshall, I need you to hold it together. Can you do that?"

The man nodded, unable to speak out of fear.

Sarge took him by the shoulders. "Here's what we're going to do, okay." He led Marshall into the wrought-iron-enclosed courtyard and pointed across the street toward the five-story brownstone. Its doors had been broken in two weeks ago, and several windows on the second floor were broken. "I'm going to run across the street and take up a position on the rooftop. Julia has done the same upstairs. I want you to stay inside the doorway and shoot anyone who comes in, except me, of course. Got it?"

"I think so," said Marshall. "I'll stay in the building until you come for me."

"Good. Crouch behind the reception desk but keep the gun pointed at the door. These guys are wearing black and silver football jerseys. I think they're a gang from Roxbury. If we do our job, you'll never see them. But, be ready, Marshall. Now is not the time to check out."

"I'm good," he said as he returned to the entryway.

Sarge checked the street and quickly darted behind the disabled U-Haul truck left there weeks ago by Steven. Finding the street clear, he ran through the crosswalk and up the eight stairs to the entrance of the building, which appeared to be vacant. *Where did everybody go?*

Sarge's heart was racing. He never imagined that he and Julia would be protecting 100 Beacon by themselves. The key was to prevent access to the building. If he could reach the rooftop, he would have mobility, the element of surprise, and the height advantage.

Sarge ran inside and looked for the stairwell. It was locked. *Dammit!* He needed another way up. He remembered the fire escape on the front of the building. He poked his head back out and didn't see anyone. He hopped over the railing and ran through the last remnants of hostas in the flower bed. Using the brick windowsill for assistance, he climbed his way up into an elm tree. Like a spider monkey, Sarge gradually made his way to the height of the second floor, where he could reach the railing, but it was just out of grasp.

He decided to climb higher into the tree where he could jump down onto the steel grate landing of the fire escape.

He made the jump, but landed with a thud and rolled into the red brick wall. Pain shot through his shoulder that took the brunt of the blow. Julia's voice came over the two-way radio.

"Hey there, Spiderman, aren't you a little old for that?"

Sarge looked up to the top of 100 Beacon and then his middle finger was raised upward.

Julia commented, "So rude."

Shaking off the pain of the fall, Sarge climbed the stairs and reached the roof. He swung his legs over the edge and found a solid surface. He took a moment to gather himself and catch his breath.

He looked up and down Beacon Street. The building housing Starbucks was fully engulfed in flames now. There were no fire trucks responding. Afternoon showers had rolled through Boston yesterday afternoon, but the skies were clear now. To the west, several cars drove slowly in front of the buildings containing the attackers. Periodically, a Raiders-clad thief would run out of the building carrying some form of loot. He would deposit the goods in the car and run in for more. The occasional gunshot was an indication that a resident had attempted to thwart the gang.

"Now we wait," said Sarge into the two-way. The two groups were working their way up the street, but the group on his side was advancing faster. He hadn't considered this. He'd secured a position with the intent to secure 100 Beacon. Now, he found himself protecting this side of the street first.

"Do you copy?" he asked Julia.

"Go ahead."

"This side is advancing faster than your side. I doubt they'll come to the rooftop. Do we make our presence known and defend this building first, or wait and see how it develops?"

Julia hesitated before responding to Sarge. "It's getting late. I don't think these guys will want to conduct these raids in the dark, do you?"

"No," replied Sarge. He glanced at the progress of the other group. They were approaching Fisher College, the long stretch of buildings next to 100 Beacon. "They're operating by force and intimidation. By wearing their gang colors and blasting their way indoors, they send a clear message to the building's occupants. *Stand down, or die.*"

"If that's the case, the end of our block is a natural stopping point for them," said Julia. "The next building down from you takes them to Arlington and Boston Common. On my side of the street, they'll be in the next block where the fire is getting worse."

"Stand by," said Sarge. He would prefer to take them separately. Ideally, one group would be preoccupied in a building while he and Julia took the other group out in the crossfire. If the others rushed to their side, then Sarge and Julia, taking advantage of the confusion, could pick them off as they made their way down the sidewalk. Several gunshots to his left interrupted his thoughts.

"Sarge, they're coming," said Julia.

Sarge's heart was racing. He needed the groups to split in two. The men were running in and out of the building next to his location. He looked west on Beacon, and then the decision became clear. The gangbangers broke through the entry doors to Fisher College. They faced a maze of hallways, corridors, and classrooms. Unlike the residential brownstones, which contained a couple of units per floor, the gang members on Julia's side of the street would be tied up for some time trying to find anything of value.

"Get ready," said Sarge. "We'll take this group first. Also, take out their vehicle. The others will come pouring out of Fisher College like a bunch of cockroaches. We don't have a very good line of sight because of the tree canopy. We'll take out as many of them as we can, as well as the trailing vehicles. There are four cars altogether."

"Got it," said Julia, adding, "Happy hunting." She had become a stone-cold killer.

Several minutes later, the last of the Raiders exited the building next to him and tossed a few fur coats into the back of an awaiting dry cleaner's van. There were five men, plus the driver. Sarge fired first, raining NATO 5.56 rounds on top of the vehicle and into the bodies of two of the men. The other men ran for cover at the back of the van, and Julia tore up the asphalt, missing them at first. Then she found her mark. The final rounds sailed through the windshield, instantly killing the driver, who slumped over the steering column, activating the wiper system.

Because the gang was clustered together, it took less than thirty seconds to kill all of them, plus the driver. The other group of looters were still inside Fisher College. The sound of squealing tires filled the air as the other three cars sped into reverse.

"Shoot the other cars!" Sarge yelled into the mic as he began shooting. He shot out the tires of the closest vehicle, and the driver attempted to exit through the passenger side. Julia shot the driver several times. One of the cars attempted to turn around and crashed into the side of a black maintenance vehicle. The driver, in desperation, backed up and pulled forward, continuing his attempt to turn around. Sarge emptied the rest of his magazine through the car's windows, killing the driver.

The last car, a Lexus *grocery-getter*, had backed out of range, using the tree canopy for protection. As predicted, the remaining five looters came out of Fisher College, but using different points of exit. Both Sarge and Julia fired on them, killing two and wounding one who rolled into a hedgerow. The other two thugs piled into the Lexus and sped away.

"Hold your position," said Sarge. "Let's make sure there are no surprises."

The last attacker lay in the bushes, screaming in pain. He was crawling through the boxwoods, trying to make his way to a descending stairwell that led to a drug counselor's office.

"What do we do with number fifteen down there," said Julia, referring to the man's blood-soaked replica of the jersey worn by Raiders' wide receiver Michael Crabtree.

Sarge adjusted his sight and shot the man in the head. He replied, "Nothing. He just retired."

CHAPTER 33

Sunday, September 25, 2016
12:26 p.m.
100 Beacon
Boston, Massachusetts

"Hey, we're out front. Over," said Steven into his two-way radio. He and Katie chased a lead on Pearson that took them toward Albany, New York, before they were turned around by the New York Army National Guard at the Hudson River. The state was experiencing an unprecedented nuclear disaster just fifty miles to the south of the checkpoint at the Indian Point Nuclear Power Plant.

When Steven and Katie were taken in for the night at Port Jervis weeks ago, a small fire department operated by a former soldier at Fort Devens named Hector took them in for the night, giving them some much-needed rest. On the next day, the entire volunteer fire department left to help their comrades put out a fire at the main transformer of Indian Point #2. Also, several transformers in unit #3 had caught fire. Apparently, the battle to put out the fire was lost.

Refugees were streaming northward along Interstate 87 towards the New York state capital of Albany, where FEMA camps had been established. The prevailing winds would carry any radioactive contamination to the east into Connecticut. When Steven encountered the checkpoint, their letter signed by O'Brien didn't grant them passage into the state, but it did allow them to fill up their gas tank for the return trip.

"Roger, come on up," replied Sarge.

"What the hell did I miss, bro? There are dead dudes all over the road out here."

"We'll fill you in. Over." When Steven checked in late last night, Sarge alluded to some visitors, but refused to elaborate over the radios, which made sense. Steven counted nearly a dozen Raiders strewn all over Beacon Street. *The dead bodies were beginning to pile up.*

Steven and Katie stopped by the kitchen to grab something to eat. They were operating their generators sparingly, but the refrigerator remained cold, allowing them to preserve leftovers from meals. They made themselves a tuna salad wrap and headed up to the rooftop, a welcome change from the MREs of the last two days.

Julia welcomed them as they walked out into the unusually warm fall day. "Greetings, weary travelers. I see you found the tuna."

"Yeah, my favorite," replied Steven with a mouthful of the wrap. He used the remainder to gesture over his shoulder. "You guys create all that carnage?" He took another bite and studied his brother. Sarge had impressed him in the past with his abilities as they trained together. But shooting at stationary targets and experiencing live rounds were different matters altogether. Over the last few years, he'd elevated Sarge's training to include real tactics that had been proven in combat and black ops. From the looks of Beacon Street, the student had digested everything and put it into practice.

"Julia did it," replied Sarge dryly.

"It wasn't all me," she protested. "Sarge started it. Those poor men were just minding their own business, and Sarge opened up on them. The welcome-wagon people fired him because of it."

Steven polished off his sandwich and started laughing. "There's broken glass everywhere, in addition to the dead guys. What were they doing?"

"The *Raiders*, as we called them, are part of J-Rock's gang," replied Sarge as he started walking toward the front of 100 Beacon. "They were forcing their way into buildings down the street by shooting up the entry doors. This form of doorbell ringing probably scared the residents into hiding, allowing the gang to have their way with any valuables."

"Like what?" asked Katie, who was leaning over the roof's parapet to get a better view.

"The last guy was loading fur coats into that van before Sarge closed down their operation," replied Julia. Then she laughed. "I guess they were getting ready for winter."

"Julia held her own, guys," said Sarge. "We lit 'em up, and when the rest of the crew scampered out of Fisher, we sent them a message as well."

"Did you get them all?" asked Steven. Regardless of the answer, his brother had stirred up a hornets' nest.

"No," replied Sarge, who hesitated for a moment before adding these prophetic words, "They'll be back."

CHAPTER 34

Monday, September 26, 2016
7:00 p.m.
Citizen Corps Region I, Office of the Governor
99 High Street
Boston, Massachusetts

O'Brien was incensed. He was too enraged to smoke a cigar. He paced back and forth through the conference room as Brad and Captain Branson made excuses for their failures.

"For over two weeks, you've promised me the military personnel I need to carry out the orders my President assigned to me!" yelled O'Brien. He would turn and face the soldiers from time to time for emphasis. "Where is my army?"

"Governor, as I have said," started Brad, "my troops have returned to their families. They are no longer available by phone or other means of contact. This is happening all over the country, sir."

"Recruit more men," demanded O'Brien. "I lost more than half of my guys because of that stupid armory fiasco."

"Sir, we aren't authorized to commission soldiers into the military," replied Brad. "Even if we could, the city is largely abandoned. The rampant crime has sent the majority of the population into the countryside."

O'Brien glared at La Rue, who sat quietly in a wing chair near the front door. He needed his *consigliere* to advise him, and he was sick of the double-talk from these two leathernecks.

"Where is Pearson? I thought you had a bloodhound after him. It's been three days!"

"Sir, our man followed Pearson into New York, but they were denied access into the state. We still believe that Pearson fled to Fort Drum." O'Brien was seeing through the lies. This charade was over.

"Would it surprise you to know that Pearson was right under our noses? He wasn't in New York! He was in Belchertown!"

Brad and Branson remained stoic. O'Brien realized that these two were not going to crack, nor would they ever obey his authority. He needed them replaced, but an alternative had to be arranged.

He calmed his nerves, and then he leaned over the table into the faces of Brad and Branson. "Get out! You two are dismissed!" *Permanently.*

O'Brien swung his arm and gestured for La Rue to follow them out. He needed to think and make a call. In the three weeks since his appointment, he'd accomplished nothing. *Nothing!* He had envisioned enriching himself and his closest friends during this opportunity that presented itself. He had plans to get even with a lot of political enemies, as well as knocking down the fat cats around here a notch or two. For weeks, he'd relied upon those idiots to provide him with the military support and weapons necessary to *set things straight* after years of oppression forced on the common man. They were just a couple of screw-ups. *Or were they?*

He stared out the window into the deserted streets of Boston. Each day, fewer people appeared and even fewer cars. Bostonians had abandoned their homes out of fear. Had he made a mistake by unleashing the gangs on the city? The lack of opposition did make it easier for his teams to clean out the upscale homes in Brookline and Chestnut Hill, but there was more to do. If he could delegate this humanitarian crap to someone else, he could take care of the business that was important to him. He needed help.

La Rue returned and interrupted O'Brien's thoughts.

"They're gone."

"Good," O'Brien gruffed. "Those two are worthless."

"No," said La Rue. "They're good at what they do, which is lie."

"Maybe."

"Just consider this, Jim," started La Rue. "Whenever they came up with an idea, their attitude was full of excitement and suggestions. But as things began to go wrong, they clammed up and offered nothing except *I don't know.*"

O'Brien dropped himself into a chair and exhaled. He considered La Rue's words for a moment and it began to dawn on him. "They've been playing me the whole time," he shouted.

"Exactly. Everything they have proposed was with the intentions of stalling your directives."

O'Brien sat up in his chair and mindlessly twirled the phone on the table. "Do you think the colonel had this planned from the beginning?"

"I do. From the training to the installation of his security team, the colonel's plan was to delay your plans while learning your intentions with a mole—Captain Branson."

"But, Marion, Branson helped with the armory raids. Wouldn't he be violating some military oath or law or something?"

"Maybe so, but his commanding officer was probably in on it," replied La Rue. "How do you punish a co-conspirator?"

"Every armory raid was a success, except…"

"Yeah, Jim, except for the fact that more than half of our people disappeared into thin air, and so did the weapons from the largest armories," said La Rue, finishing O'Brien's thought. It was starting to make sense to him now.

"The colonel hijacked our weapons and our men! Those images of the MBTA trucks rolling into New York were real, right!" O'Brien slammed his hand on the table and stood, walking back to the window. "What do you think happened?"

"I think the pictures, produced of course by Colonel Bradlee, were either faked or real. But our guys and the weapons weren't in those trucks. They're somewhere else."

"Where?" O'Brien was starting to see the importance of having another set of eyes that he could trust.

"I believe they may be in the prison camp at Fort Devens. I'll go up there tomorrow and see what I can find out."

"Take some men with you, Marion," instructed O'Brien. "I'm

gonna need you through all of this. But one more thing. Where does Pearson fit into all of this?"

"I think he was set up to take the fall," replied La Rue. "Think about it. He didn't run and hide after the armory raids went bad. He went to Belchertown to do his job, which was to get these Citizen Corps councils up and running."

O'Brien nodded his head and chuckled. "He tried to explain everything to me over the phone, but I guess I spooked him."

"I was here, remember? You were very nice to him, trying to convince him to come in and talk about it. You scared the crap out of the man, Jim." Both men laughed.

"I guess I'm not very good at *nice*," said O'Brien. The laugh enabled O'Brien to steady his nerves, and he lit up a cigar. "Marion, thank you for helping me make sense of this. We can get on track now, and I think I know how. Go home, get some rest, and find out what the hell is going on at Fort Devens. But don't take any chances. I'll have help on the way soon."

As La Rue left the conference room, O'Brien took another deep draw on his cigar. He hesitated a moment before he finally picked up the phone. He dreaded making this call because he didn't want it to be perceived as a sign of weakness. The President had placed his confidence and trust in him. It was not just the embarrassment that concerned him, it was the fear of replacement. In normal times, O'Brien knew it was damn near impossible to fire a government employee. These weren't normal times, and he worked for a President who expected results. He wiped his sweaty palms on his pants and made the call.

CHAPTER 35

Monday, September 26, 2016
7:15 p.m.
Prescott Peninsula
Quabbin Reservoir, Massachusetts

John Morgan understood the quest for power and control. His entire life's work centered on the use of money and advantage to increase his wealth and that of the Boston Brahmin. He was a master of the arts of manipulation and intimidation as tools to achieve his goals. These talents had served him well, but now he was feeling outmaneuvered by a petulant President who suddenly grew a set of balls. Using the well-known quote by Job in the Bible as an analogy, Morgan knew that what he gave, he could take away. It was time to take down this President.

Morgan understood Vladimir Putin. He was ridiculed for his deception and was frequently ostracized by most leaders of the free world. His economy was frequently in shambles, only to be rescued by rising oil prices in times of turmoil. He was often thwarted in his schemes to enrich his political allies by the rule of law or international sanctions. But he never gave up.

For all of the setbacks, Putin remained in undisputed control of the Kremlin. While his adversaries, namely the United States and the West, were successful in these insignificant skirmishes, they were losing the war with Russia over Putin's real goal—reconstituting the former Soviet Union.

Morgan understood Putin's intentions for Ukraine. Domesticating Ukraine through his routine tactics of threats and bribery was his first preference, but the military invasion had side benefits. It demonstrated the costs of insubordination to Mother Russia. Putin thought Ukraine's government was merely a puppet of the West, and the conflict had usefully shown who was boss in Russia's backyard.

When Morgan agreed to conspire with Putin to create a false-flag event in December of 2015, he knew it would have serious ramifications for global financial markets. Uncertainty could provide opportunities for large profits for those who were certain of the outcomes. Both Morgan and Putin were certain of the outcome of Steven's mission that cold winter day.

Morgan and the Boston Brahmin profited immensely from the crashing currencies. Putin successfully rallied support for his plans militarily by creating a false-flag event that convinced all of Russia to support him. Best of all, it sowed discord among Putin's adversaries—among Europeans, and between them and America.

As such, a single false-flag event fractured the West's approach to Russia's expansion. The Europeans no longer supported Washington's approach and stood idly by as Putin advanced into the Arctic. The European Union and NATO were Putin's real targets. To him, Western institutions and values were far more threatening than any army.

If the truth were to be told, Putin would have ordered the cyber attack. Putin was notorious for using criminal groups and other hackers with no overt links to the Russian government. Russian cyber operations against Ukraine on December 23, 2015, Georgia in 2008, and Estonia in 2007 appear to have been carried out for the most part by unassociated, so-called patriotic hackers—although the affected governments and independent security researchers charged a relationship exists.

The President of the United States knew this perception existed. He also knew that the Russian troop movements in the Arctic, as well as their naval operations off the U.S. coasts, made headlines daily. Morgan gave kudos to the President for pointing the finger of blame at Putin in his address to the nation the other day. The President, using the power of his megaphone as the leader of the free world, effectively generated a false-flag event out of thin air.

Morgan wanted to reduce the effectiveness of this brilliant geopolitical chess move. It was time to make a deal with the devil. Morgan had two choices. He could ask Putin to withdraw on all fronts, making the President look foolish in the process. Or he could repeat history.

France had been secretly aiding the American colonies since 1776 because the French were angry at Britain over the loss of colonial territory during the French and Indian War. In 1776, the Continental Congress sent their top diplomat, Benjamin Franklin, to France to secure a formal alliance.

France agreed to aid the colonists by providing military arms and financial assistance. Spain and the Netherlands joined France, making it a global war in which the British had no major allies. In the 1777 Battle of Saratoga, France's support deepened after the Americans beat the British, proving that the colonists were committed to independence and worthy of a formal alliance.

During the American Revolution, France sent an estimated twelve thousand soldiers and thirty-two thousand sailors to the American war effort. By 1778, Franklin was in France, signing the Treaty of Alliance, which formerly made the fledgling nation and France allies against Great Britain. In addition, the Treaty of Amity and Commerce recognized the U.S. as an independent nation and promoted trade between France and America. The French supported the revolutionary-minded colonists in their military efforts until they gained full independence from Great Britain.

The key to Morgan's decision was the United States military. He needed to trust the assurances of General Sears that the military would not raise arms against American citizens. He was aware of the growing rift between the commanders. Perhaps the President was aware as well, hence the growing presence of United Nations forces on American soil.

Another unknown was the effectiveness of the President's Citizen Corps program. *Were Americans turning on each other?* Clearly, that was the desired effect. Currently, the military was preoccupied with the potential threat from Russia, who had now surrounded America's borders. *If the military can't stand up to the President, his newly created Citizen Corps and a possible United Nations force, who can?*

Chapter 36

Tuesday, September 27, 2016
12:07 p.m.
Prescott Peninsula
Quabbin Reservoir, Massachusetts

"I'm told that the United Nations ships left Morocco on Friday and are now approaching Bermuda," said Brad. "At first, intel indicated that the ships were destined for Mexico, possibly to beef up the U.N. troop levels at the Texas border. My friend at NORAD told me today they changed course last night. Their destination now appears to be our northeast coast."

"Do you have any indication as to which port?" asked Donald.

"No, not yet," replied Brad. "My source also tells me that the ranks of the so-called U.N. peacekeeping force has risen dramatically."

"What does that mean?" asked Morgan.

"The U.N. peacekeeping function is not a full-time job," replied Brad. "They pull personnel from all over the world to conduct law enforcement matters and to draw on military experts. These functions make up only about ten percent of the one hundred thousand or so total troops. The other ninety thousand come from countries like India, Pakistan, China, and various African nations."

"I'm surprised we're not a bigger part of their operations," said Donald.

"Believe it or not, there are less than a hundred American contributors to the U.N. forces," said Brad.

"We constitute three-quarters of NATO troops, but rest assured, we pay for the United Nations contingent," added Morgan. "In this case, an operation of this size was undertaken at the behest of the President and paid for with American money."

"That's the other point I need to make," continued Brad. "The size is well beyond the normal UN contingent. The troop contributions have quadrupled. The peacekeeping force is now four hundred thousand strong, thanks to large increases in the Chinese, Indian, and Pakistani contingents."

"Are you saying that the UN troop numbers have grown to four hundred thousand?" asked Donald.

"Based upon our best intel, yes," replied Brad.

"How many troops do we have on active duty in the U.S.?" asked Morgan.

"Although there are over a million military personnel stationed at home, only a fraction are combat troops," replied Brad. "Of those, I am guessing that less than twenty percent are on duty now. The number absent without leave are unfathomable."

"Are we outgunned?" asked Donald.

"If the intel numbers are accurate, yes, we are," Brad replied.

Gunny Falcone and CWO Shore drove into the clearing where Brad was talking with Donald and Morgan. He paused, allowing the four-wheeler to come to a halt. He waved them over.

"Sitrep, gentlemen," said Brad.

"Sir, the lake traffic has increased substantially," said Gunny Falcone. "The western inlet of the reservoir has been quiet, but there has been a lot of activity on the shore from fishermen."

"They're not catching anything, sir," interjected CWO Shore. "They are spread out down the shore incrementally and are observing us. I've placed our own observers inside the tree line, and in some cases, our personnel are in makeshift tree stands."

"What about on the main body of the reservoir?" asked Brad.

"There has been a major escalation in boat traffic," replied Gunny Falcone. "Three or four days ago, we might see half a dozen fishing boats scattered around the lake. Now, there are a dozen in view during the daylight hours."

"The other interesting thing, sir, is this," added CWO Shore. "No one has approached our shoreline or the front gate since the encounter with Pearson and that guy named Archibald. It's as if they are waiting for something."

"Thank you, gentlemen, that is all," said Brad as he dismissed his men. He turned to Donald and Morgan, who spoke first.

"It appears that matters are reaching a boiling point, both locally and on a national level. Are you gentlemen comfortable with your plan to protect Prescott Peninsula?"

"Yes, sir," replied Brad. "It will come with bloodshed, primarily for the locals. As a military man, I need to make sure I understand the rules of engagement. We have been warning intruders and turning them away as they get close."

"But based on the increased activities and the information received from Steven and Katie, it is apparent that the residents of Belchertown intend to attack us," said Donald. "How do we avoid bloodshed?"

"Is diplomacy out of the question?" asked Morgan.

Brad shook his head and sighed. "I'm afraid that any interlude toward a peaceful solution will only raise more questions and possibly invite inquiry from this new governor or higher up."

"At this point, they view us as a private security force," added Donald. "Perhaps Pearson convinced them otherwise. Either way, we can't allow them on Prescott Peninsula. If they don't heed our warning, most of them will die."

Morgan suddenly became quiet and began to massage his left arm. Brad looked at Donald, who became concerned. "Mr. Morgan, are you feeling okay?"

"It's this damned diet, Mr. Quinn," said Morgan. "The constant meals of beans and rice are not what my digestive tract is used to." He continued to massage his arm, but his face reddened, and his eyes appeared to be bloodshot.

"Sir, why don't we have J.J. take a look at you?" said Brad.

Morgan held his hands up to cut off further debate. "I'm fine. You two are as bad as my daughter. Just make sure my friends are well protected. I'm going to lie down for a while." Morgan slowly walked away as Susan approached the group.

"Is he okay?" asked Susan. "He looked a little shaky."

"I guess so," said Donald. "Listen, the girls are having a good time. May I take Brad for a moment?"

"Sure, I'll be here." Donald turned to Brad.

"There are a couple of things that you need to see," said Donald as he led Brad into 1PP. An hour later, Brad was introduced to the force multiplier and enough precious metals to buy an army, or start a new country.

Chapter 37

Tuesday, September 27, 2016
9:00 a.m.
100 Beacon
Boston, Massachusetts

Julia rubbed Sarge's shoulders as the two stood on the rooftop of 100 Beacon for their morning watch. Steven and Sarge got in late from a reconnaissance mission with the Mechanics to the local food bank. They confirmed that O'Brien was hoarding the supplies received from FEMA. He was not distributing them to the remaining citizens.

For the last several nights, the sounds of gunfire filled the relative quiet. Car traffic was virtually nonexistent now, as most residents had either fled the city or didn't have any gasoline. Reports were being received that moving vehicles were being attacked as they approached blocked intersections. Even if you were one of the fortunate few with gasoline, you were in danger of losing your vehicle to marauders.

"Tell me about the rest of the country," started Sarge. "How are other cities dealing with this?"

Julia took a sip of coffee and kissed Sarge. "Thank you for the coffee, honey."

"Let's enjoy it while we can," he said. "I think we need to cut down on our generator usage. It's so quiet, it might draw attention."

"You mean more attention than the dead bodies that are piling up around the building?" She laughed.

"Yeah, that's true. So, what've you heard?"

"The reports are varied," Julia replied. "In the big cities, chaos is the word used most often to describe the aftermath. In the locations where the Citizen Corps governors' offices are located, some semblance of order is being restored. In the midsize cities, it's a bloodbath in some cases. The law enforcement personnel of the smaller towns are abandoning their jobs to protect their families. The military personnel, or what's left of them, are being redeployed to gain control of the major cities. In some cases, they are clamping down hard."

"Like where?" asked Sarge.

"Chicago, New York, and Philadelphia, for example. The military has been accused of firing indiscriminately on unarmed citizens. FEMA's supplies are running low and being redirected at the discretion of the newly appointed regional governors. Some residents have attempted to stage protests, and it's become ugly."

"Donald and Susan used to think the Jade Helm exercises were intended to prepare the military for civil unrest," said Sarge. "Those opinions would have been laughed at a month ago. Now look." Something caught Julia's attention to their north.

"The groundwork for dealing with a catastrophic event like this one has been in place for years," he continued. "These executive orders, both before and after the cyber attack, allowed the government to exercise absolute control over every aspect of a citizen's life."

Julia looked through the binoculars at an altercation between two men on the river side of Storrow Drive below them. It appeared they were fighting over a liquor bottle. She offered the binoculars to Sarge, who simply shook his head.

She continued. "In other parts of the country, the ranks of the Citizen Corps have swelled to huge numbers. With the promise of food, shelter in the form of confiscated homes, and power to bully their fellow Americans, the formerly worthless members of the population are now able to flex their muscles."

"These executive orders made no effort to justify the destruction of our freedoms, and no effort to explain how their idea of totalitarian control would stop the rioting, looting, and murders," said Sarge. "Soon, they will begin to experience corruption and bureaucratic infighting. This occurred in similar situations in fascist Italy, Nazi Germany, and the old Soviet Union."

"Guess what happened in all of those instances?"

"You bet," replied Sarge. "The oppressive governments collapsed. Their efforts at totalitarian control provoked more political turmoil, and eventually the people rose up against the governments, or they were destroyed by a greater enemy, like us."

Another man joined the fray below them. Sarge raised his weapon to get a closer look through his scope. There was now a three-man battle for the last bottle of vodka in Boston.

"Citizens are being detained in the rural areas for refusing to comply with the Citizen Corps rules ordering them to relinquish their weapons and stored food," said Julia. "The dreaded *FEMA Camps* are coming to fruition."

"I was afraid of that."

"Well, it gets worse, Sarge. Apparently the rumored *Enemy's List*, which was supposedly maintained at the direction of the President, is very real."

"Are you talking about *Main Core*?" asked Sarge.

"Yes. The database is huge, having been compiled with intelligence information from the NSA, FBI, CIA and other governmental agencies, including ATF."

"I read the list includes Americans who have been considered *unfriendly* and thus enemies of the state."

"That's right. It's being utilized now by the Citizen Corps. I'm receiving reports the gun confiscations are being directed at people with concealed-carry permits and who have registered their weapons. This is making it very easy for the President to locate the firearms of law-abiding citizens."

"Naturally." Sarge shrugged. "It's too difficult to disarm criminals."

"It also includes people based upon their social media posts, voting records, and even those who hold ham radio licenses."

"You're kidding, right?" asked Sarge.

"No," she replied. "I am sure to be in the Main Core database for a number of reasons, including being a HAMR."

"How would that be dangerous?"

"From my experience, most ham radio operators are libertarian or conservatives politically. That puts you in the crosshairs of this president. I monitor the radio waves every day, and almost all of the transmissions come from people like us. Anyone who obtained their ham call letters is a potential target."

"Should we have anticipated something like this?" asked Sarge. "We knew the government tracked everything."

"Hindsight is twenty-twenty," she replied. "But if we had it to do over again, we would never buy our weapons through a licensed FFL, using only online sources like Armslist. I rarely used my ham radio before the cyber attack. I should have purchased the equipment, stored it in a Faraday cage, and left it alone. As for social media, I can think of dozens of so-called patriotic pages and groups that I frequented that placed me on the Main Core lists."

"It's hard to stay off the government's radar," said Sarge.

"I know, but we didn't have to make it easy for them."

The two stood in silence for a moment as they contemplated the all-reaching, all-knowing big-brother government that controlled their lives prior to the grid going down. Now, Julia wondered when they would show up at their door.

"Fortunately, they haven't visited us, yet," she added.

"Brad's deception on the new governor worked well while it lasted. We've been fortunate to hold him off. Brad knows that he's been made and that he might be in danger of losing his oak leaves."

"How will he take it?" asked Julia.

"He'll be fine," replied Sarge. "We just need to provide him a new group of patriots to command."

CHAPTER 38

Wednesday, September 28, 2016
8:49 p.m.
630 Washington Street
Boston, Massachusetts

The Mechanics entered the second floor of 630 Washington as Sarge sat quietly on top of an old wooden desk, dangling his feet and gently kicking the sides with his heels. He thought of the famous quote by George Santayana—*those who cannot remember the past are condemned to repeat it.* Sarge was feeling philosophical, which was good in view of the circumstances. His beloved country was falling apart—prey to an overreaching government and victim to a cyber attack that reeked of conspiracy.

Sarge was a student of history and knew that the next days and months would be written about for centuries. When you were in the moment, part of something unfolding, you didn't recognize the impact that your decisions and actions might have on the course of history. When the Sons of Liberty, led by Samuel Adams, began to meet under the Liberty Tree or down the street at the Green Dragon Tavern, they were nothing more than wharf rats, tavern mongers, and seedy characters looking to cause trouble. Their ire was directed at the British government and their cause became *no taxation without representation.*

Groups like the Boston Caucus Club or the Loyal Nine later became well-organized patriot political organizations. Shrouded in secrecy, the Loyal Nine evolved into larger groups, including the Sons of Liberty. Leaders emerged—men who later became known as statesmen and Founding Fathers. They were the men who were acknowledged throughout history for their efforts.

But the unsung heroes of those early days from 1765 through the Declaration of Independence were the Mechanics. They were the insurgent arm of the Loyal Nine. When it was time to incite Boston's patriots into action, it was the Mechanics, not the statesmen, who gleefully did the dirty work that led to the American Revolution.

Sarge believed it was raw emotion, not knowledge, that was the impetus for change. The men and women who filled this room shoulder to shoulder had to want change. It was up to Sarge to create the passion necessary to bring knowledge to a boil.

Suddenly, the room became quiet as Steven asked the group to quiet down. Sarge, still sitting on the desk, looked into the eyes of the men and women who would be called upon to risk their lives, and the safety of their families, to fight to preserve the freedoms just as their forefathers did two hundred and fifty years ago.

Sarge took a deep breath and spoke. "Freedom comes at a price. Men and women just like you came together in places like this or taverns down the street to express their desire to break away from tyranny. They enthusiastically shouted that it was their solemn responsibility to pay any price to secure the freedom of a fledgling nation." Sarge stood to address the tightly packed group of a hundred or so patriots.

"That time has come again, my friends. History shows that the path to liberty invariably involves conflict. Whether it was the American Revolution, which involved taking up arms, or political movements, which required the banding together of like-minded Americans to fight for our Constitutional rights, the course of American history was set by people like you.

"These conflicts demand a very steep price from those who fight them. Oftentimes, when expressing your political opinions, you were demeaned or ostracized by those who disagree with you. When you chose to make your voices heard by banding together as Tea Party Patriots, you were quickly denounced and then ultimately abandoned by the very politicians you helped elect.

"Today, we find ourselves in the same shoes as the Sons of

Liberty, in a far greater conflict than the mere exchange of political dialogue. There is a battle for the heart and soul of America looming. Just like our forefathers, we face a tyrannical government that has empowered those who wish to profit from this catastrophic event, both financially and through the stifling of dissent.

"Throughout history, governments have demonstrated their willingness to trample on individual liberties without regard to the long-term consequences. We've seen this happen during our lifetimes, and now tyranny has reached new heights in this country." Sarge paced the floor as he spoke. He stopped from time to time to speak directly to one of the Mechanics.

"Prior to the attack, we lived in a nation where the government became more and more intrusive in our lives. They thought average American citizens were incapable of making decisions for themselves. They told us what we could and could not put in our bodies. They were able to declare us unfit parents, at their sole discretion, for the horrific crime of homeschooling. They told us when and where we were allowed to exercise our second amendment rights.

"They instilled fear in us with reports of angry men in caves or a threatening menace in the deserts of the Middle East. They frightened you with things that go bump in the night. Then our benevolent government offered solutions that took away your freedoms, in the name of keeping you safe. Ironically, their solutions never involved taking care of ourselves." Sarge unconsciously held the top of his holstered .45 as he spoke.

"My friends, those issues are trivial to the current despotism of this President. Many of you have experienced this firsthand. Americans' arms are being confiscated. Your food storage is being declared excessive. Some of you have been forced out of your homes for the benefit of the government's chosen few. Moreover, all of you have been denied access to life-saving food and medical supplies because of your prior political affiliation or your refusal to bow down to a newly appointed government official.

"The President claims he is doing his duty by acting in the interest of protecting the American people. He quickly pointed out it was his number one responsibility to keep Americans safe. He hasn't learned from history, or the Constitution, although he supposedly taught constitutional law.

"He took an oath, like all governmental officials, to support and defend the Constitution of the United States against all enemies, foreign and domestic. His first responsibility as President is to uphold the principles of freedom that define our nation. He has broken his oath of office by trampling on the Constitution for the illusion of security.

"There are many Americans who welcome this because they are afraid. Their security is threatened. I believe this short-term thinking creates a much more menacing state of affairs in the long term. By doing nothing, our implied acquiescence to these intrusive government actions results in another stone laid on the path to tyranny."

Sarge paused and looked around the room. The eyes of his fellow patriots gave him the answer he sought.

"Our price," he started and then hesitated. "Our price to be paid is making the difficult choice between security and liberty. We have to choose fear or freedom. But I must caution you, my friends, freedom isn't free."

CHAPTER 39

Wednesday, September 28, 2016
7:15 p.m.
Citizen Corps Region I, Office of the Governor
99 High Street
Boston, Massachusetts

O'Brien stood alone atop 99 High Street. The cool fall air chilled him slightly, so he fastened his jacket. It had been a productive and interesting day. He was starting to feel the euphoria of power that had enveloped him three weeks prior. Lighting another cigar, he was anxious to get started. But first, there were some important decisions to make.

He heard the rooftop door slam and turned to see La Rue escorting Pearson to the table. A bottle of whisky awaited the men. Pearson, who had eluded capture, had spoken with O'Brien yesterday. He was very grateful to clear up the misunderstanding and was anxious to report his information to O'Brien. La Rue had details of his missing men as well. O'Brien poured a glass of whisky for each of them and took a swig, swallowing hard as he downed the glass completely. He quickly poured another.

"Gentlemen," said O'Brien, raising his glass, "enjoy."

"Thank you, Governor," toasted Pearson. "It's good to have our problems resolved."

"It is, Pearson," said O'Brien. "Let's try to move forward and put things back on track."

"Agreed," he replied. "I have some information that relates to our colonel. Apparently, he's known as a wild card, frequently bucking command when he sees fit. He is tolerated because of his stellar combat record and connections in high places."

"How high?" asked La Rue, taking a sip of the whisky.

"The highest," replied Pearson. "He has passed over several cross promotions to commands that would have given him more visibility within the Corps. My source tells me he was in line for a full bird anyway. He must have clout in the Pentagon or the White House."

"Is he untouchable?" asked La Rue.

"No."

"Governor, I have confirmed our suspicions," said La Rue. "Our missing men are being held at Fort Devens under armed guard at the former federal prison camp there. I have men observing Devens round the clock. They recognized some of their buddies through a window. They are not allowed outside of the building where they are housed."

"What about my guns?" asked O'Brien.

"I can't say with certainty, but I know the MBTA vans are not there," replied La Rue.

"I can help you there," interrupted Pearson. "The images you told me about on the phone are real. The trucks were found abandoned in various wooded locations on the west side of the Hudson. The trucks were moved across the state line into the Albany area before the borders were closed due to the Indian Point meltdown."

"This is one sly operator," said O'Brien. "How does all of this relate to the Quabbin Reservoir?"

Pearson looked at La Rue, who gestured for him to go first in responding.

"Back in the spring, Quabbin Reservoir was acquired by a trust, and the area specifically located on the Prescott Peninsula was supposedly designated to be a safe haven for abused mothers and children."

O'Brien looked from Pearson to La Rue and back to Pearson. "Well, was it?"

"We don't know for certain," replied Pearson. "No one has seen the facility. In fact, no one has been allowed on the Peninsula since a very well-orchestrated campaign event, which included Hillary and Senator Morgan."

O'Brien studied the two for a moment and then asked, "Is there any reason to believe it's not a home for wayward souls?"

"It's the level of security, Governor," replied Pearson. "The place is crawling with either active-duty military or former private contractors. These guys are real pros and have the gear to support the theory that they are former members of the armed forces."

"I think Colonel Bradlee has something to do with this," added La Rue. "I find it very suspicious that he's lost so many men to defections. And how did he hijack our guys and the trucks. He had to have a lot of help to pull that off."

"So you think Bradlee is holed up at Prescott Peninsula, hiding under the skirts of widows and orphans or something like that?"

"There may not be any widows and orphans, Governor," replied Pearson. "I think it's a ruse for something bigger."

O'Brien poured another drink. "How are we going to get to the bottom of this?"

"Archibald, your Citizen Corps leader in Belchertown, is planning a raid on Prescott Peninsula," said Pearson. "He's coordinating with hundreds of local men to raid the shores by boat and storm the front gates. They think there's food being protected, and they're hungry."

"Good," said O'Brien. "I heard a saying once, the rich swell up with pride, but the poor rise up from hunger. Let the people take what they need and deserve." He stood and poured the last of the whisky into his glass.

"Marion, I want my men back," started O'Brien.

"I understand, Governor," he replied. "But I need more than what we have. Do you want me to load up the gangbangers and unleash them on Fort Devens. That could get really ugly, fast."

Suddenly, the eastern sky lit up as if Fenway Park had sprung to life for a night game. O'Brien abruptly turned to look over the roof's half wall.

"Right on cue, gentlemen," he said, gesturing toward Boston Harbor and the wharfs along Seaport Boulevard. "Help has arrived."

Six Watson-class prepositioning ships were making their way to dockage at the piers. Provided to the United Nations by the administration years before as part of its downsizing program, these vessels contained the unique all-white paint and distinctive U.N. logo in black. The ships, manufactured by Cabot Industries, were each capable of carrying three hundred troops with a nearly four-hundred-thousand-cubic-foot cargo area for all types of vehicles.

A Russian-made, all-white Mi-26T helicopter flew up and down the harbor from the North End to Castle Island Park. The sound of the rotors was deafening as the noise reverberated off the skyscrapers of Boston. A slightly smaller gunship, the Mi-24, moved at a lower altitude, buzzing northward toward the Charlestown Navy Yard and back again.

A variety of armored vehicles began to slowly disembark onto the wharfs. Medical trucks towed howitzers from the cargo hold. Finally, the Indian Army T-72 tanks rolled out of the bowels of the ship. O'Brien began to laugh.

"Boys, now I've got my army."

CHAPTER 40

Thursday, September 29, 2016
6:00 p.m.
Town Hall
Belchertown, Massachusetts

Archibald stood alone in the shadows of the town hall, pulling his jacket closed as the night air began to displace the day's unusual warmth. Residents from the surrounding areas came to hear his final speech before the anticipated raid upon Prescott Peninsula.

Pearson was already sitting on the stage. When Archibald first received the wanted poster, he thought something was amiss. Pearson hadn't acted like a man who should be on the run for treason. Archibald was never accused of allowing Pearson the opportunity to escape, but it was not his intention to detain the man either. As a result, he gained a friend in Pearson and an alliance, of sorts.

Belchertown was perched atop a hill overlooking the Connecticut Valley to the west and the Quabbin Reservoir to the east. The Church of Christ's spire, which was nearly the eighty-foot height of the town's water tank, was visible for miles in all directions. Originally settled as part of the Connecticut Western Reserve, the surrounding lands were granted to Jonathan Belcher, who later became the royal governor of Massachusetts.

Belchertown made history in 1774 as the first municipality in the country to refuse to pay its taxes to the Loyalist English government in America. Archibald studied the history of his small town. It was storied. On a night just like this one, in 1774, the people of Belchertown came together and created a militia, a small fighting force, under the leadership of Captain Caleb Clark. They proudly marched east to join their fellow patriots the day after the Battle of Lexington. Over half of the men residing in Belchertown saw service in the Revolution, and the other residents, although poverty stricken and hungry, were active in supporting the fight for freedom by giving their time and what belongings they had.

While their cause was noble, the aftermath of the Revolution for the citizens of Belchertown was devastating. The men returned home from the War broke, and their farms were damaged from neglect. The fledgling government faced enormous debt and financial challenges. Washington's solution was to levy taxes upon the farmers' land. The farmers' solution, true to their predecessors' penchant for rebellion, was to refuse to pay the tax and take up arms.

At the time, Massachusetts was plagued with bad harvests and economic depression. The high taxes and enforcement procedures of the federal government threatened farmers across the union with the loss of their farms. A former captain in the Continental Army, Daniel Shays, recruited men from across the state, including many from Belchertown. At first, Shay encouraged his followers to harass local merchants, lawyers, and supporters of the state government. In late 1786, the men of Shay's Rebellion made an ill-fated attempt to capture the federal arsenal at Springfield. The state militia successfully defended the armory, crushed the rebels in several engagements, and the rebellion was over.

Although Archibald knew Shay's Rebellion never seriously threatened the stability of the United States, it greatly alarmed politicians throughout the nation. Archibald needed to lead his people on a rebellion of a similar nature. It was a rebellion against an unknown enemy. He had to rely on limited planning, but hope for raw emotion. He needed to prepare them for battle, much like Captain Clark did on the Belchertown common two hundred and thirty years before.

He walked alone across the fading green grass as it became dormant for the winter. The crowd of primarily men gathered around the stage. Some carried their weapons and others held the hands of their wives. *Do they know the risks of rebellion?*

"Everyone, please gather around. We need to get started." The crowd pushed closer to the stage, which had become a permanent fixture in front of the town hall. Once again, as in the eighteenth century, the center of a community's universe became the town's common.

"Thank you all for coming this afternoon," started Archibald. "After the cyber attack, our world became much smaller. There weren't any more planes to catch or buses to ride or cars to drive to the Hampshire Mall over in Amherst. Except for those few who still have gasoline, our world has become limited to the distance we can travel on foot or by horse or on a bicycle.

"We have always been a close-knit community, and today, the importance of community has never been greater. My friends, the days of driving into your garage and quickly closing the door behind you in order to avoid a conversation with your neighbor are over. Now, you must rely on your neighbor for protection and perhaps to save your life.

"We have rallied as a community and attempted to rely on help from our government to survive. We've all come to the realization that help is not coming anytime soon. It's time to help ourselves!" Archibald raised his voice to a few cheers and shouts of approval.

"One of our own, Jimmy Fulks, who is a neighbor, a friend, and a family man, was gunned down by armed men right over there on Prescott Peninsula." Of course, Archibald, and only two other men, knew that Jimmy fired the first shot at the woman standing guard at the gate. But he needed to rally his constituents and give them a cause. Creating a martyr out of Jimmy Fulks was the perfect pretense to rally his people to fight. "Doesn't Jimmy deserve justice?"

"Yeah," came a chorus of shouts from the crowd. Archibald allowed them to settle before he continued.

"We're all hungry. We've seen the elderly die of starvation and our children suffer from lack of nutrition. I look into your eyes and see the despair that is frankly un-American. This needs to change!" he shouted. "We've observed enough about the people on Prescott

Peninsula to know that they're well fed and properly housed. Can we say the same about ourselves or our neighbors?"

"Nooo," shouted the crowd. He was inspiring them.

"In times like these, it is not fair for some Americans to live high on the hog while others die of starvation. It is not fair for some to have a comfortable roof over their head while the rest of us face the uncertainty of a harsh winter without heat. It is not fair for someone to get away with murdering one of our own!"

Archibald stood back and took in the shouts of encouragement. He glanced back at Pearson, who nodded with approval.

"Are you with me?" he shouted.

"Yes!"

"What I see before me is a whole community coming together in defiance of death. I see men and women who agree that it is time to take what we need to survive. Why should a few have so much when they can help so many?"

The people were cheering now. *They're ready.*

"You've come here as a community. Will you fight as a community to survive?"

"Yes!" they shouted.

He allowed their screams to die down once again. Archibald breathed deeply and exhaled before finishing.

"Tonight and tomorrow, I want you to rest. Spend time with your families. Steady your nerves and ready your mind. The time for planning is over. The time for starving is over! The time to fight for our fair share has come!"

Archibald stood back from the podium and raised his hands, encouraging the crowd to cheer. Now, he was a leader of men.

CHAPTER 41

Thursday, September 29, 2016
5:30 p.m.
Mount Zion
Quabbin Reservoir, Massachusetts

"Come on, it's gettin' dark out here," said Will Allen to his younger brother, M.C.

"No kiddin', Sherlock, and cold too. Ain't we got enough already?" replied M.C. as he sloshed through the muck along the shore of the Quabbin Reservoir. He stumbled slightly and got a little too close to his brother, who reacted quickly.

"Be careful, dude. You gotta pay attention with this," Will said as he stood to the side. He decided to follow his brother to the edge of the shore. As they approached the aluminum flat-bottom boat pulled onto the muddy beach, the faint sounds of yelling carried across the serene water of the lake. They both placed their contributions into the boat and went back into the woods for more.

"I know, we do this for a livin'. Well, at least we used to."

"We're getting' paid, Mikey, in the new form of currency," said Will.

"Yeah, food. BFD. How much we gonna git, you think?" asked M.C. Then he added, "And stop calling me Mikey. You did that in front of that fellow yesterday."

"Whatever. Listen, we're gonna get more than them others, and we don't have to worry about gettin' our asses shot off Saturday." Will continued deeper into the woods, using his retractable snare pole as a walking stick.

"I ain't arguin' with the gig. I'm just sayin' we've been at it all day.

That fella ain't gonna know how many we got so far. The only folks that'll know are the ones across the way." M.C. swung his forty-inch hook over his shoulder to point toward Prescott Peninsula, narrowly missing his brother.

"Dammit, Mikey," Will shouted. "I'm gonna throw your dumb ass in this hole up here if you don't straighten up. Now bring that light so I can see."

"Look there at them babies. I see their eggs too."

"Shhhh," cautioned Will as he steadied himself. M.C. shined the light, illuminating the rock outcroppings that made up a den of dozens of timber rattlesnakes. "Look at 'em all."

In the spring, Massachusetts Division of Fisheries and Wildlife had relocated hundreds of timber rattlesnakes to this fourteen-hundred-acre island in the middle of the Quabbin Reservoir. The timber rattlers were becoming extinct around the state and the head of the department elected to use the island as a breeding ground to prevent the timber rattler from going extinct. The rattlesnakes were relocated from all of the surrounding states to Mount Zion, much to the dismay of the residents of Belchertown.

During public hearings, the townspeople showed up in droves. The residents pointed out that rattlesnakes could swim and might find their way onto public access lands that were used for fishing and hiking. Others asked valid questions like "when the inevitable happens, and a hiker gets bit by a rattler, who's responsible?"

The environmental groups who supported the project were represented by the only environmental law attorney in the county—Mr. Ronald Archibald. Archibald conducted his own research. Although he allowed the proceedings to continue without comment because he didn't want the snakes over there either, he readily supplied the ammunition to gain public approval to his proxies.

Several residents came to his aid. One pointed out that timber rattlers were generally timid and only strike when provoked. Another, a longtime nurse in the community, testified that she had never seen a rattlesnake bite at the local clinic. A third argued humans were a bigger threat to the *harmless* timber rattlesnake than vice versa.

Archibald and the Allen brothers also knew the timber rattlesnake was the most dangerous snake in North America due to its long fangs, impressive size, and high venom yield. Despite their timidity, they would strike if startled. If their bite was not treated within hours, limbs were lost. Within a couple of days, lives were lost as well.

Archibald and Pearson had instructed the Allens to fill a boat with the deadly snakes, which had now multiplied many times over on Mount Zion. They were awaiting orders to make a special delivery—to Prescott Peninsula.

CHAPTER 42

Thursday, September 29, 2016
5:30 p.m.
Prescott Peninsula
Quabbin Reservoir, Massachusetts

Donald received the call over the radio that Sarge had arrived at the front gate with the others. Sarge and Steven cautioned against leaving 100 Beacon unoccupied, but after installing several families of the Mechanics in the lower floors, they considered the building well protected.

This was the first gathering of the Loyal Nine together since the cyber attack. Donald, and especially Susan, was distressed over the purpose of the meeting at 1PP, but it was necessary. They gathered for the first time to discuss the potential false-flag events and the ramifications of Morgan's involvement. They needed to trade notes without emotions getting in the way. Therefore, the initial meeting didn't include Abbie.

Donald walked into the kitchen, where Susan and Brad were talking with Stella Peabody. The girls were having their dinner of mac and cheese at the kitchen table.

"Stella, would you mind watching these hellions for a little while?" asked Donald.

"Oh my, of course I wouldn't mind, Donald," she replied. Stella patted their heads as they continued eating their beloved mac and cheese. Donald thought the girls were oblivious to the *hellions* reference. "They are adorable angels, young man."

Penny looked up at her dad and smiled.

They hear everything. "Yes, the adorable hellions, then. Thank you. We'll be back in a couple of hours."

Donald looked at Susan and Brad, nodding his head to indicate it was time to meet. He wasn't sure where Abbie was, which was just as well. He didn't want to lie to her about where they would be. Not telling her about the meeting was a big enough lie. They jumped into the four-wheeler and headed toward the front gate. When they met Sarge's OJ-40, they would pull into a quiet place to talk.

As the eight of them greeted one another and exchanged a few pleasantries, Donald nervously picked up some pinecones and tossed them into the woods. This was going to be a difficult conversation, but nothing compared to the one to follow with Abbie and her dad.

"Well, we all know why we're here," started Steven. "Let's get on with it."

Sarge stepped into the middle of the group and spoke. "J.J., I'll ask one last time because I know this subject is going to touch a raw nerve with you. Are you sure you wanna be a part of this?"

"I am, guys," replied J.J., looking at his friends. "I love Sabs and I'll never forget her. But you guys are my family, as is Abbie. This cloud is hanging over our heads, and we'll all be better off when it can be dealt with. My feelings toward Morgan may never change, only time will tell. But I won't let my animosity towards him cloud my judgment, or yours."

Susan gave J.J. a hug, and Donald patted his friend on the back. J.J. had accepted the loss of Sabs, and now they were a group again.

"Okay, good," said Sarge, looking at Steven. "Steven and I have known John Morgan all of our lives. He's our godfather and has been a dad to us since we lost our parents. We're also grown men and understand the implications of what we think we've concluded. Because decisions have to be made, we need to make sure we all understand what we think we've observed."

"I agree, Sarge," said Donald, who picked up more pinecones to help him with his nerves. "Based upon what I've heard from everybody, Katie should go first. Chronologically, it makes sense."

"Everybody knows my job was to be Mr. Morgan's mole in the

White House," said Katie. "I certainly doubt I was the only one. His reach into the deepest, darkest closets of Washington politics is the stuff of a Tom Clancy novel. He insisted that I report every piece of information that I learned during my briefings. At times, he told me to withhold intel for several days without explanation." Katie dusted off a large boulder and sat on it, then continued.

"After Abbie's computer was hacked, I took it upon myself to learn what happened. Normally, that is a job for the secret service, but Abbie, Steven and I agreed to conduct our own examination. My analysis of Abbie's laptop crossed paths with my investigation of the cyber attack on the Las Vegas power grid, leading me to Andrew Lau and the Zero Day Gamers."

"Katie, when you advised Abbie of their involvement, was there any appearance of recollection by Abbie of Lau's name or the ZDG?"

"None at all," replied Katie. "I can't remember whether I ever discussed them with Abbie prior to that one time. She didn't ask me to hide my findings either."

"Okay," said Sarge. He joined Donald in the pinecone-toss game. "As I understand it, you first mentioned this to Mr. Morgan over the telephone, right?"

"Yes," replied Katie. "But it was not the first time I had discussed the Zero Day Gamers with him. Back in the spring, I briefed him on their activities, and he instructed me to bring him any information on them I could find. So I called him to reveal the hack on Abbie's computer."

"Then what?" asked Susan.

"Nothing," she replied. "We had a very short phone conversation about it, and he appeared to be excited about what I discovered. Then I heard nothing from him for almost two weeks."

"Weird," mumbled Donald. He wiped his hands of the debris and focused on the conversation.

"Out of the blue, he summoned us to his office," said Steven. "He had an Aegis team surveilling Lau and his people. I thought it was odd because he would normally include me in an operation like that.

Then he revealed his plan to us."

"He sure did," added Katie. "He and Malcolm Lowe put into place an elaborate ruse to employ the ZDG."

"I've met Lowe only once," said J.J. as he pulled down his shirt sleeves. It was getting darker and a fall chill was in the air. "He doesn't seem like a covert-ops guy."

Steven spoke up. "He surprised me too. Not only did he think out the plan thoroughly, he carried it off flawlessly. We caught Lau totally off guard. In fact, I barely said a word. Lowe negotiated with Lau and ostensibly hired the Zero Day Gamers for some kind of hack to gain leverage on a legislative matter important to Mr. Morgan. Hell, I fell for it too."

"Did you know what he was up to?" asked Brad.

Steven paused before answering. He allowed two ATVs to pass on the gravel road to their east. "Not really, Brad. Hell, you know how it is. Good soldiers take orders and do their thing. Then things got interesting."

"How so?" asked J.J.

"I got a call from Lowe to come up to 73 Tremont. Mr. Morgan told me to assemble my team with the instructions to snatch Lau and those gamer geeks. Lowe had set up this state-of-the-art computer center in an old abandoned warehouse for the geeks to finish the job—whatever it was."

"Wait. I have to know. Wasn't Drew Jackson part of your team? Did he know about this?" asked Susan. Donald touched her arm to calm her down. She seemed agitated.

"No, no, Suzy Q," said Steven. "Slash, I mean Drew, was on Abbie's security detail full time at that point. He wouldn't know anything about it. I'm sure the guys wouldn't have a need to let him know about the op."

"Okay, sorry," said Susan. "I feel bad for what happened to him. I'm glad Drew wasn't involved."

"That's okay, Susan," said Julia. "Then what happened, Steven?"

"Well, this was the last day of August, a Wednesday, I think. Lowe and I continued to play the game, telling the geeks that it was for their own protection. Lowe took over from there, and his own team handled the operation the rest of the way."

"That was three days before the cyber attack," stated Donald. He looked around at everyone. "Has anybody had any contact with Malcolm Lowe since then?" They all shook their heads, indicating they had not. Then Julia spoke again.

"We've seen Lau, however," said Julia. "Sarge and I went to Mass General to help out after the pipeline explosion. We didn't know who Lau was or his possible involvement in the cyber attack. It was purely coincidental. I took a liking to him, out of pity, mainly. He was burned pretty bad and incoherent."

"When Katie and I went over to the hospital a day or so later, Julia gave us the name of a patient to check on," said Steven. "It turned out to be Lau. I about crapped myself when I saw him. This guy holds the answers to this whole freakin' thing."

"Did you speak to him?" asked Susan.

"Not really," replied Katie. "He was still out of it and bandaged up. Plus a nurse was hovering around."

"Do you guys think Morgan orchestrated this cyber attack?" asked J.J., looking at Sarge and Steven.

"It's too coincidental," replied Steven.

Donald knew it was time to disclose to the Loyal Nine the final pieces of the puzzle. "There's more, and I apologize for not telling you sooner. You guys had your hands full at 100 Beacon and I felt the rest of this story needed to be told in person. Today was the first available opportunity."

"What is it, Donald?" asked Julia, looking at Sarge, who was also puzzled.

"Susan overheard a conversation between Mr. Morgan, Walter Cabot, and Lawrence Lowell. Right, honey?"

"Yes. On the night of the martial law declaration, I was back by the bungalows and I heard voices from the edge of the woods. It clearly wasn't the security guys, so I went to check it out. The three of them were discussing what the President's address would be about. I heard words like *going according to plan* and *double-cross.*"

"Are you saying they knew about the martial law declaration in advance?" asked Steven.

"I think so," replied Susan. "But I never heard them say anything about the cyber attack."

"What does *according to plan* mean?" demanded J.J. He appeared to get angrier with every new revelation. "It sure sounds to me like those three were a part of something."

"Hang on, J.J.," said Brad. "We don't know that."

J.J. backed off.

"There's more," interrupted Susan. "Mrs. Lowell has acted withdrawn and angry at times. I know her, and this is not normal. I think she knows something."

"We noticed it too," added Julia. "She was that way when Sarge picked them up. Her anger was directed at her husband. Maybe he let something slip?"

It was getting darker. Also, they had been gone for a while. Donald needed to move this along.

"It's possible, but we need to wrap this up and make a decision," said Donald.

"Listen, I'm not gonna defend the old man," said Steven. He folded his arms defiantly. "He's had me do some crazy ops this year which defy explanation. But I haven't heard anyone say he arranged this attack."

Donald rubbed his face with both hands and spoke. "Now, we need to tell you about Abbie."

Susan placed her hands on his shoulders and smiled. "Let me," she said. "Abbie was having nightmares about Drew when they arrived at 1PP. They were falling in love prior to that night, but the ordeal brought them closer together. When Mr. Morgan insisted upon leaving in the helicopter with her, Drew was being brutally beaten. She was crying hysterically, and she initially recalled Drew shouting out to her *I love you, I love you.*"

"She must be devastated," interjected Julia. "It must be horrible for her to relive that nightmare over and over again."

"It still is difficult for her," said Susan. "But now for a different reason."

"We understand this is a difficult time for her, Susan, as it is for J.J.," said Katie. "But what does this have to do with Mr. Morgan's involvement?"

"She kept playing the whole event in her mind because of Drew's words," started Susan. "She was troubled because she couldn't seem to confirm what he said. She wasn't certain he was saying *I love you.*" Donald moved closer to his wife to give her support.

"If it wasn't that, what was he saying?" asked Sarge.

Susan looked them all in the face before speaking. "Drew was shouting *he knew, he knew.*"

CHAPTER 43

Thursday, September 29, 2016
7:00 p.m.
Prescott Peninsula
Quabbin Reservoir, Massachusetts

"I'll see you down there in a minute," said Sarge as he leaned into the window to give Julia a kiss. As the car slowly pulled away, the gravel crunched beneath the tires until he and Steven were alone in the dark. The brothers began the fifteen-minute walk to 1PP in silence before Steven spoke.

"Are you sure about this, bro. We can just let it go. Move on. Screw it, right?"

Sarge didn't answer immediately. He had wrestled with this decision since the thought first crossed his mind—weeks ago. The information he just received confirmed his suspicions. John Morgan was capable of many things, but he certainly underestimated the impact of this. *Or did he?*

"What's the last memory that you have of Pop?" asked Sarge.

"Look," Steven replied as he pointed up to a meteorite soaring across the southern sky. "You think that was him?"

"Shut up, seriously."

"You know, I was a lot younger than you when he died," said Steven. "I can't really say I have a last memory. I remember when I found out he was gone. But most of my childhood memories are of Mr. Morgan."

"Exactly. He stepped into Pop's shoes and looked after us like we were his own. Abbie was his blood, but we were his sons."

They continued down the road as Sarge thought about his words. *We are family.*

"Are you saying we give the old man a break?" asked Steven.

Sarge hesitated for a moment. "Not necessarily. I'm just making sure I know what the purpose of this is. What do I hope to accomplish?"

"Calling him out isn't gonna change anything," replied Steven. "We might get more answers, and then we might piss him off. How would that you make you feel?"

"Pretty damn lousy considering what he's done for us," replied Sarge.

"And *to us*, bro. Don't forget, he may have helped us along the way and bankrolled all of this preparedness stuff. But he's the one who brought this hell storm down on our heads too."

Sarge laughed as they rounded the bend and the final fifty yards to 1PP. "Did you ever get the feeling we were like a bunch of lab rats being experimented on?"

"Yeah. Like a damn puppet on a string." Steven held his hands high in the air to imitate a puppeteer.

"He's the puppet master, and we're the dancing toys on the stage," said Sarge.

Steven stopped as the two men stared at Morgan's bungalow. "I guess it's showtime."

They walked to the tiny house shared by Abbie and her father. She would be there, but Sarge wouldn't ask her to leave. He didn't like excluding her from the earlier conversation, but allowed everyone to speak freely. He knew Abbie, and he was certain she had no knowledge of this beforehand. In fact, bringing it out in the open would help ease the burden on her shoulders. *She knows he knew.*

"Hi, Sarge," greeted Abbie. "And Steven too. I didn't know you guys were coming. Is everything okay?" She gave them both a hug, and then Sarge felt her eyes probing for an explanation.

"Yeah, everything's fine," replied Sarge. "We're all here, in fact." *Damn, this is going to be hard.*

"Hello, Henry," said Morgan, who was sitting in a simple wooden dining chair at a small two-person table at the back of the bungalow. This was the first time Sarge had been in one of the bungalows built for the Boston Brahmin when they were occupied. It was pedestrian compared to the opulence to which Abbie and Morgan were accustomed. *He knew, yet he has sacrificed too.*

"Hello, sir," announced Steven as he fit his large frame through the doorway. "Wow, this is very old school. This is the first time I've seen the inside." The open floor plan helped mask the cramped quarters shared by two adults.

"It is *quaint*," said Morgan dryly. "Is this strictly a social call?" *He knows.*

Sarge's palms began to sweat. Was he capable of confronting one of the most powerful men in the world about the biggest false-flag event in the history of mankind? Morgan was not as intimidating as in his normal surroundings at 73 Tremont. He was not wearing his usual Armani suit, opting instead for khakis and Bass Weejuns. He looked like a regular guy. *But he's not a regular guy.*

"No, sir. It's not," started Sarge. He looked around for a place to sit. He didn't want to tower over his godfather—the man who had provided him so much after his dad died. Abbie stared at Sarge and then over at Steven, who led her by the arm to a small sofa. Sarge pulled up a chair at the dining table and sat across from one of the greatest negotiators on the planet.

"What's on your mind, Henry?" said Morgan, leaning back in his chair with a glare. He seemed to dare Sarge to speak his mind.

"Sir, we need to talk about the events surrounding the cyber attack—before and after."

Morgan leaned back and crossed his legs while tapping his fingers on his knee. "Let's talk, then. Go ahead, Henry."

Sarge took a deep breath and brought up his courage. *Out with it!*

"Sir, did you know about the cyber attack before it happened?"

Morgan managed a small smile and gently nodded his head without losing eye contact with Sarge. "What difference does it make if I did?" *A question with a question.*

"Well," started Sarge, leaning forward on the table, "you must admit the world has been turned on its head, and it is human nature to seek answers. Wouldn't you agree?"

"Ahh, Henry, curiosity killed the cat. Is an inquiry such as yours necessary or in anyone's best interest?"

"Are you denying your involvement?" asked Sarge, who was now emboldened because Morgan was toying with him. He could feel Abbie's glare with the eyes in the back of his head.

"Sarge, really?" she asked. "Is this absolutely necessary?"

Without turning, Sarge responded, "It is, Abbie. Regardless of motivation, the time to get this out in the open is now." He returned his focus back to Morgan.

"Satisfaction brought it back," said Sarge, referring to the curious cat.

"Indeed." Morgan laughed, appearing to relax. He was up to the challenge. "What would satisfy *you*, Henry?"

"It's not just me, sir. It's for all of us, including all of the lives who we take responsibility for here on Prescott Peninsula. The truth will satisfy me, and then I can satisfy others. Let me ask you again. Are you denying your involvement?"

"Okay, Sarge. That's enough!" shouted Abbie as she got off the sofa. "This isn't some courtroom or police interrogation room. My father's not on trial."

Steven reached out to her. "Abbie, please," he said. "Let's get this out of the way."

Abbie began to tear up and then relented. She sat down next to Steven with her arms folded, staring at the pine floors.

Morgan stood and began to pace. He was assuming his position of authority. *His comfort zone.* "Henry, I will allow you this conversation one time. I've loved both of you boys as if you were my sons. This is my family, here in this room. But my family includes everyone in my charge. Here, and all over the world. I owe them a duty as well. That said, this conversation stays here. Does everyone agree?"

"Yes, sir," replied Steven, with Abbie nodding as well. Sarge remained stoic, staring at the man who had been instrumental in

Sarge's success. He nodded his head once at Morgan, indicating his acquiescence.

Morgan continued to stand with his hands in his pockets, staring down at Sarge. "You have said many times, Henry, that all empires collapse eventually. You have expressed in your teachings, and books, that America is no exception. You were right. America has collapsed."

"Sir, did you help it along?" asked Sarge.

"It has been collapsing for decades, socially and economically," he replied. "This nation is a far cry from what our blood relatives, the Founding Fathers, intended for this great country. It is a nation conceived in self-reliance, built on the back of freedom-loving patriots who were willing to make the sacrifices necessary to survive and thrive. It is a nation that has lost its way."

"I don't disagree, sir," interrupted Sarge. "America had certain founding principles, including the freedom to succeed and fail. But failure should occur on its own, not at the behest of others. Some empires collapse when they are defeated by a greater enemy. I'm trying to ascertain who the enemy is."

Morgan fired back. "Well, it certainly isn't me! You saw the signs. All of us did. America was a nation in decline politically, economically, and especially socially. There were no signs of America correcting its course of destruction."

"It was not up to you to set its course," said Sarge. "I, too, have been dismayed over the state of our country. But I have confidence in the American people to rise up and right the ship. The cyber attack was too much."

"Perhaps, but that is your opinion, Henry. I, along with many of our friends, believed drastic measures were necessary to put America back on sound footing. I have said many times that I don't believe America's best days are behind her. The Founding Fathers would be appalled at how our nation's freedoms and ideals have been squandered."

"Sir, the Founding Fathers also agreed that a system should be established to course correct. When a mighty empire like the United

States is failing, our ancestors had confidence in their fellow Americans to follow a process that includes elections, a judiciary that upholds the constitution, and executive leadership seeking the best interest of the nation."

"Very idealistic, and naïve, young man," said Morgan. "I'm surprised that you believe that dribble. Elections are rigged. The judiciary is stacked with activist judges. The executive branch is wrought with corruption."

"The Sons of Liberty effectuated change against all odds, did they not?" asked Sarge.

"Yes, they did," replied Morgan. "But they didn't do it without a catalyst to spark the fight for independence. The Boston Tea Party was the stimulus for the Revolution."

"Very true. But the Boston Tea Party was not as extreme as the cyber attack."

"Henry, a reset was in order. A catalyst was required. Otherwise, our country was headed into a deeper decline that would result in some version of European Socialism, erasing all of the hard work of the Founding Fathers."

"How can you justify this? The cyber attack will result in millions of people dying!"

Morgan's face became red with anger. He started to shake and unconsciously massaged his left arm. "Now you listen to me. A reset was in order. I know it will be painful for many, as change often is. But our forefathers knew, as should you, that revolutions are nasty business. In the case of our country, a violent, forceful, and extreme event is exactly what this country needed to have the desired effect."

"People are dying as a result," said Sarge, shaking his head.

"No, the herd is being culled. The weak and the takers may die, but the strong and the makers will survive. America will be placed on solid footing once again!"

Now Sarge understood. The man he admired and looked up to since the death of his own father considered himself a steward of America's freedoms. John Morgan's heart was in the right place with the best of intentions. His methods, however, might have been misguided.

Or were they? Sarge doubted America could be restored to its former greatness through a series of election cycles. America's culture was lost to moral deprivation and the expectation of entitlement. More than half of Americans depended on the government to take care of them in some manner. This sense of entitlement was pervasive throughout their society. Those who were self-reliant were ridiculed and punished through taxes that were redistributed to those who professed to be entitled. It was a vicious cycle that needed to be broken, but was never addressed by the elected officials. Welfare was not only the third rail of the American political system, it had become the main rail.

Sarge's mind went back to Morgan's immediate response, which was *what difference does it make if I did?* After considering Morgan's reasoning, Sarge began to agree it didn't make a difference. The real question was *where do we go from here?*

CHAPTER 44

Thursday, September 29, 2016
8:00 p.m.
Prescott Peninsula
Quabbin Reservoir, Massachusetts

Sarge was the first to notice something was wrong with Morgan. His face seemed contorted, as if it were *uneven*. He appeared to become confused and unaware of his surroundings. Morgan momentarily lost his balance, but then steadied himself against a wall. He reached for the chair but was several feet away.

"Sir, are you okay?" asked Sarge.

"Daddy!" shouted Abbie.

Morgan tried to speak, insisting that he was okay, but he slurred his words as if he were drunk.

Sarge rushed to his side and led him to the chair. Morgan winced as he attempted to hold his head. He was unable to communicate and his eyes glossed over. Abbie was shouting for her father, but he could not respond.

"Get J.J.!" shouted Sarge to Steven, who immediately bolted out the door.

Morgan again attempted to speak, saying words that resembled *my head*.

"Sir, sir!" yelled Sarge, trying to get Morgan to focus on Sarge's face. "Can you smile for me? Please, try to raise your eyebrows." The right side of Morgan's face responded, but the left side did not.

"Whaaaa ung," said Morgan, still barely coherent.

Sarge turned to Abbie. "Listen to me, Abbie. Your dad is having a stroke. Are you with me? Can you help me?"

Abbie was crying uncontrollably, but she nodded her head.

"Help me get him to the sofa. We need to prop him up on the pillows." Sarge and Abbie helped Morgan lie down. They made sure to keep his head and shoulders raised. Abbie unbuttoned his shirt in an effort to loosen his clothing. She lovingly wiped his mouth with her shirt sleeves.

"Daddy, don't worry. Help is on the way. You be comfortable, all right."

He attempted to look in her eyes and smile, but managed only a skewed grin. He gripped her arm with his right hand.

"Keep talking to him, Abbie," said Sarge. "Keep him awake. Try to have him focus on squeezing your hand." Sarge heard loud voices and shouts heading toward the bungalow. He ran out to grab J.J. A crowd immediately surrounded the building.

"What happened, Sarge?" asked J.J. pushing his way past and inside.

Sarge followed him and answered, "Stroke, I think. The symptoms started about five minutes ago. He became unsteady on his feet, and he has been slurring his words. He is able to grip Abbie's hand with his right arm, but he hasn't moved his left. Also, he seems to have a headache."

Steven entered the bungalow, followed by Lowell, Cabot and Susan Quinn. The space was overcrowded, which drew a quick response from J.J. "Everybody out. Too many people in here for the man to breathe. Susan, you stay. Abbie and Sarge, please move back."

Steven led everyone outside except for Abbie. J.J. shouted at him before he left, "Steven, get Brad. Find out where the helicopter pilot is."

"I'm on it," replied Steven.

"Susan, get me my bag and the portable defib. Also, bring the blood pressure cuff. Hurry."

"What can I do, J.J.?" asked Abbie through her tears. Sarge handed her a Kleenex, and he provided J.J. both a warm, wet towel and a dry one.

"Let me ask you some questions about his health. Has he ever had a stroke or a heart attack before?"

"No."

"He's not diabetic, is he?"

"No."

"What about medications, especially for high blood pressure, cholesterol, or artery disease?"

Abbie went to a kitchen cabinet and found her father's Lisinopril bottle, which was a common high blood pressure medication. She handed it to J.J. "He's been out of his normal meds. This was the best we had available."

Brad and Steven returned. "Damn it," said Brad as he saw Morgan stretched out on the sofa. Some of the women gathered outside were crying.

"Where is the pilot?" asked J.J.

"He's at Fort Devens. I can have him here in about an hour."

"Crap. Listen, get him back and be ready to fly out of here."

"To where?" asked Sarge.

"I don't know, Mass General is in shambles," replied J.J. "We'd have to find another hospital."

"Excuse me, Brad," said Susan as she forced her way inside. Brad immediately turned and left to contact the helicopter pilot.

Morgan was groaning and attempting to reach for his head. His face was still drooping on the left side.

"Stay with me, Mr. Morgan, while I check your vitals," said J.J. "Thank you, Abbie, let Susan slide in here to assist me, please."

"What do you want me to do?" asked Susan, who took out the stethoscope and the blood pressure cuff. J.J. immediately checked Morgan's blood pressure and pulse.

"Keep him comfortable and wipe away any secretions from his mouth. Make sure his airway stays clean and open. Use these towels to wipe his brow. Use a patting motion, don't rub or cause his head to swivel unnecessarily."

J.J. took another moment to examine Morgan's eyes with a pocketscope and listened to his breathing with the stethoscope. Satisfied, he put the equipment in his bag. He stood up and whispered to Susan, who smiled and continued watching over Morgan.

"Come over here," started J.J.

"Did he have a heart attack?" asked Abbie frantically.

"No, Abbie. I believe—" said J.J. before Abbie interrupted him.

"He's been under so much stress. This whole scene tonight was unnecessary. This could have been avoided, Sarge!"

Sarge looked at Abbie and then caught Julia looking at him through the doorway. He felt terrible. He didn't mean for anything like this to happen.

"I'm sorry, Abbie," pleaded Sarge. "I didn't know he had a condition with his heart." He folded his arms and stared at Morgan. Sarge tried to reach to Abbie, but she pulled away from him.

"Let me finish, please. Nobody caused this tonight. Nobody is at fault here. This was a ticking time bomb that he's been carrying inside him for some time. This was not necessarily triggered by any argument or stress."

"What has happened to my daddy?" asked Abbie, who began to recover from crying.

"I believe your dad had what's called a transient ischemic attack—*a ministroke*. If I am right, and there is no way to be certain without a full medical evaluation, this will be just a brief episode."

"He's going to be okay, right?" asked Abbie.

"Yes, for now. Unlike an actual stroke, a TIA doesn't result in permanent brain damage. The blood flow to his brain was temporarily interrupted by a blood clot that blocked a vessel or artery. Eighty to ninety percent of strokes are ischemic. Only a very small percentage are considered hemorrhagic, which are caused by a blood vessel in the brain that breaks, resulting in bleeding."

"That's good news," said Sarge, trying to stay positive.

Abbie managed a nod.

"He's not out of the woods yet," cautioned J.J. "TIAs are strong predictors of a future stroke event. About five percent of victims will experience a true stroke within forty-eight hours. Although it is tempting to ignore his ministroke once the symptoms disappear, the attack should be considered a warning sign that a full-blown stroke is possible."

"What's the next step?" asked Sarge.

"He can stay here and rest. I will remain with Abbie and Susan. We'll keep him calm and monitor his vitals. The more time that passes, the better his potential for averting a major stroke will be."

"Okay," said Sarge, looking past J.J. to the crowd outside. "What can I tell the others?"

J.J. turned to Abbie. "Why don't you join Susan and keep your dad calm? Have him squeeze your hand and let him know you are there. Talk to him, Abbie. He needs to hear your voice."

Abbie hugged J.J. as the tears welled up again in her eyes. "Thank you for helping him, J.J."

"Of course," he replied. "I'll be with you guys in a moment."

Sarge leaned into J.J. and whispered, "Did you sugarcoat anything?"

"Not really," replied J.J. as he lowered his voice. "The next twenty-four hours will be critical. Sarge, you know how I feel about him."

"I know, J.J. I can't argue with you. But he is—"

J.J. interrupted. "I hold him responsible for Sabina's death. She and I should be sitting at home watching Netflix right now. Instead, she's dead, in large part due to his actions. Don't worry. I will treat him as my patient. It is my duty to keep him alive and nurse him back to health."

Sarge placed both hands on J.J.'s shoulders, hugged him, and said thank you. There was no time to carry hatred or animosity. One never knew what the next day would bring.

CHAPTER 45

Friday, September 30, 2016
10:16 a.m.
Prescott Peninsula
Quabbin Reservoir, Massachusetts

"I'm alive, my dear friends, and I plan to stay that way," said Morgan to Lowell and Cabot. He'd sent Abbie to request his longtime trusted confidants join him. He had dodged a bullet, but it was the closest call of his life. Morgan dealt in the shadows of banking, geopolitical affairs, and the military-industrial complex. The bullets he had dodged in the past were related to political advantage or monetary gain. He had never come close to death. It was a defining moment in his life.

After a stroke, many victims experienced communication challenges known as aphasia. Some people had difficulty speaking while others had trouble understanding words spoken by others. Over time, those communications skills would improve, although the level of improvement was unpredictable.

Throughout his life, Morgan believed in the maxim that luck could result when preparation met opportunity. In his dealings, Morgan believed he made his own luck through planning. But the stroke was different. One couldn't plan for achieving any measure of *luck* after a stroke. Luck was also believing you're lucky, and John Morgan was. His stroke, while a shot across the bow, left him with very few adverse problems. J.J. advised him to rest and relax. J.J. further cautioned him his recovery would take months.

Morgan contemplated the ramifications of his near death and the potential for a more devastating stroke in the near future.

"John, you gave us quite a scare, old friend," said Lowell as he sat down and gave Morgan's hand a squeeze. "It is good to see you awake and alert."

"Yes, John," said Cabot, smiling. "I dreaded having to find another bridge partner. You have a way of staring down our opponents into making mistakes. It's a gift, you know."

Morgan smiled and motioned them to come closer. He whispered, "I love you old fools like brothers. I need you to stand with me now more than ever."

"Of course, John. Tell us what you need done. Walter and I can help."

Morgan, his voice weakened but fully coherent, explained his request to his friends. For the next several minutes, Morgan reflected on his life, his friendships, and the successes the Boston Brahmin had achieved together. Cabot and Lowell listened attentively to their dear friend.

"John, this is deathbed talk," started Cabot. "Where are you going with this?"

"I want you to support me," replied Morgan. He attempted to push himself upright onto the sofa cushions. Lowell quickly assisted him to a more comfortable, seated position.

"How's that?" asked Lowell. Morgan nodded and patted his arm. "We've always stood by your side, John. What will you have us do?"

Morgan spent the next several minutes finding the words, and the strength, to tell his trusted friends his wishes. At times, he paused to find the words before continuing. Cabot and Lowell were very patient with him, sometimes finishing his sentences to allow him to gather his thoughts.

"Will you do this for me?" asked Morgan.

"Of course, John. Lawrence and I will support you in every way."

"Bring them in, please," said Morgan, waving his arm toward the door.

Outside the Morgan bungalow, a vigil was being held by all of the Boston Brahmin and their wives. Every member of the Loyal Nine was present as well. Many prayed for Morgan throughout the night.

They were there to comfort Abbie as well. Morgan had earned the love and respect of them all for his strength during this close call.

One by one, the Boston Brahmin entered the bungalow at Cabot's insistence. Peabody, Bradlee, Winthrop, and Endicott joined their comrades and closed the door for privacy. The four newcomers paid their respects to the man who shepherded the Boston Brahmin through times of turmoil and peace.

For several minutes, they listened as he struggled to speak. Glances were exchanged, and emotions were released.

Morgan, in his weakened state, troubled them all. But his words were unequivocal. His request left no doubt in their minds.

"Now, please," said Morgan. He motioned toward the door, and Lowell exited as instructed. A moment later, the hushed whispers in the bungalow ceased, and all heads turned to the door closing, and Sarge, who entered sheepishly.

"Come, sit with me, Henry," said Morgan, who took a deep breath before continuing. "I promised your father that you would do great things. I promised to be your guardian, your mentor, and protector. For all of these years, I have ushered you through life, keeping a watchful eye over you as if you were my son."

"Yes, sir, I know," said Sarge, who was welling up with emotion.

"I am not a dying man, but I am tired. A tired man can do nothing easily, and we still have work to do, Henry." Morgan attempted to push himself up again, and he was assisted by Sarge.

Morgan continued as he addressed the room. "I thank God that I have done my duty in upholding the ideals and vision of our forefathers. I've done all of the business I am capable of doing on this earth." He turned his attention to Sarge.

"Patriotism is not enough, Henry. I see compassion in you I never had. You recognize that our fellow man must not be forgotten."

Morgan again looked into the faces of the Boston Brahmin. "I intend to live, my friends. You can't dispatch me that easily.

"We must finish what we started, but it requires a younger man. It needs a different vision, one capable of looking beyond the creation of wealth, but to the creation of a new nation. My role now is that of teacher—the grand master to the student." He turned his attention to Sarge and struggled as he reached out to grasp his shoulder.

"It is time for me to step aside. The Boston Brahmin must be led by the next generation of patriots. Henry, I am entrusting you to take the reins and accept your destiny as the new head of the Boston Brahmin."

The saga will continue in THE MECHANICS.

Continue reading to get a sneak peek at the first few chapters.

THANK YOU FOR READING FALSE FLAG!

If you enjoyed it, I'd be grateful if you'd take a moment to write a short review (just a few words are needed) and post it on Amazon. Amazon uses complicated algorithms to determine what books are recommended to readers. Sales are, of course, a factor, but so are the quantities of reviews my books get. By taking a few seconds to leave a review, you help me out, and also help new readers learn about my work.

And before you go…

SIGN UP for Bobby Akart's mailing list to receive special offers, bonus content, and you'll be the first to receive news about new releases.

eepurl.com/bYqq3L

VISIT Amazon.com/BobbyAkart for more information on his next project, as well as his completed words: the Doomsday series, the Yellowstone series, the Lone Star series, the Pandemic series, the Blackout series, the Boston Brahmin series and the Prepping for Tomorrow series totaling nearly forty novels, including over thirty Amazon #1 Bestsellers in forty-plus fiction and nonfiction genres.

Visit Bobby Akart's website for informative blog entries on preparedness, writing, and a behind-the-scenes look into his novels.

BobbyAkart.com

READ ON FOR A BONUS EXCERPT from

THE MECHANICS

Book Five in The Boston Brahmin Series.

Best Selling Author of *The Pandemic Series*

BOBBY AKART

THE MECHANICS

The Boston Brahmin Series . Book Five

Excerpt from *The Mechanics*

Chapter 1

Saturday, October 1, 2016
1:11 a.m.
Prescott Peninsula
Quabbin Reservoir, Massachusetts

It was now October, and the autumn chill of the New England air began to set in. So did reality. The fire, dying down now with only a few glowing embers, had served its purpose. It provided warmth, light, and a distraction when the voices of his friends needed to be compartmentalized away from his thoughts.

"*It is time for me to step aside. The Boston Brahmin must be led by the next generation of patriots. Henry, I am entrusting you to take the reins and accept your destiny as the new head of the Boston Brahmin.*"

Sarge's mind replayed the words of John Morgan over and over again. *Entrusting. Destiny.* He knew this day would come. But not now, and certainly not under these circumstances.

Sarge finished off the last of the Moulin-à-Vent Beaujolais and studied the red Solo cup as he chuckled to himself. *A hundred-dollar bottle of wine in a ten-cent cup. King Henry the VIII, I am not. Where's my silver chalice?*

His thoughts were interrupted by Donald, who tossed his cup into the fire as he slid off the top of the picnic table. "Well, guys, it's been real, but I'm gonna turn in."

Sarge lifted himself out of the Adirondack chair and hugged his friend. In normal times, he would lean on Donald heavily as he managed the massive global financial holdings of the Boston Brahmin. He doubted his life would ever be *normal* again.

"Good night, buddy," said Sarge as he hugged Donald. "It's been a helluva day."

"No kidding." Donald laughed. "There's a lot to talk about, and I'm sure Mr. Morgan will want to be a part of our conversations if he's up to it. Listen, there's a whole lot more that I don't know than what I do know. Make sense?"

"It's pretty damned overwhelming," replied Sarge. "Where the hell do we start?"

"Let's not worry about it now," Donald replied. "Global finances are not a high priority at the moment. We'll get a handle on things on the fly."

Sarge patted his friend on the back and led him out of the circle of chairs that surrounded the fire. They walked toward the steps of 1PP.

Sarge leaned in and whispered into Donald's ear, "Do you think he'll tell us everything?" One of the lingering doubts in Sarge's mind was whether the secretive John Morgan was truly ready to turn over the reins of leadership and power.

"He has to sooner or later," replied Donald. "This was inevitable. It's just that the circumstances suck."

Sarge stopped and looked Donald in the eyes. "I'm gonna need you to guide me through this. I can only imagine how vast their holdings are."

Donald laughed and replied, "No worries, Sarge. It's only money. If you squander a few hundred million here and there, who cares, right?"

"Thanks for the vote of confidence, *Mr. Quinn*," Sarge said, using his best impression of Morgan. "Good night."

"Good night, Henry," Donald replied, using his best John Morgan Brahmin accent.

Sarge shook his head and returned to the remainder of the Loyal Nine gathered around the dying fire—Julia, Steven, and Katie.

"There's a little more wine, honey," said Julia as he approached. She held up the last of the bottles the group had polished off during the evening. There might be a few headaches in the morning from the celebration. Steven had suggested popping a few corks of champagne, but Sarge quickly put that idea to rest. He was not sure whether this was an event to celebrate. Not only because of the stroke that led to the decision. But Sarge also knew that the eyes of the Boston Brahmin would be upon him during this period of transition. Sarge was accepting his new role reluctantly, and a champs-fueled celebration was inappropriate.

"I'm good, thanks," he replied. He was tired and desperately wanted to speak with Julia alone. They'd been surrounded since the announcement earlier, and he needed his best friend to analyze the events with him.

Sarge eased back into the chair and sat in silence, staring at the last of the burning embers. Inwardly, he hoped that Steven and Katie would go to bed.

The quiet had the desired effect. "Well, I guess we'll hit the bunks too," announced Steven. He stood and helped Katie out of her chair. Sarge started to rise and Steven stopped him. "No, please sit, your highness. Allow me, your humble knave, to kiss the ring of the king once more." Steven bent on one knee in front of Sarge and attempted to kiss his hand.

"Screw you, knave!" Sarge swatted at Steven's head several times, and he easily avoided the blows like Sugar Ray Leonard in the boxing ring. The girls laughed, clearly enjoying the playful banter between the brothers.

"As you wish, your highness," said Steven. "Will you join us on the hunt in the morning? We are in search of the wildebeest who roams the forest." Steven stood and struck a *Game of Thrones* pose.

"Maybe," replied Sarge.

"Or perhaps your highness would prefer to sleep in with the fair maiden here and create an heir to the throne?"

“Away with you, knave, before I give the order.” Sarge laughed. “Off with his head!” Sarge stood and gave his brother a hug. He also hugged Katie.

“Congratulations, Sarge,” she whispered in his ear. “Good luck.” Katie broke their embrace and she walked off into the darkness toward the bungalows. Sarge smiled and nodded at his brother, who was standing awkwardly alone. He watched them for a moment as Steven gradually turned to a ghostly figure disappearing into the darkness.

CHAPTER 2

Saturday, October 1, 2016
1:30 a.m.
The Quabbin Visitor Center
Quabbin Reservoir, Massachusetts

Ronald Archibald paced the floor in front of his handpicked lieutenants. He had no military or law enforcement experience, but he stood alone as the leader of the Belchertown raiding party. Joseph Pearson had offered little assistance in the planning of the raid on Prescott Peninsula. The raid was Archibald's baby, and he intended it to be a success.

Archibald had successfully recruited and trained nearly three hundred men for the task. Lack of intelligence about the current inhabitants of Prescott Peninsula was a concern, but he was confident in his ability to overrun them with overwhelming force and surprise.

His troops, as he called them, consisted of ordinary citizens from the surrounding areas. They included the local pharmacist, an auto mechanic, an unemployed car salesman, and a retired postal worker. They were different in most respects, from their occupations to their race and gender. But they all had one thing in common—they were hungry, for food and revenge.

The day before, Archibald had whipped them into a hatred-driven frenzy. The residents of Belchertown were now convinced that the enemy consisted of the unknown faces on Prescott Peninsula. These mysterious opponents had food and supplies to save their families. Archibald convinced his *troops* to risk their lives to attack and claim the supplies for the benefit of the town. Archibald did not reveal to his troops, however, that the enemy was likely made up of seasoned military personnel. That minor detail would have doomed the mission to failure before it started.

"Okay, gentlemen, let's get down to business," announced Archibald, calling the group to attention. "Let's take a look at the map and go over the plan one last time."

He grabbed one of the men and whispered, "Raise the Allen brothers on the radio. Tell them we're on time. They'll know what to do."

The assistant nodded his head and left the room.

Archibald turned his attention to the room and walked in front of a bulletin board hung on a wall. Above it, on a particle board shelf, sat a stuffed beaver, an owl, and an otter. Under their watchful eyes, Archibald rapped his knuckles on the map.

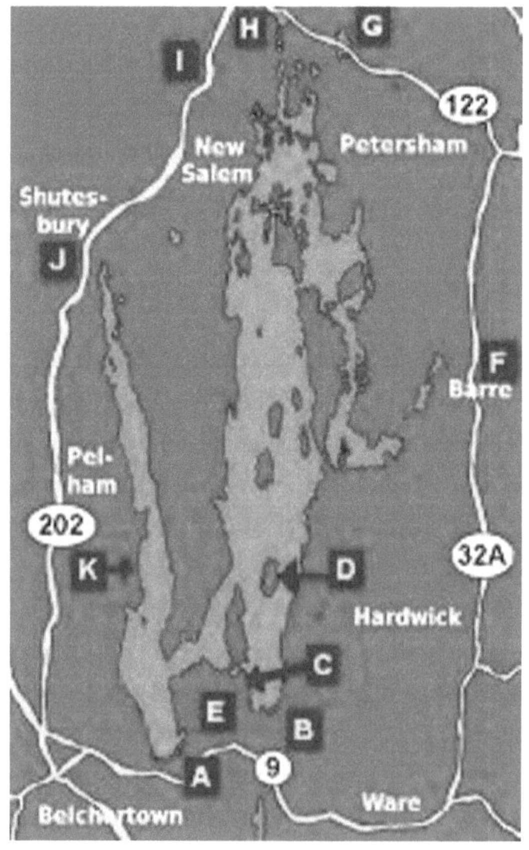

"We've gone over this, but this will be the last time, as we'll be giving the order to start this party. Sunrise is around 5:00 a.m. and everyone needs to be in position."

Archibald turned and looked at his men. The murmur of nervous conversation died down when he spoke. He pointed to the letter *A* on the map.

"This is the Visitor's Center, which will be used as our fallback position and for wounded triage."

The group began to whisper again, and Archibald quieted them down. He could sense their trepidation. "Gentlemen, make no mistake, we will take some casualties. I hope not, obviously, but for our families to survive, we must take risks. In the lobby, we have our most capable health care providers and all the medical supplies we could muster. While the success of our mission is paramount, the lives of our friends and neighbors are just as important. If you or the man next to you gets wounded, come back here immediately for medical attention."

Archibald laid out the plan, first pointing to the letter *E*. "I will be taking up a command and control position here, on Quabbin Hill, at the Observatory Tower. Those of you assigned to the power boats will convene here, at the launch that I've marked as letter *C*. Gentlemen, you will be the second phase of the attack."

He moved across the map to point to the left side identified as Pelham. "Just south of Pelham, at letter *K*, the pontoon boats will be at the ready to cross this narrow stretch of the lake onto the west shore of Prescott Peninsula. You will be the third phase of the attack."

Next, he slapped his hands at the top of the map, on top of the letter *J*. "This is where we get their attention—the front gate. Jimmy Fulks was murdered there. The front gate is where the battle begins."

The men in the room cheered, clearly ready for the task at hand. He allowed the celebration to go on, and then he moved to calm them. He pointed to the other letters on the map designated *B, F, G, H,* and *I*. "We have established roadblocks at these remaining locations. We don't want them to be able to call in any reinforcements. *Mano a mano*, right, gentlemen?"

"Yes, sir!" they shouted as they patted each other on the back.

"Okay, before I send you out to get into position, does anyone have any questions?"

One hand rose in the rear of the room. "I do, sir."

"What is it?" asked Archibald.

"We've never discussed letter *D* on the map. What is that for?"

Archibald looked at the tiny island in the middle of the Quabbin Reservoir and grinned. "I've got a special surprise in store for these people, and our men who will be carrying it out have been in place for a couple of days. It has already been set into motion, my friends."

CHAPTER 3

Saturday, October 1, 2016
1:35 a.m.
Mount Lizzie
Quabbin Reservoir, Massachusetts

"Showtime," said Will Allen to his younger brother, M.C. He was cold and tired. They had spent forty-eight hours camping on the Quabbin Reservoir. Their first stop was Mount Zion to their north, gathering up a skiff full of timber rattlesnakes. The Allens camped on the island the first night, then in the early morning hours of Friday, they rowed past Walker Hill and along the eastern shore of the Quabbin Reservoir until they reached Mount Lizzie.

Prior to 1939 when the flooding of the Quabbin Reservoir began, Mount Lizzie was the home of the small town of Greenwich. The oldest of the four towns flooded by the Quabbin Reservoir project, Greenwich was incorporated in 1754 under land grants to immigrants of Scottish and Irish heritage following the Indian Wars.

Once known as the Plantation of the Quabbin, the name of a revered Nipmuc Indian, the town was renamed for the Scottish Duke of Greenwich. This was a once thriving town, boasting the first church in the area, the first post office, and one of the first public libraries. Progress, in the form of the Quabbin Reservoir, flooded the historic town eight days after its one hundred and eighty-fourth birthday.

Today, it was one of the smallest islands in the reservoir, but it stood the tallest at an elevation of nearly nine hundred feet. During the day on Friday, the Allen brothers made camp at the summit of Mount Lizzie and observed the activities on the eastern shoreline of

Prescott Peninsula through binoculars. They kept their boats and the cargo hidden from view on the east side of the island. They also kept quiet, as voices carried on the water. They were only a mile away from the shore of Prescott Peninsula and the uninhabited Little Quabbin Hill island to their southwest.

"I'm ready," said M.C. "I'm more than ready to get this over with and get home to the missus. This better be worth it, brother."

"It will be," replied Will. "You're hungry, aren't you?"

"Yeah, hungry enough to eat them rattlers."

"Then let's do this," said Will. "It'll take a couple of hours to make our way around the island. Thank God there ain't a moon tonight. We'll use the dark skies and Little Quabbin Hill for cover. Then we'll work our way up towards that point." He directed his brother's attention to the pronounced stretch of shore that was nearest Little Quabbin Hill.

"How far do we have to carry the snakes before we release them?"

"I'm not sure, probably a mile or so," replied Will. "It'll take us a couple of trips. C'mon. We need to get in position for the signal."

The two men folded up their camping gear and headed down the eastern slope of Mount Zion to their flat-bottom aluminum boats, which were pulled onto the rocky shore. Although their skiff had a trolling motor, in order to approach undetected, they would have to row the entire distance—not an easy feat when pulling another boat full of dozens of large rattlesnakes.

Over the next two hours, they made their way across the half-mile stretch of lake undetected. The Allens sought cover on the banks of Little Quabbin Hill while they rested. They could easily row the last few hundred yards in less than fifteen minutes. Their orders were to wait for the signal.

M.C., out of boredom, broke the silence. "How will we know when it's time to get started? What's the signal?"

"Don't worry. We'll know."

CHAPTER 4

Saturday, October 1, 2016
1:52 a.m.
Prescott Peninsula
Quabbin Reservoir, Massachusetts

Julia broke Sarge out of his half-conscious, hypnotic state. He got a chill and attempted to shake it off.

"Honey, are you ready for bed?" asked Julia. "Maybe we should produce an heir to the throne?"

Sarge rolled his neck and released some tension. He took a deep breath, exhaled and sat back in the chair. He realized that he had been on edge all day. This was his first opportunity to relax—alone with Julia.

"Let's polish off this bottle and talk," he said.

"Are you okay?" asked Julia. She poured the last of the wine into her cup and handed it to him. She reached over into Katie's chair and grabbed Sarge a blanket. The temperature was in the upper forties.

Sarge smiled and reached over to hold her hand. "Yeah, it's been a long day and my brain is tired. I've wanted to talk with you alone, and we've never had the chance."

"Suddenly, you're a very popular guy."

"I know, Julia, and my mind has been racing all day. I've known Mr. Morgan my entire life, but I've never really contemplated what he does every day." Sarge covered himself with the blanket and took another sip of wine. He allowed the fruit flavors to soak into his mouth before swallowing it. Julia studied him and allowed him to continue.

"Am I still a professor? Do I go to work every day at 73 Tremont? Does any of that matter anymore now that the country has been thrown back into the 1800s?"

Julia reached for her wine and emptied the cup, which she put in the pile of empty wine bottles. "No wonder you're brain-dead. It's difficult to answer any of those questions or establish a game plan when the world is collapsing around us. Since the cyber attack, we've been *reacting*. Right?"

Sarge allowed the statement to soak in. For the past four weeks, their lives had been a whirlwind of activity—acting in response to a particular situation rather than creating it or controlling it.

"That's a great point," said Sarge. "Our survival instincts kicked in, and we hunkered down. Fate keeps throwing us curveballs and . . ."

"We hit it right back at 'em," added Julia, finishing his sentence.

Sarge nodded in agreement. "It may be this way for a while, but at some point in time, we need to rebuild our lives." He stretched out his body and clasped his hands behind his head. "I've had quite a bit of wine, and as you know, I can get real philosophical at times."

"Really? Nah." Julia laughed.

"You know me," said Sarge, adding in his best Southern drawl, "I do my best thinkin' when I'm drinkin'."

Julia nudged the pile of empty wine bottles and laughed.

"Hey, I didn't drink all of those!" protested Sarge. She reached over, and he held her hands, which were soft and warm. "You and I have always talked in terms of fate, destiny, and even karma."

"That's true."

"I guess, deep inside, I've known this was my destiny," said Sarge. He stared up at the stars. The new moon allowed faint objects such as galaxies and star clusters to shine unimpeded. *We're such an insignificant part of the universe, yet we are the center of our own.*

"You're not afraid, are you?" asked Julia, indicating unease for the first time that day.

Sarge quickly eased her concerns. "Oh, no, not at all," he replied reassuringly. "I've got a job to do and a whole lot of lives to be responsible for. I'm not sure where to start."

Julia was briefly quiet and then spoke. "Sarge, Mr. Morgan is not going to leave you out here flailing on your own. It could be worse, you know. He could be dead."

This reality struck Sarge like a ton of bricks. *He could be dead.*

"I'd really be crappin' my pants then," Sarge said with a chuckle.

"Sarge, he's going to be very supportive of you. You're the chosen one, so to speak. He will not set you up for failure."

"I know, I know. It also seems like the others were on board. Cabot and Lowell gave me the impression they were pleased with Mr. Morgan's decision."

"I agree," said Julia. "As I talked with them, and especially Mrs. Lowell, they were enthusiastic in their praise for you and your abilities. Mrs. Lowell hasn't been happy during this entire ordeal until now."

"How about our guys, the Quinns, J.J.?" Sarge's voice trailed off.

Julia let go of his hand and sat up in her chair. "They love *and respect* you, Sarge. We've never had a defined hierarchy, but it was always assumed that you were our fearless leader."

"Ha-ha, the fearless leader who is over here shakin' in his boots," said Sarge. He laughed with Julia at his self-deprecation.

"I think it's natural to be apprehensive, Sarge. But you know everyone will support you as you take on this new role. We all have our roles, and now you have the ability to be the final decision maker on everything. You hold the power and the purse strings."

"Julia, I'll control billions of dollars in assets worldwide. I'll be able to pick up the phone and call world leaders. Hell, Morgan has a direct line to the President. All of that power and responsibility rests squarely on my shoulders now." Sarge also sat up in his chair and started to contemplate the magnitude of his new role.

"We can do great things, my love," encouraged Julia. "Let it all soak in and don't look at this as some daunting, overwhelming task. You've been given the unique opportunity to shape world events in your vision."

Sarge thought about this. *What is my worldview? I used to lecture about this at Harvard. Now I feel like Sarah Palin in her first ABC interview with Charlie Gibson—dumbfounded.*

"Absolutely," said Sarge. "Our country, hell, the world faces a serious catastrophe. I'm taking the reins of the Boston Brahmin at an opportune time. I don't think we can solve this crisis by using the same way of thinking that helped put us here in the first place."

"Now you're talkin', Sarge. You have to be optimistic about this opportunity you've been given. Besides, you can always cry about it later."

CHAPTER 5

Saturday, October 1, 2016
4:52 a.m.
Prescott Peninsula
Quabbin Reservoir, Massachusetts

"Alpha One, this is Bravo Two. We've got a vehicle approaching the front gate, sir," said Corporal David Morrell into his comms. Morrell led a six-man patrol that guarded the front gate and perimeter fence on a twenty-four-hour basis. Because of the unusual hour and the heightened state of awareness his team was practicing, Morrell felt it necessary to notify his immediate superior officer, Chief Warrant Officer Kyle Shore.

"Roger, Bravo Two. Is it hostile?" asked Shore, still groggy from the early wake-up call.

"Unknown, sir," replied Morrell. "The vehicle is approaching slowly. I've called in two men from the shore patrol to assist, if necessary."

"Roger that, Bravo Two. Stay on mission. Alpha One en route," replied Shore.

The vehicle came to a halt one hundred yards from the protective cover of the HESCO barriers at the front gate. Morrell gestured for the two soldiers to flank him left and right and take cover positions. They waited. In the distance, he heard the sounds of four-wheelers approaching.

"This is private property!" shouted Morrell to the stopped and idling vehicle. Because the headlights blinded him, he couldn't discern the make or model, although it appeared to be a pickup or SUV.

He shouted again, "Stop. This is private property. Exit the vehicle with your hands over your head and state your business!" There was no response.

Then the vehicle began to roll forward, slowly crunching the gravel under its tires. The truck was closing on the entrance. *Seventy-five yards. Fifty yards.*

Morrell crouched lower behind the barrier. He shook his head and frowned.

"I don't like this," he mumbled to himself. The four-wheelers were approaching from his rear. The truck was inching closer. He had to make a decision.

"Light it …" he yelled until the sound of his voice was muted by a massive explosion. The pickup truck's payload of fifty-five-gallon drums containing oil, gasoline, and shrapnel was detonated by shots fired from a high-power rifle in the distance. The first two rounds punctured the drums, and the third round ignited the mixture.

A deadly barrage of broken nails, screws, bolts, and ball bearings tore through the gatehouse, obliterating the windows. The soldier closest to the gatehouse was killed instantly. The approaching Marines were knocked off their four-wheelers from the blast. The soldier to Morrell's right was safely behind the fortified mesh container designed by HESCO for this type of blast.

Morrell received shrapnel wounds to his left arm, which he'd used to shield his face from the blast. He was bleeding but was able to continue.

"Alpha One, this is Bravo Two," shouted Morrell into his radio. He repeated, "Alpha One, this is Bravo Two."

"Roger, Bravo Two. I'm two klicks out," responded Shore. The radio erupted with activity. Orders were directed to all of the patrols as responses came fast and with a clear sense of urgency.

"Charlie Two, this is Charlie Six. Over."

"Go for Six," a voice squelched back on the radio.

"This is Charlie Six. Vehicle approaching through the woods at fence post five. Repeat. Vehicle approaching at fence post five. Over."

Morrell crawled to check on the young private who survived the blast. He was huddled behind the barrier, holding onto his M4 with a death grip.

"Are you hurt, soldier?" asked Morrell. The sound of several four-wheelers could be heard in the distance.

"Not too bad, sir," replied the young man. He wiped the blood off his face with the sleeve of his wounded left arm.

"Let me see this," said Morrell as he examined the arm. The soldier winced with pain as he turned his arm over and back. "You'll be fine, soldier. I've got the same problem." He showed the young man his shrapnel-torn left arm.

Morrell looked to his left and saw Shore dismount from the ATV and approach him in a low crouch. He could see the worry on his CO's face. Things weren't right. Shore checked in by radio with the other patrols along the front gate.

More four-wheelers were approaching from 1PP, as it was all hands on deck. Shore instructed them to reinforce the western boundary of the front gate. He turned his attention to Morrell.

"What happened?" he asked.

"Sir, the truck stopped about a hundred meters out," replied Morrell. "I instructed it to stop, and then it began rolling forward again."

"I thought I heard gunfire," said Shore as he continued to look nervously back and forth.

"Yes, sir. They punctured and then detonated an explosive device contained in the back. It was dark, sir, and I was blinded by the headlights."

They were interrupted by the squawk of the radio. "This is Bravo Six. Vehicle is approaching slowly. Now half a click. Permission to open fire!" the soldier shouted.

"Hold your position," replied Shore. "They are out of range at this point. Draw your aim on the vehicle's tires. Repeat. Shoot the tires."

"Roger that, Alpha One. Range now two hundred meters, sir."

"Open fire. Shoot the tires!" yelled Shore. The rapid fire of the soldier's automatic weapon filled the air. Then another explosion lit up the sky to the west, and a fireball quickly ascended above the tree line.

"Bravo Six, this is Alpha One," said Shore into his radio. Morrell caught Shore's glance. There was silence for a stressful moment. Shore repeated the request. "Bravo Six, Alpha One. Over."

"Go for Six."

"Sitrep."

"Vehicle exploded, sir. Roughly two hundred meters from our position. No casualties, sir."

Shore leaned against the barrier and responded, "Stay frosty, Bravo Six."

"Roger that, Bravo Six out."

More soldiers arrived at the front gate, and Shore quickly dispatched them along the front entrance. The sun was rising in the east and visibility would improve.

The wounded soldier spoke up. "Sirs, you might want to take a look at this."

Morrell and Shore turned their attention from the radio and looked over the HESCO barriers. There was movement across the clearing and beyond the still-burning skeleton of the pickup truck. Armed men were scurrying from tree to tree, taking up positions across the gravel entry road.

Shore alerted the others on the front gate patrol. "Bravo Six, Charlie Three, this is Alpha One. Over."

"Charlie Three. Go, Alpha One."

"Go for Six."

"We're being approached by hostiles," instructed Shore. "We are under assault. Lethal force authorized. Repeat. Lethal force authorized."

"Roger that. Charlie Three out."

"This is Bravo Six. Hostiles approaching—" ***crack crack crack*** "—moving through the woods … four-wheelers approaching. Open fire!"

More Marines were arriving from 1PP, and they were immediately directed to lend support to Bravo Six along the western fence line.

"Sir," interrupted the soldier, grabbing Morrell's attention. "They're moving closer." Morrell looked up and saw the approaching armed men moving quickly through the woods and into the clearing.

Shore gave his orders. "Open fire!"

Morrell lifted his M16 over the barrier. The large weapon thumped in a quick report as it poured round after round into the approaching attackers. The bullets tore through their bodies, leaving bloody masses of death in the gravel. The young soldier followed his lead and began firing upon the remaining assailants hidden in the woods. Their rounds ripped flesh and shredded the bark of the trees that were being used for cover.

Humvees were approaching from the south as Shore moved away from Morrell to greet them. From the turret, a gunner lit up the forest across the way. The fifty-caliber rounds from the Ma Deuce ripped saplings in half and cut down the retreating men with ease. Shore called for them to cease fire, and additional troops were posted along the two-mile long perimeter fence and the front gate. Except for the smoldering trucks and the smell of spent rounds, the scene became eerily still.

But then a high-pitched whine could be heard in the distance. Morrell looked up, thinking it was a drone. The noise grew louder.

"Sir, are those drones?" asked Morrell.

Shore looked up and then around their perimeter. "No," he replied. "Those are boats!"

THANK YOU FOR READING THIS EXCERPT OF The Mechanics, book five of The Boston Brahmin Series. You may purchase THE MECHANICS on Amazon or by visiting www.BobbyAkart.com

SIGN UP FOR EMAIL UPDATES and receive free advance reading copies, updates on new releases, special offers, and bonus content. You can contact Bobby directly by email (BobbyAkart@gmail.com) or through his website www.BobbyAkart.com

APPENDIX

False Flags Throughout History

Throughout history, false flags have been used as a tool of military advantage, and political manipulations. Here are a few examples.

(1) Japanese troops set off a small explosion on a train track in 1931 and falsely blamed it on China in order to justify an invasion of Manchuria. This is known as the Manchurian Incident. The Tokyo International Military Tribunal found that several of the participants in the plan, including Lieutenant Colonel Hashimoto—a high-ranking Japanese army officer, have on various occasions admitted their part in the plot and have stated that the object of the Manchurian Incident was to afford an excuse for the occupation of Manchuria by the Kwantung Army.

(2) A major with the German Schutzstaffel, the Nazi SS admitted at the Nuremberg trials that under orders from the chief of the Gestapo, he and some other Nazi operatives faked attacks on their own people and resources which they blamed on the Poland, justifying the German of the eastern bloc nation.

(3) Nazi general Franz Halder also testified at the Nuremberg trials that Nazi leader Hermann Goering admitted to setting fire to the German parliament building in 1933, and then falsely blaming the communists for the arson.

(4) Soviet leader Nikita Khrushchev admitted in writing that the Soviet Union's Red Army shelled the Russian village of Mainila in November of 1939 – while blaming the attack on Finland – as a basis for launching the Winter War against Finland. Many years later, Russian president Boris Yeltsin acknowledged that Russia was the aggressor in the Winter War.

(5) The Russian Parliament, current Russian president Vladimir Putin, and former Soviet leader Gorbachev all admit that Soviet leader Joseph Stalin ordered his secret police to execute twenty-two thousand Polish army officers and civilians in 1940, and then falsely blamed it on the Nazis.

(6) The British government admits between 1946 and 1948 it bombed five ships carrying Jews attempting to flee the Holocaust to seek safety in Palestine. The Brits set up a sham group called Defenders of Arab Palestine, and then had the DAP falsely claim responsibility for the bombings.

(7) Israel admits that in 1954, an Israeli terrorist cell operating in Egypt planted bombs in several buildings, including U.S. diplomatic facilities, then left behind evidence implicating the Arabs as the culprits, In that operation, one of the bombs detonated prematurely, allowing the Egyptians to identify the bombers, and several of the Israelis later confessed.

(8) The U.S. Central Intelligence Agency admits that it hired Iranians in the 1950's to pose as Communists and stage bombings in Iran in order to turn the country against its democratically-elected prime minister.

(9) The Turkish Prime Minister admitted that the Turkish government carried out the 1955 bombing on a Turkish consulate in Greece, also damaging the nearby birthplace of the founder of modern Turkey. The Turks blamed the bombing on Greece—using it for the purpose of inciting and justifying anti-Greek violence.

(10) The British Prime Minister admitted to his defense secretary that he and American president Dwight Eisenhower approved a plan in 1957 to carry out attacks in Syria and blame it on the Syrian government as a way to effect regime change.

(11) The former Italian Prime Minister, an Italian judge, and the former head of Italian counterintelligence admit that NATO, with the help of the Pentagon and CIA, carried out terror bombings in Italy and other European countries in the 1950s and blamed the communists, in order to rally people's support for their governments in Europe in their fight against communism. As one participant in

this formerly-secret program stated: "You had to attack civilians, people, women, children, innocent people, unknown people far removed from any political game. The reason was quite simple. They were supposed to force these people, the Italian public, to turn to the state to ask for greater security". Italy and other European countries subject to the terror campaign had joined NATO before the bombings occurred. They also allegedly carried out terror attacks in France, Belgium, Denmark, Germany, Greece, the Netherlands, Norway, Portugal, the UK, and other countries.

False flag attacks carried out pursuant to this program include – by way of example only:

•The murder of the Turkish Prime Minister (1960)

•Bombings in Portugal (1966)

•The Piazza Fontana massacre in Italy (1969)

•Terror attacks in Turkey (1971)

•The Peteano bombing in Italy (1972)

•Shootings in Brescia, Italy and a bombing on an Italian train (1974)

•Shootings in Istanbul, Turkey (1977)

•The Atocha massacre in Madrid, Spain (1977)

•The abduction and murder of the Italian Prime Minister (1978)

•The bombing of the Bologna railway station in Italy (1980)

•Shooting and killing 28 shoppers in Brabant county, Belgium (1985)

(12) In 1960, American Senator George Smathers suggested that the U.S. launch "a false attack made on Guantanamo Bay which would give us the excuse of actually fomenting a fight which would then give us the excuse to go in and overthrow Castro".

(13) Official State Department documents show that, in 1961, the head of the Joint Chiefs and other high-level officials discussed blowing up a consulate in the Dominican Republic in order to justify an invasion of that country. The plans were not carried out, but they were all discussed as serious proposals.

(14) As admitted by the U.S. government, recently declassified documents show that in 1962, the American Joint Chiefs of Staff

signed off on a plan to blow up AMERICAN airplanes using an elaborate plan involving the switching of airplanes, and also to commit terrorist acts on American soil, and then to blame it on the Cubans in order to justify an invasion of Cuba.

(15) In 1963, the U.S. Department of Defense wrote a paper promoting attacks on nations within the Organization of American States, such as Trinidad-Tobago or Jamaica, and then falsely blaming them on Cuba.

(16) One U.S. Department of Defense official, who suggested covertly paying a person in the Castro government to attack the United States, said: "The only area remaining for consideration then would be to bribe one of Castro's subordinate commanders to initiate an attack on Guantanamo."

(17) The NSA admits that it lied about what really happened in the Gulf of Tonkin incident in 1964, openly admitting that it had been manipulating data to make it look like North Vietnamese boats fired on a U.S. ship so as to create a false justification for the Vietnam war.

(18) A U.S. Congressional committee admitted as part of its Cointelpro campaign, the FBI had used many provocateurs in the 1950s through 1970s to carry out violent acts and falsely blame them on political activists.

(19) A top Turkish general admitted that Turkish forces burned down a mosque on Cyprus in the 1970s and blamed it on their enemy. The General explained: "In Special War, certain acts of sabotage are staged and blamed on the enemy to increase public resistance. We did this on Cyprus; we even burnt down a mosque." In response to the surprised correspondent's incredulous look the general said, "I am giving an example".

(20) A declassified 1973 CIA document reveals a program to train foreign police and troops on how to make booby traps, pretending that they were training them on how to investigate terrorist acts:

The Agency maintains liaison in varying degrees with foreign police/security organizations through its field stations by:

a. Providing trainees with basic knowledge in the uses of commercial and military demolitions and incendiaries as they may be applied in terrorism and industrial sabotage operations.

b. Introducing the trainees to commercially available materials and home laboratory techniques, likely to be used in the manufacture of explosives and incendiaries by terrorists or saboteurs.

c. Familiarizing the trainees with the concept of target analysis and operational planning that a saboteur or terrorist must employ.

d. Introducing the trainees to booby trapping devices and techniques giving practical experience with both manufactured and improvised devices through actual fabrication.

In addition, the program provides the trainees with ample opportunity to develop basic familiarity and use proficiently through handling, preparing and applying the various explosive charges, incendiary agents, terrorist devices and sabotage techniques.

(21) The German government admitted that, in 1978, the German secret service detonated a bomb in the outer wall of a prison and planted "escape tools" on a prisoner – a member of the Red Army Faction – which the secret service wished to frame the bombing on.

(22) A Mossad agent admits that, in 1984, Mossad planted a radio transmitter in Gaddafi's compound in Tripoli, Libya which broadcast fake terrorist transmissions recorded by Mossad, in order to frame Gaddafi as a terrorist supporter. Ronald Reagan bombed Libya immediately thereafter.

(23) The South African Truth and Reconciliation Council found that, in 1989, the Civil Cooperation Bureau—a covert branch of the South African Defense Force—approached an explosives expert and asked him to participate in an operation aimed at discrediting the African National Congress by bombing the police vehicle of the investigating officer into the murder incident, thus framing the ANC for the bombing.

(24) An Algerian diplomat and several officers in the Algerian army admit that, in the 1990s, the Algerian army frequently massacred Algerian civilians and then blamed Islamic militants for the killings.

(25) In 1993, a bomb in Northern Ireland killed 9 civilians. Official documents from the Royal Ulster Constabulary, an arm of

the British government, showed that the mastermind of the bombing was a British agent, and that the bombing was designed to inflame sectarian tensions.

(26) The United States Army's 1994 publication Special Forces Foreign Internal Defense Tactics Techniques and Procedures for Special Forces, as amended, recommends employing terrorists and using false flag operations to destabilize leftist regimes in Latin America. False flag terrorist attacks were carried out in Latin America and other regions as part of the CIA's Dirty Wars program.

(27) Similarly, a CIA psychological operation manual prepared by a CIA contractor for the Nicaraguan Contra rebels noted the value of assassinating someone on your own side to create a martyr for the cause. The manual was authenticated by the U.S. government. The manual received so much publicity from the media, namely, the Associated Press, Washington Post and other news coverage that during the 1984 presidential debate, President Reagan was confronted with the question on national television.

(28) An Indonesian fact-finding team investigated violent riots which occurred in 1998, and determined that elements of the military had been involved in the riots, some of which were deliberately provoked.

(29) Senior Russian Senior military and intelligence officers admit that the KGB blew up Russian apartment buildings in 1999 and falsely blamed it on Chechens, in order to justify an invasion of Chechnya.

(30) As reported by the BBC, the New York Times, and the Associated Press, Macedonian officials admit that the government murdered seven innocent immigrants in cold blood and pretended that they were Al Qaeda soldiers attempting to assassinate Macedonian police, in order to join the war on terror.

(31) At the July 2001 G8 Summit in Genoa, Italy, black-clad thugs were videotaped getting out of police cars, and were seen by an Italian MP carrying iron bars inside the police station. Subsequently, senior police officials in Genoa subsequently admitted that police planted two Molotov cocktails and faked the stabbing of a police

officer at the G8 Summit, in order to justify a violent crackdown against protesters.

(32) The U.S. falsely blamed Iraq for playing a role in the 9/11 attacks – as shown by a memo from the defense secretary – as one of the main justifications for launching the Iraq war. Even after the 9/11 Commission admitted that there was no connection, Dick Cheney said that the evidence is "overwhelming" that al Qaeda had a relationship with Saddam Hussein's regime, that Cheney "probably" had information unavailable to the Commission, and that the media was not 'doing their homework' in reporting such ties. Top U.S. government officials now admit that the Iraq war was really launched for oil ... not 9/11 or weapons of mass destruction. Despite previous "lone wolf" claims, many U.S. government officials now say that 9/11 was state-sponsored terror; but Iraq was not the state which backed the hijackers. (Many U.S. officials have alleged that 9/11 was a false flag operation by rogue elements of the U.S. government; but such a claim is beyond the scope of this discussion. The key point is that the U.S. falsely blamed it on Iraq, when it knew Iraq had nothing to do with it.)

(33) Although the FBI now admits that the 2001 anthrax attacks were carried out by one or more U.S. government scientists, a senior FBI official says that the FBI was actually told to blame the Anthrax attacks on Al Qaeda by White House officials. Government officials also confirm that the white House tried to link the anthrax to Iraq as a justification for regime change in that country.

(34) According to the Washington Post, Indonesian police admit that the Indonesian military killed American teachers in Papua in 2002 and blamed the murders on a Papuan separatist group in order to get that group listed as a terrorist organization.

(35) The well-respected former Indonesian president also admits that the government probably had a role in the Bali bombings.

(36) Police outside of a 2003 European Union summit in Greece were filmed planting Molotov cocktails on a peaceful protester.

(37) Former Department of Justice lawyer John Yoo suggested in 2005 that the US should go on the offensive against al-Qaeda, having

"our intelligence agencies create a false terrorist organization. It could have its own websites, recruitment centers, training camps, and fundraising operations. It could launch fake terrorist operations and claim credit for real terrorist strikes, helping to sow confusion within al-Qaeda's ranks, causing operatives to doubt others' identities and to question the validity of communications."

(38) Similarly, in 2005, Professor John Arquilla of the Naval Postgraduate School – a renowned US defense analyst credited with developing the concept of netwar – called for western intelligence services to create new "pseudo gang" terrorist groups, as a way of undermining "real" terror networks. According to Pulitzer-Prize winning journalist Seymour Hersh, Arquilla's pseudo-gang strategy was, Hersh reported, already being implemented by the Pentagon:

"Under Rumsfeld's new approach, I was told, US military operatives would be permitted to pose abroad as corrupt foreign businessmen seeking to buy contraband items that could be used in nuclear-weapons systems. In some cases, according to the Pentagon advisers, local citizens could be recruited and asked to join up with guerrillas or terrorist"

The new rules will enable the Special Forces community to set up what it calls action teams in the target countries overseas which can be used to find and eliminate terrorist organizations

(39) United Press International reported in June 2005:

U.S. intelligence officers are reporting that some of the insurgents in Iraq are using recent-model Beretta 92 pistols, but the pistols seem to have had their serial numbers erased. The numbers do not appear to have been physically removed; the pistols seem to have come off a production line without any serial numbers. Analysts suggest the lack of serial numbers indicates that the weapons were intended for intelligence operations or terrorist cells with substantial government backing. Analysts speculate that these guns are probably from either Mossad or the CIA. Analysts speculate that agent provocateurs may be using the untraceable weapons even as U.S. authorities use insurgent attacks against civilians as evidence of the illegitimacy of the resistance.

(40) Undercover Israeli soldiers admitted in 2005 to throwing stones at other Israeli soldiers so they could blame it on Palestinians, as an excuse to crack down on peaceful protests by the Palestinians.

(41) Quebec police admitted that, in 2007, thugs carrying rocks to a peaceful protest were actually undercover Quebec police officers.

(42) A 2008 US Army special operations field manual recommends that the U.S. military use surrogate non-state groups such as "paramilitary forces, individuals, businesses, foreign political organizations, resistant or insurgent organizations, expatriates, transnational terrorism adversaries, disillusioned transnational terrorism members, black marketers, and other social or political 'undesirables.'" The manual specifically acknowledged that U.S. special operations can involve counterterrorism and terrorism (as well as "transnational criminal activities, including narco-trafficking, illicit arms-dealing, and illegal financial transactions.")

(43) The former head of Secret Services and Head of State of Italy (Francesco Cossiga) advised the 2008 minister in charge of the police, on how to deal with protests from teachers and students:

"He should do what I did when I was Minister of the Interior … infiltrate the movement with agents provocateurs inclined to do anything …. And after that, with the strength of the gained population consent, … beat them for blood and beat for blood also those teachers that incite them. Especially the teachers. Not the elderly, of course, but the girl teachers, yes."

(44) At the G20 protests in London in 2009, a British member of parliament saw plain clothes police officers attempting to incite the crowd to violence.

(45) Egyptian politicians admitted that government employees looted priceless museum artifacts in 2011 to try to discredit the protesters.

(46) Rioters who discredited the peaceful protests against the swearing in of the Mexican president in 2012 admitted that they were paid 300 pesos each to destroy everything in their path. According to Wikipedia, photos also show the vandals waiting in groups behind police lines prior to the violence.

(47) A Colombian army colonel has admitted that his unit murdered 57 civilians, then dressed them in uniforms and claimed they were rebels killed in combat.

(48) On November 20, 2014, Mexican agent provocateurs were transported by army vehicles to participate in the 2014 Iguala mass kidnapping protests, as was shown by videos and pictures distributed via social networks.

(49) The highly-respected writer for the Telegraph Ambrose Evans-Pritchard says that the head of Saudi intelligence, Prince Bandar, recently admitted that the Saudi government controls Chechen terrorists.

(50) High-level American sources admitted that the Turkish government – a fellow NATO country – carried out the chemical weapons attacks blamed on the Syrian government and high-ranking Turkish government admitted on tape plans to carry out attacks and blame it on the Syrian government.

(51) The Ukrainian security chief admits that the sniper attacks which started the Ukrainian coup were carried out in order to frame others. Ukrainian officials admit that the Ukrainian snipers fired on both sides, to create maximum chaos.

(52) Burmese government officials admitted that Burma (renamed Myanmar) used false flag attacks against Muslim and Buddhist groups within the country to stir up hatred between the two groups, to prevent democracy from spreading.

(53) Britain's spy agency has admitted that it carries out digital false flag attacks on targets, framing people by writing offensive or unlawful material and blaming it on the target.

(54) U.S. soldiers have admitted that if they kill innocent Iraqis and Afghanis, they then drop automatic weapons near their body so they can pretend they were militants.

(55) A former U.S. intelligence officer recently alleged most terrorists are false flag terrorists or are created by "our own security services".

(56) Unmarked Israeli fighter jets and unmarked torpedo boats attacked a U.S. ship off the coast of Egypt in 1967 called the USS

Liberty. The attack started by targeting communications on the ship so that the Americans couldn't radio for help. The Israelis then jammed the ship's emergency distress channel, and shot at escaping life rafts in an attempt to prevent survivors from escaping.

Transcripts of conversations between the Israeli pilots and Israeli military show that Israel knew it were an American ship. Numerous top-level American military and intelligence officials – including Admiral Thomas H. Moorer, former Chairman of the Joint Chiefs of Staff – believe that this was a failed false flag attack, and that Israel would have attempted to blame Egypt if the Israeli military had succeeded in sinking the ship. Indeed, President Lyndon Johnson dispatched nuclear-armed fighter jets to drop nuclear bombs on Cairo, Egypt. They were only recalled at the last minute, when Johnson realized that it was the Israelis – and not the Egyptians – who had fired on the Liberty.

The actions were arguably an admission that Israel intended to frame Egypt for the attack, and didn't want the Liberty's crew to be able to tell the world what really happened, such as: (1) using unmarked jets and boats, (2) destroying the Liberty's communication equipment and jamming the Liberty's emergency distress channel, and (3) trying to sink the ship and destroy all life rafts.

Thank you to our friends at Washington's Blog for their assistance in compiling this list.

www.ingramcontent.com/pod-product-compliance
Lightning Source LLC
Chambersburg PA
CBHW020936310726
48980CB00007B/793/J

* 9 7 8 0 5 7 8 4 8 5 5 5 3 *